DEADHEAD AND BURIED

THE ENGLISH COTTAGE GARDEN MYSTERIES
BOOK ONE

H.Y. HANNA

CONTENTS

H.Y. HANNA

CHAPTER ONE

Poppy Lancaster rushed out of the train station and paused as her eyes fell on the opposite street corner. Her heart sank. The queue at the popular espresso bar was usually pretty long, but this morning it stretched out of sight around the block. She glanced at her watch—she was definitely going to be late if she joined that line—then she remembered the terse message on her phone and, taking a deep breath, crossed the street to take her place at the end of the queue.

"Looks like you're going to be in for a long wait, luv," said a kindly faced, middle-aged woman standing on the corner. She had a cardboard tray in one hand, filled with brightly coloured pins, and a collecting tin in the other. A sash emblazoned with the logo of a well-known cancer charity covered her chest.

She smiled hopefully at Poppy. "Fancy buying a pin while you're waiting?"

Poppy gave the woman a shamefaced look. "I... I'm really sorry. I don't have enough change—"

"Oh, that's all right, luv. Some other time then," said the woman cheerfully, making Poppy feel even worse.

She bit her lip and almost reached into her handbag—but she thought of the small pile of change in her purse and knew that she wouldn't have enough to spare. Sighing, she joined the queue and dutifully shuffled along the pavement, getting slowly closer to the open window where a barista was busily taking orders and handing out cups of fragrant, steaming coffee. When it came to her turn, she reeled off the order she had learned by heart:

"A decaf, non-fat, no foam, soy cappuccino with raw sugar and extra whipped cream, please."

"Bloody hell—what kind of order is that?" grumbled the man in the queue behind her. He looked at his watch with exaggerated impatience and blew a loud sigh. "Can't you order something simpler? That's going to take ages!"

"Um... it's not for me," Poppy mumbled.

The barista frowned at the man, then turned back to Poppy and said with a smile: "And what about you? What would you like?"

Poppy watched the other baristas at the huge espresso machine, filling jugs with frothy milk, sprinkling chocolate flakes over creamy cappuccinos, whilst steam billowed in great clouds around them. The heavenly aroma of freshly brewed coffee filled her nostrils and she wished desperately that she could order a cup. But she knew that takeaway coffee was a luxury she couldn't afford.

She raised her chin and gave the barista a wan smile. "Nothing, thanks."

Poppy paid and waited for her order, trying to ignore the scowling businessman behind her, who kept sighing and making irate noises whilst constantly looking at his watch. Then all of a sudden, he cursed loudly, glared at Poppy, and left the queue, shoving her aside roughly. He barged down the pavement, knocking into the charity volunteer standing on the corner and sending her tray flying, scattering pins everywhere. The woman cried out, but the man didn't even give her a backward glance as he rounded the corner and disappeared.

"Here you are..." The barista leaned over the counter.

Poppy mumbled her thanks, grabbed the cup, then hurried over to the charity volunteer. "Are you all right?" she asked.

"Y-yes... fine. Just got a nasty surprise."

The woman took a few calming breaths, then crouched down painfully to begin gathering the spilled pins. Poppy glanced at her watch and hesitated, then placed her coffee on a nearby ledge and dropped to her knees to help.

"Oh... ta... that's really kind of you, luv," said the woman, beaming at her. "It would have taken me ages... and I've got a bit of a dodgy knee..."

It took longer than expected to gather all the pins, but finally they were all safely back in the tray. Poppy picked up her coffee cup again, noting uneasily that it no longer felt so hot anymore, and was about to leave when the woman caught her arm.

"Wait, luv... here... as a small thank you." The woman smiled and handed her a pin.

Poppy looked down and realised that the pin was actually fashioned in the shape of a sprig of heather, with feathery lavender-coloured blooms along the grey-green stem. Despite being made of papier-mâché, it was incredibly lifelike and beautiful.

"Flowers have meanings associated with them, you know," said the woman. "Heather symbolises transformative change—from the mundane to the extraordinary. It's a lovely meaning, don't you think?"

"Yes," said Poppy with a smile, touching the tiny flowers with her fingertips.

"Here... it will look beautiful on your lapel... and it really brings out your blue eyes," said the woman, reaching out to pin it on her.

"Oh... but I don't have any money to give you—" Poppy protested.

The woman waved a hand. "You've done more than enough to deserve a pin. Take it, dear—and I hope it brings you luck."

Poppy looked down at the pin, then smiled at the woman. "Thank you. I will treasure it." Then she glanced at her watch again and gasped. "Oh my God—I've got to go! It was lovely to meet you—and good luck with the collection!"

Giving the woman a wave and clutching the coffee cup to her, Poppy hurried away. Several minutes later, she raced into the foyer of a small office block and jabbed frantically at the button for the lift. It seemed to take an interminably long time to arrive and as she waited, shifting from foot to foot, she noted anxiously that the cup in her hands now felt distinctly lukewarm. By the time she arrived on the seventh floor and rushed through the open-plan office to the large executive desk in the corner, she was breathless and tense with nerves.

A tall, thin woman looked up from the desk and regarded her coldly. "What time do you call this?"

"I'm sorry, Amanda. I know I'm a bit late but there was a terribly long queue at the espresso bar and then—"

"Spare me your excuses! All I expect is for my assistant to pick up a cup of coffee for me in the mornings—is that too much to ask for?"

"No, but—"

"And if you know there's going to be a queue, then it's simply a matter of leaving your place a few minutes earlier to account for the wait. Surely even someone with your lack of education can figure that out?"

Poppy winced. It was a low blow and it wasn't the first time that her boss had jeered at her anaemic qualifications, but she didn't feel that she could make any comeback. She knew that her background was weak compared to most other working women her age and that she had been lucky to get this position, considering her lack of training and professional skills. So she swallowed the retort that sprang to her lips and instead said meekly:

"I'm sorry. It won't happen again. I'll make sure to leave earlier from now on."

Amanda held out one hand. "Well... is that my coffee?"

"Oh—oh, yes..." Poppy stepped forwards to place the coffee on the desk, then watched nervously as her boss raised the cup to her lips.

"It's stone cold!" Amanda cried, curling her lips back in disgust.

"I'm sorry... There was this man who knocked a lady over—a charity volunteer—so I had to stop and help her; she'd dropped all her..." She trailed off as she met Amanda's contemptuous gaze. Everybody in the office was watching and she felt her cheeks flush.

"You're paid to be my assistant, not some bloody Mother Teresa on the streets," Amanda snapped.

"So I'm supposed to just sit here waiting while you're busy doing your good works?"

Again, Poppy opened her mouth, then took a deep breath and shut it again. She counted slowly to five, then said in a neutral voice:

"Would you like me to make you a fresh coffee in the kitchen?"

"Ah... forget it! And take this away!" Amanda gestured to the paper cup in disgust.

Poppy picked up the unwanted cup, then hesitated by the desk. "Um... Amanda? The money for your coffee... well, you didn't give me any petty cash..."

Amanda looked at her blankly.

Poppy felt her face burning with embarrassment, but she continued doggedly, "I... um... I thought you would reimburse me—"

Amanda rolled her eyes. "For God's sake, it was only a couple of quid."

"Actually, it was a bit more than that... and the coffee wasn't for me..." Poppy gritted her teeth. "It's just that... I don't get paid until the end of next week and I'm quite low on cash..."

Amanda regarded her coldly. "Really, Poppy, considering that you were late and the coffee was cold and totally undrinkable, I'm amazed you have the cheek to ask for the money. Anyone else would have seen it as a justified forfeit."

Poppy's hands clenched, and she felt something hot and angry surge in her chest. She opened her mouth to speak, then a voice screamed in her head: *You can't afford to lose this job!* The words trembled on her lips, then she shut her jaws with a click.

Taking a deep, shuddering breath, she turned and was about to walk away when Stan from Accounts rushed up, holding a potted plant. Stan was a small, fussy man who seemed only able to have a functional relationship with his calculator; he rarely left his office, avoided eye contact, and never spoke to Poppy unless he had something to say about her wages. Now, however, he was looking at her accusingly as he shoved the pot towards her.

"Look! Look at this!"

Poppy stared at the plant in dismay. It was drooping badly, its leaves curled and brown. She reached out to touch one shrivelled leaf and gasped as it fell off into her hands. It was limp and soft, almost mushy. There was a faint musty smell rising from the soil in the pot.

"They're all like this! All the plants in the office," said Stan. He looked at Amanda and pointed at Poppy: "*She* was supposed to be looking after them!"

Amanda rounded on her. "Did you forget to water them?"

"No, no! I watered them every day!" cried Poppy.

"What? *Every* day?" Stan spluttered. "For heaven's sake, don't you know anything about plants? That's why they're dying—they've been completely overwatered! Do you realise how much potted plants like these cost? We bought advanced specimens so that they would instantly green up the office and it'll cost a fortune to replace them. I haven't got the money in the budget."

"I... I didn't know... I mean..." Poppy stammered.

"Well, they'd better not die," said Amanda, narrowing her eyes. "Or the cost of replacing every plant in this office will be coming out of your wages!"

CHAPTER TWO

Poppy flinched and stared at Amanda in horror. Pay to replace every plant in the office? That could run to hundreds of pounds!

"No... please, I..." she started to protest, but Amanda had already turned away, obviously dismissing her, and begun texting on her phone.

Stan gave a disdainful sniff, then turned and stalked off. Poppy was left standing, trembling with humiliation. She could feel the eyes of all the other staff on her as she walked slowly back to her desk. As she sat down, however, she heard a voice speak beside her:

"Amanda's a right cow."

She looked up with surprise to see Chloe, one of the secretaries, lean over from the desk next to hers and give her a sympathetic smile. Poppy felt a flash of gratitude for the girl's support.

"What am I going to do?" she whispered, feeling on the verge of tears. She was already struggling to pay her rent and the bills, not to mention the minimum payment on the credit card each month. She just couldn't afford to lose any part of her wages.

Chloe snapped her fingers. "I tell you what—I'll ask my Dad how to fix these plants. I'm sure he'll know what to do. He's got an allotment and he's really into gardening." She laughed. "In fact, I'm getting him this really cool garden toolbelt for Father's Day next week. He's been wanting it for ages. I can't wait to see his face when he opens his present!" She looked at Poppy. "So what have you got your dad for Father's Day?"

"Oh... um... I don't really... I never knew my father," Poppy mumbled.

"You mean—he died when you were a baby?"

"No, I mean..." Poppy flushed. "I... I don't know who he is."

Chloe's eyes rounded. "Seriously? Like... your mum never told you?"

Poppy hesitated. She didn't normally talk about this, but she was also incredibly touched by Chloe's show of support. Maybe it was time she started opening up a bit about herself—it might mean that she'd finally make a friend.

"Um... my mother was a bit of a wild child in her teens and she... well, she was a groupie over in the

States for a while."

Chloe's eyes went even rounder. "Ooh! You mean, those girls who get to hang out backstage with the band and travel around with them, going to all the parties? The whole sex, drugs, and rock 'n' roll thing?"

Poppy shifted uncomfortably. "Yeah, I guess…"

Chloe squealed. "Oh my God—so your dad could be an American rock star?"

Poppy glanced around the office to see if anyone else was listening. She was beginning to regret opening up to Chloe.

"I can't believe your mother never told you anything about him! Didn't you ask her?"

"Of course, I did," said Poppy, a bit tartly. "I tried to ask her loads of times but all she would tell me was that he was one of the musicians in the bands she was following around, and that he never knew about me. She left and came back to England when she got pregnant with me."

"Well, do you know which bands? You could check out their members and see if you look like any of them!" said Chloe excitedly. "That's what I'd be doing! I mean, imagine if you find out that your dad is some big rock star who's got this mansion in LA and you could go and live with him and go to all these parties and meet celebrities… wouldn't that be *brilliant*?"

Poppy looked away. She was too embarrassed to admit that those were *exactly* the things she had secretly been wishing for all her life. Ever since she had been old enough to ask about her father and understand her background, she had dreamt of an older man turning up on her doorstep one day, giving her a hug, and sweeping her off to a new glamorous life in Hollywood. No more overdue credit card bills to worry about, no more nasty boss, no more boring, dreary life in England...

But she knew they were just dreams and never likely to happen, and it was this bitterness which made her say, more sharply than she intended:

"I've got more sense than to indulge in stupid dreams like that!"

Chloe pulled back, her expression cooling. "Oh. Well, I think it's nice to dream sometimes," she said stiffly.

Poppy bit her lip. "I'm sorry. I didn't mean—"

"It's all right. I've got to get on with this email anyway." The other girl turned away.

Sighing, Poppy turned to her own computer. The morning dragged on and she was relieved when lunchtime finally rolled around. *Maybe I'll pick up something for Chloe—like a chocolate muffin or something, as a peace offering*, thought Poppy. After shelling out for Amanda's coffee, she had precious little cash left in her purse, but if she chose a cheaper sandwich, she'd have enough money left over for a small treat.

As she was walking to the sandwich shop, however, Poppy caught sight of the bookshop across the street and her feet moved as if of their own accord, carrying her over to the shop window. She stared longingly at all the glossy book covers displayed under a sign saying: "New Releases!" Books were another luxury that she could rarely afford—she had to rely on the free offerings from her local library—but that didn't stop her often coming to the bookshop to browse through the shelves and wistfully read the blurbs on the backs of the novels.

The shop was normally fairly quiet during lunchtimes on a weekday. Today, however, she was surprised to find it filled with customers, all milling about in an excited fashion. Curious, she stepped inside and peered over the heads of the crowd to see what the commotion was about. A table and chair had been set up in the far corner, next to a stack of hardback novels, and there was a large poster featuring a book cover and the words "*Nick Forrest's thrilling new bestseller!*" splashed across it in bold letters.

The name sounded vaguely familiar, although Poppy didn't think she had read any of his books. From the picture of the cover, it looked like a dark, gritty crime thriller and she usually preferred lighter reading—fantasy stories that allowed her to dream and escape. Still, looking at the line of people around the room, all clutching copies of novels for him to sign, this author was obviously incredibly popular.

A murmur of excitement rippled through the crowd and, the next moment, a tall man entered the store from the rear entrance, flanked by the store manager and several other people, like a king accompanied by his entourage. He carried himself like a king too—there was a commanding brusqueness to his manner as he strode across the room and sat down behind the table.

So this is Nick Forrest, the bestselling crime writer. Now that she thought about it, she *had* read about him in a couple of magazines. The articles had gushed about him as "the sexy face of crimewriting", in a way which had made Poppy roll her eyes. She eyed him critically from across the room. *It's not as if he's really handsome,* she thought. Well, okay, there *was* something about him, if you liked the dark, brooding Heathcliff type—not that she did, she reminded herself. He was younger than she had expected—somewhere in his late thirties, she guessed—with silver edging the black hair at his temples and a cynical expression in his dark eyes. Poppy noticed several women in the crowd elbowing each other and giggling as they gave him coy looks, and she felt herself instantly dislike him. Maybe it was a silly reaction—she didn't even know the man—but she couldn't help it. The more hyped up a book, movie, or celebrity, the more she took against them. Perhaps it was a subconscious thing, not wanting to become like her mother—a groupie slavishly following others like sheep, to worship at an idol's feet.

Now, she watched askance as the store manager clapped his hands for attention and gave a short speech, detailing the crime writer's impressive book sales and awards. Poppy felt her irritation growing. When the manager finally finished, she seized the chance to leave, but she hadn't gone a few steps when a masculine voice stopped her in her tracks.

She turned involuntarily around to look back at the table. Nick Forrest was reading from his book and his deep voice was mesmerising, conjuring up vivid pictures and fascinating characters from the words on the page. She had stood listening for several minutes before she realised it. Annoyed with herself, Poppy turned resolutely once more towards the door, and this time managed to push her way through the crowds and leave the bookshop.

CHAPTER THREE

"Poppy, is that you, dear? The dragon keeping you late at work again, is she? And probably not for any proper office business either. That woman is a selfish cow! I'll have words with her one day—see if I don't!"

Poppy paused inside the door of the shabby terraced townhouse and smiled as she heard the motherly voice.

"Are you hungry? Did you get a proper lunch? You probably just rushed out this morning without eating any breakfast, as usual. It's not right, you know. Breakfast is the most important meal of the day, they say, and besides, you need some fattening up. Look at you—you're practically skin and bones! Being too thin is terribly ageing, you know, and it will ruin your looks. And then how are you going to get a man?"

The speaker of this torrent of words came bustling down the hallway, stepping into the light of the dusty bulb in the foyer. She was a woman in her sixties, with grey hair curling in a halo around her head and plump cheeks split by a wide smile. Poppy thought again how lucky it was that she had met Nell Hopkins. When her mother had become ill and they'd needed a place to live that was close to the hospital, this run-down sublet had been the only place they could afford. Poppy had been nervous about who they'd have to share the small townhouse with and when she had first met the talkative cleaning lady, she had been taken aback.

But she had soon discovered that Nell's loquacious manner was matched by a generous spirit and a warm heart. In fact, she didn't know how she would have got through the final months of her mother's illness if it hadn't been for her kindly landlady. Nell had helped to provide the home-nursing that her mother had needed; her job as a cleaner for many of the businesses in town meant that she worked in the evenings, after offices were closed, and was free for most of the day—a perfect arrangement that enabled Poppy to go out to work.

And when Holly Lancaster had passed away, Nell had stepped into the motherly void with ease, nagging Poppy to eat properly and constantly worrying about her (non-existent!) love life—as she was doing now:

"...and I know you're only in your twenties, Poppy, but it won't be long before you're over thirty and you know what they say: everything goes downhill after thirty! What are you going to do if you don't meet a nice man by then?" Nell wagged a finger. "Don't you roll your eyes at me, dear—you need someone in your life. Someone to cuddle and look after and give you a baby to bounce on your knee—"

"Nell!" Poppy burst out, with an exasperated laugh. "Which century are you living in? Women don't need men in their lives to feel fulfilled and happy."

"Ah... that's what they all say but I'm telling you, no one's truly happy until they have someone to love—and you never know when it's going to happen! That's why you need to be open to the possibilities. I mean, you could meet the love of your life when you least expect it! I knew a girl who was travelling in Australia and got bitten by a poisonous spider. She ended up in hospital in a coma and the doctor who was looking after her found a notebook of poetry that she'd written in her bag. Well, he started reading it to her, while she lay unconscious, and he fell in love with her—just through her words! And then when she woke up a few days later, he asked her to have dinner with him." Nell gave a dreamy sigh. "And they got married a year later."

"Is that really true or is it from the latest

romance novel you're reading?" asked Poppy suspiciously.

Nell looked a bit cagey. "Well, all right, it was from a book—but that doesn't mean it couldn't happen!" she added quickly. "Mrs Simpson from next door told me that her daughter Jilly met her boyfriend while she was working as his nurse at the hospital. Jilly wasn't in a coma, of course, but she did have the flu and she fainted right into Stuart's arms when they were operating in theatre together—so romantic, don't you think?—and now they're getting engaged..."

Poppy hid a smile as the older woman rambled on. If there was one thing Nell loved more than anything else, it was a romance—whether in real life or in the pages of a novel. In fact, her landlady seemed to spend all her free time speculating about the love lives of various neighbours... when she wasn't fussing around Poppy like an anxious mother hen.

"Well, now... I've just boiled the kettle; you'll have a cuppa, won't you?" said Nell, turning to lead the way to the kitchen on her side of the house. "And you can tell me about your day. Here, give me your bag..." Nell reached out and dragged Poppy's handbag off her shoulder. "Oh my lordy Lord, Poppy, what are you carrying in here? It weighs a ton! You really need to sort out your handbag and take all the junk out. I watched this programme on telly that said women's handbags have more bacteria than the average toilet... I couldn't believe it but they'd done tests and everything..."

Poppy felt a mixture of affection, exasperation, and gratitude as Nell started up again, fussing and worrying. In a way, Nell was more of a mother than Holly Lancaster had ever been. Even after giving birth to a baby, her mother had remained very much the same reckless teenager who had run away from home to become a rock-star groupie. Poppy had spent most of her childhood on the move, drifting around England as her mother chased the next "big dream" that was going to make their fortunes.

And in the meantime, Holly had thought nothing of putting impulsive, extravagant purchases on the credit card. As a little girl, Poppy had loved her mother's "fun surprises"; it was only as she'd got older that she started to worry about how they could afford them, and it wasn't until after her mother's funeral that she realised how many bills were outstanding, how much debt was unpaid.

Which is why I can't give up my job, no matter how awful Amanda is, she reminded herself. Still, it helped to have someone to share her woes with, and now she followed Nell gratefully to her kitchen. She accepted a cup of tea and sat down to recount the details of her terrible day.

"I hope Chloe's father comes up with a good idea for the office plants," she said at last. "Do you think they might just dry out and recover?"

"Well, I know what to do with a pot of herbs but I'm not much good with those fancy plants they have in offices nowadays. I always keep well away from them when I'm cleaning," said Nell. "Your mother, now—she would have known what to do."

"Yes," said Poppy wistfully. "I wish I'd inherited Mum's skill with plants. She was amazing; she could make anything grow. She didn't just have green fingers—she was practically a green goddess." Poppy shook her head sadly. "Whereas me... well, I could kill a plastic plant from IKEA."

Nell laughed. "There are worse faults to have, dear." She rose from the kitchen table and went to the stove. "Now, I've made a nice leek and potato soup, and there's a fresh loaf of bread—would you like to have some supper?"

Poppy was tempted. Her hasty lunch was hours ago and she realised now that she was starving. Nell was a fantastic cook and a bowl of hot soup sounded wonderfully comforting after the day she'd had. But she felt bad about how often she ate Nell's food, and her landlady would never accept any kind of monetary reimbursement, despite the fact that Nell only earned a modest income herself from her cleaning jobs.

"No, thank you—although that's really sweet of you to offer," Poppy said with a smile as she rose as well. "I've... um... got some things in the fridge that I need to finish up."

Like a piece of mouldy cheese, she thought,

wincing internally. But she gave Nell a cheerful wave and turned to leave.

Nell put out a hand. "Oh! Hang on, dear... I nearly forgot—this came for you today."

Poppy looked curiously at the letter that Nell handed to her. It was made of heavy, expensive paper, and looked official, with a typed address and the logo of a solicitor's firm in Oxford printed in the top left-hand corner.

"For me?" she said.

Nell nodded. "It came by registered post. I signed for it—I didn't think you'd mind. Saves you having to go to the post office to collect it."

"Oh, yes, of course..." murmured Poppy distractedly as she turned the envelope over. Slowly, she peeled the flap open and drew out the single sheet of thick cream paper. It was a typed letter, with an embossed letterhead at the top and an elegant signature next to the name "Charles Mannering Esq." at the bottom. Her eyes widened as she read the contents.

"Well? What is it?" demanded Nell.

"It's... it's a letter from a lawyer," said Poppy in a slight daze.

"And? What does it say?" Without waiting for Poppy to answer, Nell leaned over her shoulder and read the letter out loud:

"...writing to inform you that as Mary Lancaster's only granddaughter, you are the sole benefactor of her estate... Please contact me at your earliest convenience to arrange a meeting to discuss—Oh my lordy Lord!" she cried, clutching Poppy's arm.

"Poppy, what have you inherited?"

CHAPTER FOUR

The next morning, Poppy risked Amanda's displeasure and delayed leaving for work so that she could ring the lawyer's office in Oxford when it opened. She asked to speak to Charles Mannering, and when she hung up again a short while later, it was as if everything had taken on a sense of the surreal.

"Well?" Nell asked breathlessly. She had been hovering in the doorway of Poppy's room, unable to contain herself, and now she came forwards eagerly. "What did he say? What are you inheriting? Is it money? Jewels? A house in the country?"

"Nell!" Poppy gave an exasperated laugh. "I'm not an heiress in a Regency romance novel!" She took a deep breath. "But in fact—yes, it *is* a house in the country. Not a grand house," she hastened to add.

"Just a cottage—a little cottage on a large piece of land in Oxfordshire. Apparently, my grandmother had a thriving garden nursery business—"

"A cottage garden nursery!" cried Nell, her eyes glowing. "Oh Poppy! Just think—you'll be able to grow your own fruit and vegetables, raise little potted plants to sell, have a beautiful cutting garden to make your own flower bouquets, and live in a quaint little cottage with gorgeous climbing roses and—"

"Nell, I can't even keep a couple of office plants alive! There's no way I'd be able to run a garden business."

"You could learn. It can't be that hard."

For a moment, Poppy indulged in a fantasy of herself as the owner of a thriving garden nursery, attached to a beautiful cottage surrounded by a wild, romantic English garden bursting with flowers, with billowing lavender lining the path and wafting perfume in the breeze...

Abruptly, she snapped out of the daydream. She remembered the yellowed, drooping plants in the office—what on earth was she thinking?

"No," she said with a sigh. "It's nice to dream but, at the end of the day, I have to be realistic. I'd be a fool to think I could do it, what with my track record with plants."

Nell pursed her lips but didn't argue. Instead, she said, "Well, you could still live at the cottage. At least you've got your own home now and—"

"Er... actually, it's not quite so simple."

"What do you mean?"

"Well, Mr Mannering said that my grandmother left a condition in her will: I can only live at the cottage if I agree to continue the family business and keep the garden nursery running. Otherwise, the property will have to be sold—although I would get the proceeds of the sale, of course."

"But that's ridiculous! It's your property now, so you should be able to do as you see fit. Your grandmother was always a hard, unreasonable woman," Nell declared. "Looks like she hadn't mellowed with age."

"Do you know anything about her?" asked Poppy, looking up in surprise. "Mum would never talk to me about her."

Nell shook her head. "Your mother never told me much either. All I know is that your grandmother was very strict and they were always at each other's throats, what with your mum being such a rebel and all. It was bad enough when Holly joined the other groupies and ran off to America, but when she got pregnant with you—well! That was the last straw! I don't think your grandmother ever spoke to your mum again." Nell made a sound of disapproval. "Imagine! Her own daughter, and with a grandchild on the way! Well, that tells you what kind of hard, unreasonable woman she was."

"But... if she never tried to contact Mum or see us in all these years, why would she suddenly think of me in her will?"

"Guilt, probably," said Nell with a knowing look. "People start regretting all sorts of things on their deathbeds. Maybe she wanted to contact you but her pride wouldn't let her. Your mum was just as bad, you know. Many's a time I told her that she should just let bygones be bygones, but she wouldn't budge. Said she wasn't going crawling back—"

"Yes, even when she became ill and we were struggling, Mum wouldn't let me try to find her family to ask for help." Poppy sighed. "I do feel a bit disloyal accepting this—"

"Nonsense! Don't you dare think like that," said Nell sternly. "Your mother was a wonderful woman, bless her soul, but she was too proud and stubborn for her own good. If your grandmother wanted to mend fences at last, then you should grab the opportunity. Don't look a gift horse in the stomach, is what I say."

Poppy smiled. "I think you mean 'mouth'."

Nell waved a hand. "Stomach, mouth, it's all the same. Take the gift and count your blessings."

"Yes... and you know what?" Poppy brightened. "It doesn't matter that I can't live there. I can just sell the place, take the money, and go travelling! Maybe even go to America and find my fa—" She broke off and hastily amended it to: "—er... well, just do all the things I could never afford to do. I'm sure I can ask Mr Mannering when I see him—"

"Well, what are you waiting for?" cried Nell, making a shooing motion. "You can hop on a train and be in Oxford in an hour."

"But I'm supposed to be at work—"

"Oh, bosh!" Nell waved a contemptuous hand. "Amanda hasn't given you any of the paid leave you're due... I think you're entitled to take a sickie."

Feeling emboldened, Poppy rang her office and asked for the day off, pleading a bad migraine, then—armed with her birth certificate and other identity documents—she jumped on a train for Oxford.

***

The lawyer, Charles Mannering, turned out to be a dapper gentleman in his early sixties with a cut-glass accent that matched his distinguished appearance. He wore a sombre three piece suit, with old-fashioned gold cufflinks at his wrists and a traditional tie-pin carefully displayed on his chest— and would have looked slightly intimidating, had Poppy not found herself instantly warming to his kind, fatherly manner. However, as he took her patiently through a long meeting full of dry legal language and dozens of forms to sign, her hopes of a sudden cash windfall were dashed as she discovered that there was very little ready money left after the outstanding bills had been settled.

"Most of the capital in the estate is tied up in the

cottage and gardens," Charles Mannering explained. "And I am afraid that it might be a tricky property to sell. You see, there have been extensive changes made to the house and grounds over the years, to support a working garden nursery, and so any family looking to move in would have to do some major renovation in order to turn the layout back into a more traditional residence." Mannering adjusted his spectacles and made a tutting sound. "In addition, the cottage itself is actually quite small, with fixtures that have not been upgraded in decades. The bathtub, I believe, could be a relic from Victorian times!"

"What about trying to sell it as a garden business?" Poppy asked hesitantly.

"Hmm... hmm... well, we could certainly try," said Mannering in a tone which suggested that it would be an even greater challenge. "However, you must be aware that a very large garden centre has just opened nearby and—as is usual with these large chains—it has the advantage of lower prices." He looked apologetic. "I must say, I have been guilty of going there myself, just because it is easier, and they have a larger range. This has been happening up and down the country, and it is difficult for small, independent nurseries to compete."

Poppy sighed. "Well, I'll leave it with you and keep my fingers crossed." She started to rise, then paused as she spotted the bunch of keys on the table in front of her.

"Those are the keys to the cottage," said Mannering. "Perhaps you would like to go and look at the property? It is in a village in south Oxfordshire."

Poppy hesitated. She knew it was silly, but despite what Nell had said, she still felt a niggling sense of disloyalty to her mother, and going to visit her grandmother's cottage in person seemed somehow to be an even bigger betrayal. Besides, if she was going to sell it anyway, what was the point?

"Um... no, I don't think so... I've... er... got to get back to London," she said.

"Well, they'll be here in the office, should you change your mind, Miss Lancaster," said the lawyer, rising as well and coming around his enormous mahogany desk to shake her hand with old-fashioned formality. "And I shall keep you informed of developments."

CHAPTER FIVE

Poppy stepped out of the train station and felt a sense of déjà vu as she hurried across the road and joined the queue outside the espresso bar. Was it only one week ago that she had been standing here, waiting to buy Amanda's morning coffee, unaware that a letter was going to arrive that day and change her life completely?

Not that much has changed as yet, Poppy reflected wryly. Nell might have had visions of her being swept off—Little Orphan Annie-style—to a glamorous makeover and a new life in a luxurious mansion, but the reality was a bit more mundane than that. In fact, very little had happened since her meeting with Charles Mannering and life seemed to have quickly returned to its dreary old routines.

She glanced idly around as she shuffled down

the line; she couldn't see the charity volunteer today—instead a flower seller had taken up residence on the street corner, with a makeshift stall and bundles of colourful flowers spilling out of plastic buckets arranged in a row. Poppy watched enviously as a woman stopped to select a generous bunch of colourful blooms. She sighed. How she would have loved to buy a bouquet herself. Other women might love jewellery or designer shoes, but for Poppy, it was fresh-cut flowers. Beautiful, romantic, perfumed—and horribly expensive—they'd always seemed like the ultimate extravagance. They were certainly a luxury that she could never afford. Even for her birthdays, she could never justify spending her hard-earned cash on something that would fade in just a few days.

A vision of a cottage garden bursting with flowers flashed in her mind and Nell's voice came back to her: *"...you'll be able to have a beautiful cutting garden to make your own flower bouquets, and live in a quaint little cottage with gorgeous climbing roses..."*

"Next!" called an impatient voice.

Poppy snapped out of her thoughts and hurried up to the counter. Once she got the coffee, she raced to get to Amanda's desk before it got cold—but to her chagrin, she discovered that her boss was not in the office that morning. *How nice of her to bother to tell me*, she thought irritably. Still, it meant that she was able to get on with her work in peace and she finished in time to leave early for her lunch break.

On her way out, she paused to examine some of the plants around the office and was delighted to see that they seemed to be recovering. A few had even started growing new leaves! Her good mood made her slightly complacent and she lingered too long over her sandwich as she sat on a bench in the sun. When she rushed back, however, she found to her surprise that Amanda's desk was still empty.

"Don't worry—Her Majesty won't be back for a while yet," said Chloe with a smirk.

"I didn't realise her meetings today would be so long," Poppy said.

Chloe made a rude sound. "Meetings? Huh! Amanda's not gone to see any clients—she's gone to a day spa."

"*What?*"

Chloe nodded. "I made the appointments for her myself. Getting some kind of micro-whatsit for her face. Y'know, when they pour on acid to burn the dead skin away... or something like that. It was some package that the spa was offering—together with a body polish and massage and this special treatment for cellulite." She looked ruefully down at her own thighs. "Wish I could afford to do that—I've got cellulite something chronic! Must be nice to just lie there and have someone massage it all away, while you're relaxing and listening to music..."

"But... I thought Amanda said... I'm sure she

told me that she would be busy going to client meetings all day," said Poppy, frowning.

Chloe gave a cynical laugh. "Well, of course she'd say that. Not going to admit that she's lounging around, enjoying massages and facials, while we're here working our arses off, is she? But I told you—I made the bookings: she's at the day spa today and she's going back tomorrow morning."

Poppy felt a surge of disgust for the woman's hypocrisy, but before she could say anything, Amanda herself sashayed into the office, her clothing slightly rumpled and her complexion suspiciously glowing. She saw the girls watching her and her eyes narrowed.

"I don't pay you to sit around and chitchat, you know," she snapped. "I've had an exhausting day, running around seeing clients, and I'd have hoped that my staff would have the decency to at least *look* like they're working when I return." She stalked past them and went over to her desk.

"Bloody hell, wouldn't I love to throw that back in her face," muttered Chloe under her breath. "But it's more than my job's worth, unfortunately."

Poppy had a few letters that she needed her boss to sign and she knew she couldn't delay. Sighing, she picked up the sheaf of typed pages and walked across the office to Amanda's desk. She found the woman sitting back in her big leather chair, with her eyes closed and an expression of weary resignation on her face, for all the world as if she really had just had an exhausting day liaising with clients. Poppy felt another surge of disgust, but she kept her expression carefully neutral as she waited for Amanda to sign the letters. As she was turning to leave, however, her boss said:

"Oh, by the way, Poppy, I'll need you to come in early tomorrow morning. There's a conference call planned with the Portugal office and I'm out at a meeting all morning. So I'll need you to take the call for me—they'll want the updated figures from the charity account and you know where the spreadsheets are—"

"Tomorrow morning? But I've asked for leave," said Poppy.

Amanda frowned. "What do you mean?"

"I asked you a few weeks ago—remember? I asked to have the morning off and you agreed."

"I don't remember that."

"You did," Poppy insisted. "I even had to speak to Accounts about it because you said I had to take it as unpaid leave and get Stan to calculate the deduction from my wages."

Amanda scowled. "Well, you'll just have to change your plans—"

"I can't. I have to go to—"

"Oh, for God's sake, I'm sure you can rearrange whatever it is you're doing."

"No, I *have* to go tomorrow. It's the anniversary of my mother's death and I want to visit her grave—"

"She's dead already! What does one more day matter?"

Poppy was so taken aback by the woman's insensitivity and rudeness that she was speechless for a moment.

"No, you don't understand—it's the *first* anniversary of her death and I made a promise to go and lay fresh flowers on her grave. It's really important to me. That's why I especially asked for leave—"

"Oh, cry me a river... you're not the first person to lose their mother, you know," said Amanda with an exaggerated sigh. "Really, Poppy, if you hope to get anywhere in your career, you'll have to start acting with professionalism. That means not letting your selfish desires or petty personal issues stand in the way of your work ethic. We all have to make sacrifices, you know."

Poppy stared at her, too shocked and furious to even reply. How dare the woman talk about sacrifices and professionalism when she was bunking off herself to go to a day spa during work hours! The hypocrisy was unbelievable! Taking several deep breaths, Poppy turned on her heel and began to walk away. But with every step she took, she felt herself seething more and more, until it felt as if her head would explode.

Suddenly she swung around and faced her boss again. "Actually, Amanda, since you mentioned it... I have been following *your* lead."

Amanda glanced up carelessly. "What?"

"Well, you set such a brilliant example of how to behave with professionalism—I'm sure you won't be sacrificing your work ethic when you're at the day spa tomorrow morning."

Amanda flushed bright red.

Poppy gave her a breezy smile. "But unfortunately, you will have to find some other mug to cover your arse—oops, I mean, take your place in the conference call—because I won't be here."

"What do you mean?" snarled Amanda. "I just told you, I'm not approving your leave—"

"That's all right. You won't need to. I won't be here because I'm handing in my notice. You'll have my resignation letter within the hour."

Her head held high, Poppy turned and strode away.

CHAPTER SIX

An hour later, Poppy walked trembling out of the office building and onto the street, her thoughts spinning. *Oh my God*, she thought. *I can't believe what I've done!* She had stood up to Amanda at last! For a moment, she felt a rush of exhilaration and a deep sense of satisfaction at finally putting the horrible woman in her place. Then she came back down to earth with a thump: she had also walked out of a job and was now unemployed with no references and no qualifications, in a time of recession, when jobs were hard to come by...

Poppy felt her heart give a sickening lurch as reality began to sink in. Then she took a deep breath and hitched her handbag higher up her shoulder. There was no point standing in the street, worrying about it. She would go home first, have some lunch, and then consider her next steps.

It was strange taking the train home: the carriages that were normally so packed during rush hour were now empty, save for the occasional pensioner or mother and toddler out on a day trip. Poppy stared out of the window and tried not to worry about the future, although now that her temper had cooled and the enormity of what she'd done was hitting her, she was really beginning to panic. Self-righteous vindication might feel great, but it didn't put food on the table.

She sighed, fiddling nervously with the buttons on her jacket, then paused as her fingers brushed something soft and feathery. She looked down. It was the pin that the charity volunteer had given her last week—the sprig of heather flowers, made of papier-mâché. She had completely forgotten that it was still pinned on her jacket. She stared at the delicate lavender-coloured blooms as the woman's words came back to her: *"...heather symbolises transformative change—from the mundane to the extraordinary..."*

Poppy pulled a face. Well, her life was certainly going through transformative change, all right, although right now it looked more like it was going from the mundane to the disastrous!

She was grateful when the train finally arrived at her stop and put an end to her brooding thoughts. She hurried the short distance back to the shabby old townhouse and let herself in, then hesitated outside the door to her own rooms, before turning and walking down the hallway to Nell's part of the house.

"Poppy!" Nell said in surprise when she saw her. "What are you doing home? Is something wrong? Are you ill?"

"No, no, nothing—I'm fine," Poppy assured her. She hesitated, then blurted, "Nell, I walked out!"

The older woman stared at her. "You what?"

"I told Amanda where to stuff it! Well, not in so many words, but she got my drift. I just couldn't take it anymore. She's an absolute selfish cow—and the most disgusting hypocrite too! She refused to let me have leave tomorrow morning to visit Mum's grave, even though I—" Poppy broke off as she realised that Nell didn't seem to be listening. "Is something wrong?"

Nell sighed, picked up a piece of paper from her coffee table, and handed it to Poppy. "This came today. It's from the owner of this townhouse... my landlord. He's claiming that I've broken the terms of the tenancy by subletting rooms—"

"But that's rubbish!" cried Poppy. "I can remember clearly having a meeting with him before Mum and I moved in. He was fine about it, as long as he got a cut of our rent."

"That's what he said on the day. Now he's denying that he ever agreed to it."

"But he can't! It must be down in writing somewhere—"

"Actually…" Nell looked slightly shamefaced. "It's not. He kept promising to bring me the amended contract but he never did and I guess I got busy and forgot about it. You know how it is—you just get on with life. You and your mum were living here anyway with no problems, and I suppose I just let things slide…"

Poppy looked down at the letter again, then said to Nell, "I've got to move out. Otherwise, he might evict you and then you'll have nowhere to live and it'll be my fault."

"But where will you go?" asked Nell worriedly. "You'll have to find somewhere cheap and that's going to be really difficult in this area. So many people have moved here now, because of the easy commute into London—they've pushed the rental prices up. And now that you're unemployed—"

"I have my grandmother's cottage," said Poppy suddenly.

Nell gaped at her. "But… but you're selling that—"

"Yes, but until it's sold, it's still mine, isn't it? I mean, I know there's a condition attached to living there but I'm sure even my grandmother wouldn't quibble if I just stayed there temporarily. It's only for a few weeks, until I find another place to live. It'll give me the breathing space I need and help save money too, since I won't have to worry about paying rent while I'm living there."

Nell still looked doubtful but Poppy smiled,

feeling a sense of certainty for the first time since walking out of her job that morning. She reached out and gave Nell's hand a squeeze.

"I'll visit Mum's grave tomorrow morning, then go up to Oxfordshire to check out this cottage."

***

As Poppy boarded the train for Oxford the next morning, she was filled with a carefree abandonment that she hadn't felt in a long time— like that delicious sense of freedom on the first day of a long summer holiday. Charles Mannering was away when she arrived at his office, but luckily his secretary remembered her and showed no surprise or curiosity when Poppy asked for the keys to the cottage. Perhaps the woman was used to clients making odd requests. At any rate, she got up from her desk without demur and want to rummage through a cabinet of drawers. She seemed to be a long time and straightened at last with a puzzled look on her face.

"Strange..." she muttered.

"Is something wrong?" asked Poppy.

"The keys don't seem to be here," said the secretary, frowning.

"Perhaps Mr Mannering has taken them?"

"No, no, he's up in London today... and in any case, he wouldn't need to. He has a second set in his office safe. Excuse me... I'll just go and fetch those for you."

She returned from the inner office a few minutes later with a set of keys clutched in her hands. "Here they are. I must let Mr Mannering know that the main set is missing. I wonder who might have taken them?"

"Is the drawer that they're kept in locked?" asked Poppy.

"No... but I'm usually here and the cabinet is behind my desk, so I would know if anyone was trying to get something."

"Perhaps someone came during your lunch break?" suggested Poppy, thinking back to her London office. The receptionist's desk there was often unattended for short periods during lunch. "Does Mr Mannering have a junior partner who might have taken the keys?"

"No, there is no other lawyer here; Mr Mannering works alone. No one else would have access except me... oh, and I suppose the cleaner who comes after office hours. I normally have my lunch here at the desk, so it's never unattended for long periods but I suppose someone *could* have come in when I popped briefly to the loo. Still, why would a stranger take the keys to the cottage?" She shook her head, then gave Poppy a smooth, professional smile. "It's certainly a bit of a mystery but no need for you to worry about it. This second set should work fine. If you could just sign for it here..."

A few minutes later, Poppy left the office, an

ancient bunch of keys clutched in her hand and an address scrawled on a note in her pocket. Her grandmother's cottage was situated in a village called Bunnington, about ten miles south of Oxford. It would probably only take twenty minutes to drive, but with no car, Poppy found that her only option was a slow local bus that seemed to stop at every town and village on the way. Still, it was a beautiful June morning and she enjoyed the ride through the pretty landscape of the south Oxfordshire countryside.

Arriving in the village at last, Poppy paused by the little Saxon church, situated at the edge of a wide triangle of grass—the traditional "village green"—and looked around. There were lots of tourists milling about and as she scanned her surroundings, she began to see why. Bunnington was absolutely picturesque, brimming with quaint timber-framed cottages and honey-coloured stone houses, as well as a mediaeval guesthouse—now doing duty as the village pub—and an ancient mill by the river that ran past the village.

There was a handy poster with a map of the village, right outside the post office, and Poppy paused to consult this. She was pleased to find that the cottage was in a lane just off the high street and should only be a short walk away. A few minutes later, she stood in front of a rickety wooden gate, hemmed in on either side by a crumbling stone wall. Overgrown vines and climbing roses draped over the wall and formed an arch above the top of the gate, leaving a gap through which to peek at the garden beyond. Poppy stepped closer and looked through the gap; she was taken aback to see a crazy profusion of overgrown bushes and shrubs, climbing vines, overhanging trees and weeds... weeds everywhere!

It was so *not* the image she'd had in mind of a neat and pretty cottage garden filled with flowers that, for a moment, she wondered if she had come to the right place. Then she noticed something on the wall next to the gate—it looked like a sign, half-covered by twining stems. Carefully, she lifted some of the leaves to get a better look and found a beautiful old mosaic plaque, the faded tiles spelling out the words:

HOLLYHOCK COTTAGE & GARDENS
Garden Nursery and Fresh Cut Flowers

The words were followed by the house number. Poppy pulled the note with the scrawled address out of her pocket and checked: yes, the numbers matched. This was her grandmother's cottage.

CHAPTER SEVEN

Stuffing the note back into her pocket, Poppy took a deep breath and pushed the gate open. It was stiff, the hinges creaky and rusty, and she had to duck under the arch of climbing vines as she entered, so that there was a sense of stepping through a doorway into another world. She found herself surrounded by a dense tangle of grasses and shrubs. In the distance, she could see a stone cottage nestled deep in the centre of the garden, but she wondered how to reach it. Then, as she pushed a few bushy stalks aside, she realised that what had looked like an impenetrable wall of green was in fact two wide borders on either side of a winding gravel path. The plants had become so overgrown that they were spilling out of the beds and obscuring the pathway.

Slowly, she began to pick her way towards the cottage, shoving and heaving plants up and out of the way. Now that she was closer, she could see that there *were* flowers poking through the greenery—clumps of yellow and white daisies growing by the path, as well as several other flowers she didn't know the names of, all mingling their bright, happy colours at her feet. In the distance, tall spires of foxgloves swayed gently in the shady corners under trees, and scattered through the tall grass were patches of vivid colour from the bright blooms of poppies.

But most of all, she saw the roses. Great big cabbage roses in shades of soft apricot and pink, romantic climbing roses that festooned the stone walls, cupped roses stuffed with petals that looked like ruffled tissues, and perfumed roses that nodded and scattered their fragrant petals in the breeze. Poppy had never seen roses like these before—they looked like the roses found in illustrated books of old fairy tales, like the antique roses that once tempted Beauty into the garden of the Beast... and somehow, they were all growing and blooming in this neglected garden.

She turned and caught sight of another climbing rose, this time clambering up a trellis on the side of the cottage, its trusses of pink and apricot blooms glowing softly in the afternoon sun. Beneath it, framing the cottage windows, was another plant with tall arching stems bearing sprays of dainty white flowers that swayed in the breeze like a cloud of white butterflies.

Poppy felt her breath catch in her throat as she stared at the scene in front of her. From this distance, the weeds and overgrowth seemed to recede, and it was as if she'd caught a glimpse of what the cottage garden could look like, of how beautiful and enchanting it could be. *How amazing it would be to restore it to its former glory*, she thought wistfully.

It was several minutes before Poppy realised that she had been standing there, gawping. Hastily, she continued along the path and arrived at last at the cottage. It was small, but quaint and charming, with low timbered ceilings, working fireplaces, and large bay windows looking out into the surrounding gardens. There were a few pieces of furniture in some of the rooms—a wooden table and chairs in the kitchen, a sagging sofa and old armchair by the fireplace in the sitting room, as well as single beds with lumpy mattresses in both the bedrooms—but most of her grandmother's personal possessions seemed to have been removed. Poppy had hoped to find some photographs or other mementos to tell her more about her mother's estranged family, but there was nothing. The mantelpiece was bare, the bookshelves empty.

She discovered that a large part of the rear of the cottage had been converted and an extension added, to create a large greenhouse working area, filled with rusty spades and trowels, old earthenware pots, stacks of empty seed trays, and an assortment of other garden paraphernalia. It was quite dusty, with cobwebs in the corners, and the whole place had the musty smell of a house that had been shut up for too long.

Still, the garden might have been overgrown, but the cottage itself seemed clean and liveable. The stove in the kitchen was in working order, and a few plates and cups, as well as some old cutlery, had been left in the cupboards. There was even an electric kettle—stained and rusty, but working—in one corner of the counter, several tins of beans, and a box of teabags left in the pantry. In the bathroom, the water ran clear and while the "H" tap, after much choking and spluttering, seemed only able to manage lukewarm at best, it was good enough for a quick bath. The bathtub itself—as Charles Mannering had said—looked ancient, but despite the cracked enamel, it didn't seem to be leaking.

In the linen cupboard, Poppy found some old but clean bedsheets, and she was just reaching for them when she paused. Was she really going to spend the night here? Shouldn't she book into a nearby bed and breakfast instead? Even if there wasn't anything available in Bunnington itself, there was still time to take the next bus on to Wallingford, where she would be bound to find accommodation. But something in her resisted. For one thing, it would save money to spend the night here, but she knew that wasn't the only reason. It was as if now that she was here, she felt a sense of ownership, a feeling of loyalty to this place which made her reluctant to abandon it for another.

Don't get too used to it, she reminded herself. *This place is going to be sold; it isn't really going to be your home.* Still, it wouldn't hurt to spend a test night at the cottage, especially if she was hoping to live here for a while.

Poppy pulled the sheets out and headed back towards the bedroom. She had barely unfolded the top sheet, though, when the peace was shattered by an unearthly shriek. She froze, then dropped everything and rushed out of the front door.

The cry came again—a blood-curdling yowl that thinned into a shrill scream. It didn't sound human and Poppy stopped in confusion, straining her ears and staring around the overgrown garden.

Another scream, this time followed by a loud growling. The sounds seemed to be coming from the rear section of the property, in the garden behind the cottage. Poppy hurried around the corner of the building, then faltered to a stop as she came upon a familiar scene of battle between two age-old enemies.

An enormous ginger tomcat stood in a face-off with a scruffy black terrier.

The cat's back was hunched, his fur standing on end, as he glared at the dog, who glowered back. The ginger tom hissed and yelled an insult, and the terrier quivered with indignation. He growled a reply, baring his teeth and lunging forwards. The cat didn't even flinch. He simply twitched his tail and gave another blood-curdling yowl. Not to be outdone, the terrier let loose with a volley of barking, hurling every canine obscenity he could think of.

"Hey!" Poppy shouted above the din, stepping forwards with her hands raised. She had never dealt with a dog-cat fight before and wasn't quite sure what to do. "Hey! Um... no fighting!" she said lamely.

The animals turned, distracted, then, to her surprise, they both came eagerly towards her. The ginger tomcat stopped beside her and sniffed her leg, then rubbed himself against her jeans. He was a handsome fellow, with a thick orange pelt, big yellow eyes and scars on his ears that showed he could take care of himself in a fight. He let Poppy scratch his chin, purring with smug satisfaction, all while shooting dirty looks at the dog on her other side. The terrier bounced up and down, wagging his tail and whining loudly, and Poppy laughed, reaching out with her other hand to pat him.

"All right, all right... you too ..." she said, rubbing the dog's scruffy head. "What's your name?"

"*Rufff!*"

Poppy noticed that he was wearing a collar but no tag. She looked around, wondering how he had got into the property. Then she saw that the soil in the flowerbed next to them had been disturbed. Had the dog been digging there?

She stood up and walked over to take a closer look. Unlike the wide borders at the front which were heavily planted with all kinds of shrubs and flowers, and had a very natural look, this rectangular bed was clearly edged in straight lines and filled with a dark, rich soil that was bare, except for several plants scattered here and there. They seemed to be growing in an odd way and, after a while, Poppy saw that it was because they were growing more or less in rows. She realised suddenly that this must have been some kind of functional garden—a vegetable patch, perhaps? She peered closer. No, not vegetables... flowers. She could see the tall stems, thick with buds, and several were already blooming.

A cutting garden, she thought excitedly. Yes, of course! She remembered the sign outside the gate. Her grandmother must have grown cut flowers to sell. These must either be the survivors of the last batch sown, or plants that had self-seeded and grown from last year's crop. She reached out to pluck a large pink bloom, then a sound made her turn quickly around.

The noise seemed to come from the front of the property; it sounded like shattering glass. From her position by the flowerbed, the cottage blocked her view of the gate and the front garden, so she couldn't see if anyone else had arrived at the property.

The tinkle of glass came again, and this time Poppy had an uneasy thought. It sounded like a window breaking... was someone trying to break in?

CHAPTER EIGHT

Poppy sprang up and ran around the side of the cottage. She reached the front garden just in time to see a dark figure lurking by one of the windows. It was a man—somewhere in his late twenties, by the look of it—with heavily gelled hair, a dark hooded top, and baggy jeans. He was holding a chisel in one hand and pushing the window frame with the other, but at the sound of her footsteps, he swung around. Poppy caught a glimpse of a narrow, sullen face before he turned and bolted for the gate. She hesitated, not sure whether to chase after him or not, and by the time she'd made up her mind and run to the gate, the lane was empty.

Slowly, Poppy walked back to the cottage and examined the window. It was an old-fashioned lattice type, with several rows of small glass panels instead of one large pane. The man had obviously been trying to lever it open but had only succeeded in shattering one of the glass panels. She tested the window—it was still solidly locked—and the broken panel was too small to allow anything bigger than a child's hand through. Besides, no one in their right mind would put their hand through that hole lined with jagged glass fragments. She decided it was secure enough for the time being, and was just wondering how to find a window repair service locally when her mobile rang. It was Charles Mannering:

"My dear... I have just returned from London and my secretary tells me that you have come up to view your grandmother's property!" he said, sounding quite agitated. "I am sorry I wasn't here to take you down myself. If I had known that you were coming—"

"Oh, don't worry, Mr Mannering," Poppy reassured him. "It was a bit of a spur-of-the moment thing, and your secretary gave me very good directions, so I found it no problem. I'm here now, actually."

"Ah! I'm afraid the gardens have been quite neglected and the cottage is not in the best state—"

"Oh, it's not too bad. In fact, everything seems to be in working order—more than good enough for me, anyway. I'm sure I'll manage fine tonight—"

"I... I beg your pardon?"

"Um... well, I was planning to stay the night here

at the cottage—maybe even a few days—"

"But my dear! I don't think it will be very comfortable—"

"Oh, don't worry—as I said, I'm used to not having a lot of mod cons. The place I sublet in London doesn't have many luxuries either. I'm sure I'll be fine."

"But what about safety? You'll be all alone... I'd heard rumours in the village about a tramp seen lurking thereabouts and furthermore—"

"I'll lock all the doors and windows, and keep all the lights on," Poppy promised. "My grandmother lived here on her own, didn't she?"

Mannering sighed. "Well... if you insist, my dear. But do be careful—especially in the garden. It has been neglected for a long time, what with your grandmother being ill and then having an extended stay in hospital. It's very overgrown and there are some prickly old roses and other shrubs with very nasty thorns. I'd hate for you to hurt yourself; perhaps it would be best if you didn't go wandering in there until—"

"I promise I won't venture too far from the cottage," said Poppy, touched by his fatherly concern.

She had meant to tell him about the strange man trying to break in the window and ask for a recommendation for a local repair service, but the old lawyer seemed so upset already, she decided not to add to his anxiety. In any case, it had probably just been some opportunistic small-time thief who had thought that the house was empty and tried his chances. With the lights on and obvious movement about the place, petty criminals were unlikely to try again.

So she assured Mannering again that she would be fine and promised to call him if she needed anything. As she hung up, she suddenly remembered the ginger tomcat and the little terrier she'd met. She had completely forgotten about them in the excitement, but now she made her way back around the outside of the cottage to the flowerbed at the rear. It was empty. Poppy turned around, scanning the area, but the dog and cat were nowhere to be seen. She shrugged. Well, they both looked too well fed and healthy to be strays. She assumed that they must have gone back to their respective homes.

Returning to the cottage, she unpacked her small overnight bag and toiletries, made up the bed, then filled the old kettle in the kitchen and set it to boil. Twilight was drawing in and she went around carefully switching on all the lights and drawing the curtains, as well as double-checking that the front door was locked. As she was returning to the kitchen, she was startled by a clatter from the rear of the house.

Poppy froze. It had sounded a bit like shattering crockery, and reminded her of the sound of the breaking glass from earlier. Surely someone couldn't be trying to be break in again? Nervously, she made her way to the large greenhouse extension at the back of the cottage and was startled to see the door leading out to the rear garden standing slightly ajar.

She stiffened and looked quickly around. The greenhouse seemed empty. Then her gaze sharpened as she saw what had caused the noise: a column of terracotta pots had toppled over, with several smashing and breaking on the worn stone floor. That must have been the sound that she'd heard. She walked over and picked the intact pots back up, restacking them on the bench again. There were several other columns of pots there and they all seemed to be secure. Why had this one suddenly toppled like that?

Something brushed against her leg and she shrieked and jumped. Then she looked down and clutched her chest in relief as she saw a large ginger tomcat at her feet, staring up at her with wide yellow eyes.

"Oh, it's you...!" she said in a shaky voice.

He meowed—Poppy had never heard any cat sound like that. He had a deep, insistent voice and sounded for all the world as if he was saying: "*N-ow... N-ow!*"

He sprang up suddenly onto the bench, so that he was closer to her face, and rubbed his chin against her shoulder. Then he walked along the bench to the stacks of pots, weaving between them.

Ah... Poppy smiled. She was beginning to have an inkling as to why the pots had fallen.

"You're a troublemaker, aren't you?" she said with a chuckle.

"*N-ow!*" said the ginger tom.

She reached out to pat him but he evaded her hands, jumping down nimbly and trotting over to the back door.

"*N-ow?*" he said, looking back at her.

She followed him to the door, wondering again why it was ajar. It was obviously how the cat had got in, but she didn't think even his feline resourcefulness extended to opening locked doors. Then she peered closer and realised what must have happened: it was a self-latching door and whoever had last pushed it shut, hadn't made sure that it had clicked into place. The door must have swung ajar again in the breeze, and the cat had pushed it open easily.

She watched as the ginger tom slipped through the gap and out into the rear garden. She was about to shut the door after him when she heard him call insistently again.

"*N-ow! N-OW!*"

What on earth does he want? Poppy stepped outside. Night had almost completely fallen and the garden was just a mass of dark shapes moving in the breeze. She hesitated, then walked farther out, leaving the door wide open behind her so that light from the greenhouse would spill out. It didn't help much, barely penetrating more than a few feet, and seemed only to make the rest of the garden beyond even blacker.

Poppy walked to the edge of the light and peered out into the darkness. She could just make out the cat—a paler shape against the black background—a short distance away.

"*N-ow!*" he called again.

Poppy wished that she had a torch, but she couldn't be bothered to go back in to search for one; in any case, she didn't know if there was one in the cottage. Besides, her eyes were acclimatising a bit now and she could make out a bit of the darkened landscape around them: the big trees at the back, the large mounds of shrubbery around, and the straight lines of the rectangular cutting flowerbed, where the terrier had been digging earlier...

"*N-ow!*" came the insistent voice.

"All right, all right... I'm coming..." muttered Poppy, picking her way carefully through the weeds.

She saw that the cat was in the middle of the cutting flowerbed, his tail twitching impatiently. Climbing over the prickly stems of some kind of bushy plant, she stepped into the bed. The soil here was softer than she'd expected and she lost her balance as the loose earth settled beneath her weight. Poppy stumbled sideways, her ankle catching against a vine of some sort, and the next moment, she pitched forwards, facedown into the dirt.

"Ommpphh!"

She lay winded for a moment, then raised herself slowly onto her elbows. There was soil on her face, neck, clothes... She sat up and tried to brush it off. "Ugh!"

"*N-ow?*" said the ginger tom, coming over and eyeing her curiously.

"It's all your fault!" grumbled Poppy, pushing herself to her knees and attempting to stand up.

The crumbly earth beneath her made it difficult and she groped around for a handhold—anything to give her a bit of support. Her fingers scrabbled through the soil, brushing against fuzzy stems and floppy leaves, and then they encountered something soft and clammy.

Poppy recoiled with a gasp. It sounded crazy, but it had felt like... *skin.*

She panicked, scooting backwards on her bum and kicking up clods of earth everywhere. The ginger tom gave a hiss of annoyance and jumped out of the way.

"*N-ooow!*" he said, looking at her reproachfully.

The cat's cry brought her back to her senses and Poppy gave a sheepish laugh. *Of course, it can't be skin! What am I thinking?*

She peered at the bed in front of her, straining her eyes in the darkness. In the faint light spilling out from the greenhouse, she could see nothing other than mounds of disturbed earth, and a few broken flower stalks. She leaned forwards and poked the soil in a few places. There was a glint of metal—it was the tines of a little handheld garden fork which had been left in the bed—but nothing that resembled any part of a human body.

Poppy sat back. It must have been her overactive imagination. The lonely surroundings of the cottage, together with the wild, overgrown garden and Charles Mannering's anxiety had combined to create an eerie atmosphere that was putting sinister ideas in her head. Getting to her feet, she brushed herself off and stepped carefully out of the bed, making sure to avoid the vine that had tripped her previously. She turned back towards the cottage, but she hadn't gone two steps when that familiar plaintive wail came again:

"*N-ow! N-ooow!*"

She whirled around with an impatient sigh. "For goodness' sake, what do you want?"

The cat trotted over and sat down at her feet, looking up at her with wide, unblinking eyes. She stood at a loss for a moment. Was he lost? Hungry? She didn't have anything in the cottage to feed him, and besides, she was sure he was somebody's pet. She bent down to examine him again, and this time she realised that he *was* actually wearing a collar— a thin leather band with a small tag attached. She turned this over eagerly and peered at the engraved information. There was no name, just an address. She was surprised to see that it was the number right before the cottage on the lane. The ginger tom belonged to her next-door neighbour!

"*N-ow!*" he said again.

Poppy stood and looked at him indecisively, wondering what to do. She didn't have the heart to just walk into the cottage and shut the door in his face. She also didn't want him to stand out here, wailing "*N-ooow!*" all night.

She made a sweeping gesture with her hand. "Shoo... Go home!" she said.

"*N-ow...?*"

"Yes, now. Go home. Go on... it's just there, over that wall..." Poppy pointed.

"*N-ow? N-ow...?*"

Poppy sighed. On an impulse, she reached down and scooped the cat up. He squirmed for a moment, and then, to her surprise, settled in her arms and even began purring. She carried him into the cottage, through the house, and out the front door... heading for the lane and the house next door.

CHAPTER NINE

The ginger tom was a big boy and heavier than she'd expected. By the time Poppy got out of the garden gate, her arms were beginning to ache and she was breathing hard with effort. She lugged him up the lane until she reached the house right before Hollyhock Cottage. She must have walked past it when she arrived yesterday, but she had barely glanced at it. Now, Poppy looked around curiously as she carried the ginger tom up to its front entrance. The gleaming iron gate opened into neat landscaped grounds, with stone steps that led up to a raised porch and an elegant panelled front door in the Georgian style.

Poppy shifted the cat's weight in her arms and reached out to press the doorbell, hoping that the owners were home. Her heart sank as long minutes passed and no one came. She pressed on the doorbell again, craning her neck to look through the windows. With the curtains drawn, it was hard to see into the house, but it looked like lights were on in the interior—although that in itself didn't necessarily mean much. People could have left the lights on and gone out, or even have the switches attached to an automatic timer.

She was just reaching out to press the doorbell again when the door was flung open and a tall man loomed out of the threshold.

"YES?" he snapped.

Poppy stared. Flashing dark eyes, strong jaw, brooding mouth... It was Nick Forrest, the crime author. He was looking much more unkempt than the last time she'd seen him, with his shirt rumpled and open at the collar, and his dark hair tousled, as if he had been running his hand through it repeatedly.

"Oh! It's you!" she said stupidly.

He stared blankly at her.

"I met you at the bookshop—I mean, we didn't really meet, but that's where I saw you give a reading... I thought you lived in London—I didn't realise you lived in Oxfordshire..." Poppy trailed off as she realised that she was babbling. She lifted the ginger tom higher to show him. "Um... I brought your cat back."

"*What?*" he said in an irritable voice. Then his eyes fell on the ginger tom. "Oh, the bloody cat.

Chuck him inside." He indicated the hallway behind him with an impatient gesture.

Poppy was slightly taken aback but did as she was bid, setting the ginger tom down and giving him a gentle nudge towards the open door. The cat paused to lick a nonchalant paw, then trotted into the house without a backward glance at her. As soon as he was in, Nick Forrest gave her a curt nod, muttered something that sounded like "Thanks" but could equally have been "Pranks!" and retreated into the house, leaving her standing on the porch, staring at the closed door.

"Well... you're welcome!" muttered Poppy. *What a rude man!*

Turning, she stalked back to the cottage in a huff. This time, she made sure that all doors—front and back—were securely locked, then took herself off for a much-needed wash in the ancient bathtub. Despite the water not being very hot, the bath was more soothing than she'd expected, and she emerged from the bathroom feeling calmer and also suddenly very tired. It had been a long day, with a lot of excitement, and she felt emotionally drained.

As Poppy towelled her shoulder-length hair dry, she wondered half-heartedly about going to the village pub for dinner. She wasn't actually very hungry—the huge sandwich she had picked up in Oxford before getting on the bus was still making its presence felt in her stomach—and she decided that it wouldn't hurt to skip dinner for one night. There was a bar of chocolate in her handbag; she could simply have that and a hot cup of tea. *Nell would be horrified but she doesn't have to know*, thought Poppy with a grin.

She was standing in the kitchen, waiting for the kettle to boil, when she heard voices. A man and a woman. The deep male voice was one she instantly recognised; she could still hear the rich baritone weaving magic with words, conjuring vivid images in her mind. Then she remembered the same voice, irritable and impatient, and her expression soured. Still, almost against her will, Poppy drifted to the open kitchen window and pulled back the curtains to peer out.

From this angle, she could just catch a glimpse of the neighbouring property through the trees. It would have been too dark to see anything, except that Nick Forrest's porch and front garden were well lit with discreet spotlights. She could see him now, standing on the front steps. There was a woman with him—a slim, elegant figure who stretched up to give him a kiss, then turned and walked towards the front gate. The woman called something back to him and Nick answered, his deep voice carrying in the still night air.

"Thanks, Suzanne. I'll see you for dinner when I get back."

The woman called something in reply, then there was the sound of a car door slamming and, a few minutes later, the soft purr of an engine, which faded slowly into the night. Nick Forrest lingered for a moment on his front porch and Poppy pulled back, feeling suddenly like she was spying on him. It was silly—it wasn't as if he could see her, and besides, she wasn't *really* interested in what he was doing. She had just been idly curious, that was all. Still, she stood watching until Nick had gone back into the house and it was only the sound of the kettle boiling that pulled her away from the window.

Half an hour later, Poppy climbed into bed with a weary sigh, placed her head on the lumpy pillow, and promptly fell asleep. Her night was filled with confused dreams: ginger cats slinking between stacks of books, toppling them over one by one, and tramps having tea and scones beneath climbing roses... and all the while, Charles Mannering stood in the background, waving a property sales contract and shouting "*N-ow! N-ow!*"

Poppy awoke with a start and looked blearily at the bedroom window. From the weak light peeking through the curtains, she guessed that it was just before dawn. Turning over, she closed her eyes again, but sleep wouldn't come. She had gone to bed so early last night, it was not surprising that she was wide awake now. She sighed and rolled onto her back, and stared up at the ceiling's exposed wood beams.

For some reason, her thoughts kept reverting to that moment last night when she had been scrabbling in the soil and had felt something cold and clammy brush against her fingers. She knew it couldn't be skin—of course not—and yet she couldn't shake the memory of that sensation from her mind. It was like a sore tooth, niggling at her, refusing to be ignored.

Finally, she sat up. This was ridiculous. There was only one way to resolve it, once and for all. It was lighter now and she'd be able to see the garden bed much more clearly. She would go down and have a look again and reassure herself that it was just her overactive imagination.

Poppy dressed quickly and hurried through the cottage. As she stepped out of the back door, she paused for a moment, drinking in the scene in front of her. The dawn light bathed the garden in a soft grey haze, lending it an almost otherworldly feel. Morning dew sparkled like jewels on the twining stems of a vine growing near the cutting flowerbed. *That must have been what tripped me up last night*, Poppy realised. It had been planted at the base of an old wooden obelisk next to the bed, but with no one to tend it, it had outgrown its support and was spilling everywhere.

She picked her way carefully around the vine and stepped into the soft earth of the flowerbed, putting her arms out to steady herself. It was easy to see where she had been scrabbling in the soil last night—there were large scrape marks and kicked piles of soil, and a depression where she obviously lain. She crouched down and reached out to dig with her hands, trying to remember where she had been groping. It was here... near these flower stalks... She remembered feeling their soft floppy leaves and then...

Poppy jerked back.

She stared at the ground in front of her. The morning sunlight slanted over her shoulder, outlining something that was protruding from a mound of disturbed earth.

It was a human hand.

CHAPTER TEN

Poppy felt disbelief wash over her. No, it couldn't be true. She had to be dreaming. She closed her eyes for a moment, then opened them again. The hand was still there.

Slowly, she picked up the little garden fork she had noticed last night, then reached out and prodded the hand. It rolled sideways, then fell back limply.

Poppy swallowed. She gathered her courage and crawled a bit closer. She used the little garden fork to gingerly scrape the earth away. The hand was attached to an arm... and the arm belonged to a man...

A dead man, shallowly buried in the middle of the cutting flowerbed.

She stood up and stared down at the body. He

had been young—somewhere in his late twenties—just a few years older than her, perhaps. Poppy swallowed again. He was wearing rough work clothes and there was dirt under his nails, and healed scratches on his arms. He also wore a tool belt of some kind, with a small apron in front that had pockets for tools, and Poppy caught a glimpse of a coil of garden twine, and some kind of small rake. Had the man been a gardener? But what had he been doing here?

She continued staring, still with that sense of unreality. She knew she should do something—call for help, call the police, maybe even just scream—but it was as if she were paralysed. All she could think about was how she had slept, unknowing, in the cottage all night, whilst out here, a dead body lay waiting...

A hand came down on her shoulder.

Poppy screamed. She whirled around, then gasped with a mixture of surprise and relief as she recognised the tall man standing behind her.

"Oh! It's you!" she said, for the second time in twenty-four hours. "You scared me half to death!"

He didn't apologise, instead saying with a frown: "What are you doing here?"

"I..." Poppy opened her mouth, then paused, at a loss over how to say it. Instead, she stepped aside so that he could see for himself.

Nick Forrest started forwards, then jerked to a stop as he saw the body. He went very still.

"Do... do you know him?" Poppy asked.

He gave a curt nod. "It's Pete. Pete Sykes. He is—was—a sort of gardener-cum-general-handyman who helped Mary Lancaster around the nursery." He tilted his head, examining the body with an almost clinical detachment. "It looks like he might have been dead for a while"

He walked around the bed, giving the dead man a wide berth, and stopped when he reached the opposite side. Poppy watched as he bent to take a closer look at the back of the man's head.

"His head's been smashed in," Nick said tonelessly.

Poppy flinched. She didn't know how he could just stand there and say that so coolly. Then she remembered that he was a crime writer. Perhaps gory dead bodies were just a daily occurrence in the pages of his manuscripts.

"Do you think he was working out here and tripped and fell... and hit his head on something?" she asked.

"This was no accident."

Poppy gave a snort of laughter at his tone. "What—you're not suggesting that he was *murdered*?"

He didn't answer, but continued to observe the body, his keen gaze taking in every detail.

"Look, I know you're a crime writer and all that..." said Poppy impatiently. "But surely you're letting your imagination run away with you?

Murders are things that happen in books and movies, not in real life."

He looked up and raised a mocking, incredulous eyebrow.

"No, I mean..." Poppy stammered. "Okay, they do happen in real life. Of course they do. People do kill each other. But in gangland shootings or... or violent robberies... or even dangerous neighbourhoods in big cities! Not in a sleepy little English village. And besides, who would want to kill a gardener?"

"You might be surprised..." Nick murmured.

"What's that supposed to mean?"

"Nothing." He walked back around the body to join her.

"Well, if... if there's really been foul play, shouldn't we call the police?" said Poppy. She turned and started for the cottage. "I'll get my phone—"

"No, let me get mine." His voice was authoritative. "I'll call Suzanne."

"S-Suzanne?" spluttered Poppy, remembering the elegant woman from the night before. "This is no time to be calling your girlfriend!"

He threw her a sardonic look. "*Ex*-girlfriend, actually."

Then, without another word, he turned and strode away, disappearing around the side of the cottage. A few minutes later, Poppy heard the sound of the front gate slamming, and then his footsteps in the adjoining property. She stood fuming for a moment, wondering what to do. She had never met anyone so infuriating! Who did he think he was? Well, she wasn't going to stand here waiting for him, like a dog told to "Stay"—she was going to call the police herself!

Whirling, she rushed back into the cottage and hurried into the bedroom, where she rummaged around for her phone. Where had she put it? She was sure she had left it on the table by the bed... She'd sent Nell a quick text message before going to bed the night before—perhaps she had put it automatically back in her handbag without thinking? *Yes.* She found the phone in the depths of her handbag, but when she pulled it out, her face fell in dismay. It seemed to be completely dead. She shook it and jabbed the power button several times, but it remained unresponsive, the screen blank.

Poppy sighed. The phone was several years old— this model wasn't even available on the market anymore—and its battery had been playing up for months now, often discharging suddenly for no reason. She desperately needed to upgrade but a new phone was something she just couldn't afford at the moment.

Now she cursed under her breath and stood undecided in the middle of the bedroom. The cottage had no phone—she'd checked yesterday—so the only option was to go next door and ask Nick Forrest for the use of his. She hated the thought of having to ask him for anything, but there was no other choice. Gritting her teeth, she left the cottage and walked next door. She had barely climbed the front steps, however, when she bumped into Nick coming in out of his house. Making an effort to keep her voice neutral, she said:

"Uh... look, I really think we need to call the police first. I was wondering if I might borrow your phone—the battery on mine is dead—or maybe you'd like to call them yourself—"

"The police are on their way."

Poppy gaped at him. "Huh?"

"The police. They should be here in a few minutes."

"Oh." Poppy felt slightly mollified. "Oh... okay. Thanks for calling them. I suppose we ought to go back and wait by the body—"

"Did you touch anything?"

"No. Well, other than last night... I think I might have brushed against it by mistake." Poppy shuddered at the memory. At Nick's quizzical look, she told him what had happened, adding excitedly, "Your cat... now that I think about it... I think he was trying to tell me about the body! He kept meowing at me and trying to get me to go out into the back garden..."

Nick shrugged. "Perhaps. Humans have a tendency to anthropomorphise everything, though."

Poppy bristled. "I wasn't imagining it. Cats are supposed to be very clever—"

"Oh, I'm not doubting his intelligence," said Nick in a dry voice.

Poppy wondered if he was implying that he was doubting *hers*, and she bristled even more. "Well, I'm telling you, if it wasn't for your cat, I wouldn't have found the body. I would never have even known that it was there!"

"Why are you at the cottage anyway?"

"Oh... It's mine. I mean, I've inherited it. My name is Poppy Lancaster. I'm Mary Lancaster's granddaughter."

His eyebrows shot up. "I didn't know Mary had a grandchild."

Poppy tried not to sound defensive. "My mother was... er... estranged from her family so I never met my grandmother when she was alive."

His voice softened slightly. "I'm sorry... I just never heard Mary talk about a granddaughter—or even a daughter."

"Did you know her very well?"

He shrugged. "Well enough, I suppose."

"What was she like?"

Nick chuckled. "Difficult. Very stern, very proud. She didn't suffer fools gladly. She would have made a great character for a book," he added enthusiastically. "I often thought of creating a character inspired by her. In real life, though, I think her manner put a lot of people off—if it wasn't for the fact that she grew such fantastic plants, she'd probably have had no customers!"

"Oh…" Poppy digested this. "Did my grandfather run the nursery as well?"

He shook his head. "I never met him. I only bought this house about ten years ago. Your grandmother was widowed very young, I believe, and brought up your mother alone. She must have had a pretty tough life—it wouldn't have been easy for a woman to be a single mother in those days."

Especially with a daughter as wild and rebellious as Holly Lancaster had been, thought Poppy. Although she was still hurt and angry that Mary Lancaster had never made any effort at reconciliation, she began to think more charitably of the woman who had been her grandmother.

As if reading her thoughts, Nick Forrest added, "She could be very prickly and she was too proud and stubborn for her own good, but she was a good woman, Mary Lancaster. She always donated plants to welfare societies to help raise funds for charitable causes, and also often gave seedlings away for free to people on limited income. She was very generous to me too: she knew that visiting her garden always helped me a lot, especially when I'm wrestling with writer's block." He chuckled. "Something about the natural, unrestrained style of a cottage garden, I think. It seems to encourage creativity. Anyway, she invited me to go over any time I liked."

"Oh… is that why you were there so early this morning?" asked Poppy.

"Yes, I've hit a snag in the plot and it's been

driving me crazy. I was working on it until late last night, then woke up early this morning and couldn't sleep. I thought a walk there might help to clear my head."

He hesitated, then cleared his throat and added gruffly, "I'm sorry if I was a bit brusque with you last night. You came over just when I was deep in a scene that I've had to rewrite several times already. I'm... er... not in the best of moods when I'm writing, especially if things are not going well."

Bloody hell, you could say that again, thought Poppy. A T-Rex with a sore head would have seemed friendly compared to him last night. Still, she acknowledged the apology and said dryly, "I'm beginning to see why you liked my grandmother. You seem to be kindred antisocial souls."

He tossed his head back and laughed, and Poppy was surprised by the change in him—with the brooding expression gone and his dark eyes alight with humour, he radiated unexpected charm.

Nick grinned. "Yes, we understood each other. We both liked our solitude and just wanted people to leave us in peace—her to her plants and me to my writing."

Poppy started to answer but was interrupted by the sound of an engine. She turned to look out at the lane, expecting to see police cars, but instead she saw a sleek grey Audi pull up in front of the house. An elegant, dark-haired woman emerged and came swiftly through the iron gate and up the front steps to join them. It was the lady she had seen with Nick last night.

She smiled at Poppy and held a hand out. "I'm Detective Inspector Suzanne Whittaker. I believe you found the body? I'd appreciate it if I could ask you a few questions."

CHAPTER ELEVEN

"...and can you remember what time you arrived at the cottage yesterday?"

Poppy frowned and shook her head. "Sorry. I don't remember exactly. I caught the two-thirty bus from Oxford and it stopped at a lot of places. It was definitely mid- to late afternoon. Maybe three-thirty... four o'clock... thereabouts?"

"And you saw nothing unusual when you first arrived?"

"No... but I don't know if I would have noticed if something *was* 'unusual'. This is the first time I've visited so I don't know what the cottage normally looks like. There weren't any smashed windows or broken locks, if that's what you're asking."

Suzanne Whittaker flashed her an appreciative look. "Yes, that *is* what I was getting at." She glanced down at her notes. "But you said later you *did* see a man trying to break in?"

"Yes, that was probably around an hour after I'd arrived. I was out the back, by the cutting flowerbed, and I heard the sound of breaking glass at the front, so I came around the front to investigate. He was standing by one of the windows and he had a sort of chisel-thing in his hand. He looked like he was trying to force the window open."

"Did you get a look at his face? Would you be able to identify him again?"

Poppy hesitated. "I... I'm not sure. He ran as soon as he saw me. I did catch a glimpse of his face and I *think* I would recognise him again, but... well, it was such a brief look, I can't be certain." She paused, then asked: "Do you think maybe that's what happened? Maybe Pete Sykes interrupted someone else trying to break in and got in a fight with them?"

Suzanne shook her head. "It's too soon to draw any conclusions, really. However, it seems likely that Sykes was struck on the head by a heavy tool— perhaps one of the large spades or garden forks in the greenhouse at the back of the cottage. So if you're telling me that the house was all locked up, with no signs of a break-in, then perhaps the murder weapon came from somewhere else."

"Or the murderer had the keys to the cottage!" said Poppy excitedly. "I just remembered something! When I went to Oxford yesterday to pick up the keys from the lawyer's office, the secretary couldn't find them. She had to give me the spare set from the office safe."

"Really?" Suzanne perked up. "That's very interesting. I'd been planning to speak to Charles Mannering shortly. As executor of the estate, he will have dealt with Pete Sykes and I was hoping he could give me more information about the dead man. I will certainly bring this up with him."

They were standing together beside the garden gate, and now Suzanne glanced towards the cottage and the back of the property. The cutting flowerbed was hidden from view by the building of the cottage itself, but Poppy could see part of the rear garden and several men in white overalls busily walking about.

Suzanne followed her gaze and said: "We'll know more once the forensics team have had a chance to process the crime scene. They will probably test each of the tools in the greenhouse for traces of human hair or tissue."

Poppy grimaced and marvelled at how Suzanne—like Nick Forrest—seemed able to talk so coolly about such gruesome details. Well, perhaps it was not surprising. As a member of the CID, Suzanne probably spent her days immersed in rapes, murders, and other serious crimes.

"Are you staying at the cottage?" Suzanne asked. "I understand that you own it now."

"Well..." Poppy hesitated. "Yes, sort of, although I

had originally been planning to head back to London today. My things are still there, you see. I'd only meant to stay one night at first, just to see what it was like."

"I'd be obliged if you could remain in Oxfordshire for the next few days at least," said Suzanne. "Do you have any friends or family nearby? Somewhere where you can stay for a while? I'm afraid you can't stay in the cottage while it's still a designated crime scene."

Poppy shook her head. "I don't know anyone hereabouts. I'd have to go to a hotel and the expense—"

Suzanne snapped her fingers. "I'll tell you what: I'll ask Nick if you can stay in one of his spare rooms. That way, you're just next door and can return easily to the cottage as soon as we're done."

"Oh no, I don't think—"

"I'm sure he won't mind. He's rattling around in that huge house by himself anyway. And he probably won't even notice that you're there—he's in a world of his own when he's deep in a manuscript," said Suzanne, chuckling and rolling her eyes. "Give me a moment to speak to the forensics team and then I'll ring him."

Poppy started to protest again, but Suzanne had already turned and walked away. She huffed with frustration. Nick Forrest had given a brief statement and left shortly after the police arrived, probably to return to his beloved manuscript. The last thing she wanted to do was impose on his solitude and she hated the thought of having to beg him for any kind of favour.

Still… Poppy's practical side asserted itself: she had to admit that it made sense and would save money. If she insisted on returning to London each night, there would be the costs of the train tickets, not to mention the hassle and time spent going back and forth, and the only other option was to spend the night in a hotel or B&B.

Suzanne took longer than expected briefing the rest of her team, and Poppy waited impatiently, conscious of a nagging hollow feeling in her stomach. In all the excitement since finding the body, she hadn't had a chance to think about breakfast and now she realised that she was starving. She hadn't had anything to eat since the chocolate bar last night and her stomach was protesting loudly.

Finally, Suzanne returned, holding her phone and looking pleased. "I've just spoken to Nick and it's settled. He's actually going away on a book tour tomorrow so the house will be empty anyway—in fact, you'll be doing him a favour, if you don't mind feeding his cat?"

"Oh, of course," said Poppy.

"Great," said Suzanne enthusiastically. "He's out this evening but I've got a spare key anyway." She glanced at her watch, then added, "If you can hang on for a bit, I'll take you over myself after I finish—"

"Actually... do you mind if I pop into the village to get some food first?" Poppy gave her a sheepish grin. "I haven't had anything to eat since last night and I'm starving."

"Oh Lord, yes. I'm sorry, I hadn't realised the time. Yes, you go and get some lunch. In fact, if you have a word with the landlord at The Lucky Ladybird, he'll put your meal on the police tab. It's the least we can do for kicking you out of the cottage," said Suzanne with a smile.

"Thanks—that's really kind of you," said Poppy, pleasantly surprised.

"And take your time, don't worry about rushing back—I'll be here..." Suzanne gestured to the back of the cottage.

***

The Lucky Ladybird was the quintessential English country pub and when Poppy arrived, she found the large, timber-framed interior already filled with locals, all buzzing with gossip about the murder. Like many villages, Bunnington had a thriving grapevine and it seemed that the residents already knew as much about the case as the police... probably more!

"...likely to be some kind of gang, I shouldn't wonder. Pete Sykes always looked like the type who would get mixed up with the wrong sort," said one middle-aged woman with a knowing look.

"Yes, I always thought so too!" said her friend, not to be outdone. "Came over to help me do some weeding once and kept offering to sell me a bunch of iPhones for cheap. All the latest models too. Where did he get them, I ask you? Wouldn't give me a straight answer when I asked him. Fell off the back of a lorry, no doubt."

The third woman at the table shook her head. "I think it was drugs. It's always drugs. D'you know, I read in the papers that drug dealers even have loyalty cards these days—like your Tesco's Clubcard—and they give you a free gram of cocaine after five orders... can you believe it?"

A man called out from the counter by the bar: "No, no, no... I'll tell you who murdered Pete Sykes: his missus, that's who."

"His missus?" The three women turned to looked at him sceptically. "What, Jenny Sykes?"

"Aye. Wanted a divorce, didn't she? But Pete wouldn't give her one."

"How d'you know that?" demanded the first woman.

The man smirked "I keep my ears open."

"But why would she want to leave him?" asked the second woman.

"She was shagging another bloke, what else?"

"Get out! Jenny Sykes? She was Pete's high school sweetheart, wasn't she? She'd never even *look* at another man."

"That's not what *I* heard," said the man with a

smug expression. "I heard that Jenny is a right little tart who—" He broke off suddenly as he noticed Poppy standing near them and turned to her with a wide smile. "Well, hello... hello! Haven't seen you around the village, miss. You visiting?"

"Er... yes, sort of." Poppy hesitated, then decided that if she was going to stay at the cottage, even for a little while, she should make some effort to befriend the locals. "I'm staying at Hollyhock Cottage."

One of the women raised her eyebrows. "You the new owner? Have they sold that place already?"

"Last I heard, old Mannering had some property developer lined up to bulldoze the place," her friend added. "Turn it into posh townhouses."

"Oh no—I heard that he's trying to sell it as a gardening business," the third woman said.

Wow, thought Poppy. *The village grapevine really is something!* Still, she was surprised that they hadn't guessed who *she* was. She would have thought the villagers would know all about the unusual terms of Mary's will and the search for the long-lost granddaughter to take over the family business. Perhaps old Mannering *was* more discreet than she'd given him credit for.

"No," she said aloud. "Actually, I'm Mary Lancaster's granddaughter and I've come to stay at the cottage for a while."

The women all turned and regarded her with bright-eyed interest, and Poppy tried not to squirm under their avid gaze.

"Mary Lancaster's granddaughter? Well, I never!" said the first woman, her eyes wide.

"I didn't know she had any family. Well, other than that nephew—you know, the real estate chap. I thought *he* inherited the place," said her friend.

The man by the bar counter spoke up again: "*I* knew she had a daughter... but Mary would never talk about her. What was her name? Harriet? Hayley?"

"Holly," Poppy supplied. "Yes, she was my mother."

"Was?" said the first woman sharply.

"She passed away last year. She had breast cancer."

"Oh no... I'm sorry, luv."

"How awful! You poor child!"

Poppy was touched by their genuine sympathy. They might have been nosy gossips, but their hearts were in the right place. They fussed over her now, inviting her to sit with them and asking her if she'd had lunch, then calling the pub owner to take her order. By the time the food came, and Poppy was able to tuck into a hearty plate of fish 'n' chips, she found that the crowd of curious villagers around her had doubled in size. She was pleased to discover, however, that several of the newcomers were from the older generation and that they remembered her mother. She asked eagerly for their recollections, keen to learn more about the early childhood that her mother would never talk about.

"Yes, I remember Holly," said one elderly lady. "A real handful, she was. Always staying out late and giving Mary no end of grief."

Another white-haired lady nodded. "She was never happy to stay at the cottage and help out in the nursery, like Mary wanted her to. Terrible scandal, it was, when she ran off to join those other girls—you know, the kind that follow musicians around... what are they called? Guppies?"

"Groupies," someone piped up.

"Yes, that's right. I remember that!" the first elderly lady cried. "And then she came back a year later, proud as you please, and announced that she was having a baby! Barely seventeen, she was... and no idea who the father was, of course."

There were tutting sounds and looks of disapproval in the crowd.

"Oh, she knew who the father was," the second old lady said. "She just wouldn't say."

"Do *you* know? Did you ever find out?" asked Poppy breathlessly.

To her disappointment, the old lady shook her head.

"I'm surprised Mary didn't force it out of her and make the boy marry her," said the man at the bar counter. "Real old-fashioned, she was. Must have been her worst nightmare to have her daughter have a baby out of wedlock."

"Well, personally, I feel sorry for the daughter,"

said one of the original three women who had invited Poppy to their table. "Can you imagine what it was like having Mary for a mother? It'd be like living in a nunnery! Up at dawn, plain porridge for breakfast, and then a day of back-breaking work weeding and digging in the garden."

"Yes, and Mary had such strict standards," said her friend, shaking her head. "I remember being at the nursery once when Pete Sykes was doing some work for her and she made him dig up all forty bulbs that he had planted and start again, just because they weren't evenly spaced enough for her liking."

"It's no wonder the girl never wanted to stay home with a mother like that," declared the first woman. Then, as if she suddenly remembered that Mary's granddaughter was sitting at the same table, she flushed and glanced at Poppy, adding hastily, "But she was wonderful with plants. Mary grew the best plants I'd ever seen. So big and healthy... and blooming continuously."

"Yes," her friend agreed. "Her hollyhocks were amazing. I don't know how she did it. Over six feet tall, flowering the first year—and not a speck of rust on them, even though she never sprayed!"

"So are you going to take over your grandmother's nursery?" the first woman asked Poppy with a smile. "It'd be wonderful to be able to buy plants in Bunnington again, instead of having to drive out to one of those big garden centres."

"Er... Well, I..." Poppy felt like the whole room was looking at her expectantly, waiting for her answer. "I'm not sure," she said at last, giving them an embarrassed smile. "I... er... I don't think I've inherited my grandmother's green fingers."

"Nonsense!" said the elderly lady who had spoken about her mother. "The Lancasters have always been fantastic with plants. It's in their blood. You've been a city girl so far, haven't you? Well, you just need to get out there in the garden and get your hands dirty. It'll come to you. You'll see."

CHAPTER TWELVE

After lunch, Poppy dawdled in the village for a while, wandering down the high street and checking out the various shops and businesses. She'd hoped to pick up a few essentials for her extended stay (such as extra underwear!), but aside from the village post office shop and a little Co-op supermarket selling mostly fresh food and produce, the rest of the establishments seemed to cater more to tourists: there was an art gallery, an antique shop, a gift shop selling knick-knacks and souvenirs, another selling handmade soaps, creams, and lotions made from locally grown herbs, a small inn providing "bed and breakfast" services next to a larger hotel with a posh-looking restaurant, and an ancient mill that now doubled as the local tourist information centre.

Poppy wandered back to Hollyhock Cottage at last and found the forensics team still combing the property. A young police constable had been posted at the gate to keep back the crowd of nosy villagers and tourists. She assumed that Suzanne was still in the cottage and was about to go up to the constable to announce herself, when she changed her mind and decided to take a stroll farther down the lane instead.

As she walked beyond Hollyhock Cottage, Poppy realised that the lane was actually a cul-de-sac, with a dead end just a few hundred metres farther down from the cottage garden gate. She was also surprised to find that there was another house tucked beyond the cottage, just before the end of the cul-de-sac. It was a small, run-down affair, mostly hidden by an overgrown hedge.

She went up to the hedge and stood on tiptoe to peer over the top. She saw a modest garden with a threadbare patch of grass and a few straggly bushes. Beyond that was an old house, with roof slates wanting repair and the walls needing painting. *Who lives here?* she wondered. As if in answer to her question, she heard an excited little bark, followed by the rumble of a man's voice in admonishment. The sounds seemed to be coming from the back of the garden, on the side which shared the wall with her grandmother's property.

Curiosity gripped her. Poppy stretched up even more on the tips of her toes and strained to see, but that side of the garden was shaded by a row of trees growing alongside the stone wall and it was hard to make out anything in their dappled gloom. She lowered herself with a frustrated sigh, then brightened as she noticed a gap to her right, just where the hedge met the corner of the stone wall. She bent down to peer through the gap, leaning forwards and sticking her head and shoulders through the hedge to try and get a better view.

As her eyes slowly acclimatised, she saw a familiar scruffy shape. It was the little black terrier she had seen fighting with the ginger tom on the first day. He seemed to be doing an odd little dance next to the stone wall, running backwards and forwards, panting excitedly and making bouncing movements—like a dog waiting excitedly outside a door for its owner. A moment later, to Poppy's surprise, a figure emerged out of the wall. She blinked and rubbed her eyes. No, she hadn't been imagining it. Where previously there had been just a dog, now there was a man standing next to him— an old man, with dishevelled clothes and unkempt grey hair.

He was clutching a large object wrapped in heavy burlap and his movements were quick and furtive. As she watched, he said something to the dog, then hurried around the back of the house, out of sight, with the little terrier trotting after him. Poppy stared at the empty space where he had been. *How had he emerged from the wall like that?*

Her curiosity really piqued now, she climbed through the gap in the hedge and straightened up on the other side. Keeping a wary eye on the back of the house, around which the old man had disappeared, she crept along the wall until she reached the place where she had seen him emerge. There, she discovered the reason behind his strange, sudden appearance: there was a large hole at the base of the wall, where one of the limestone slabs had crumbled away.

She crouched down and looked through the opening: on the other side, a tall, bushy plant with long stalks bearing white domes of lace-like flowers was growing right in front of the hole, so that it would only be visible if you leaned sideways and looked behind the plant. Any casual passer-by would never know that the gap in the wall was there. Through the leafy stalks and the tangled foliage beyond, Poppy could just catch a glimpse of Hollyhock Cottage: the side of the greenhouse attached to the back of the house and part of the rear flowerbed, where the body had been found.

The sound of voices came to her ears; one sounded familiar—she thought it might be Suzanne Whittaker—and the other was a woman's voice she didn't recognise. Poppy shifted slightly so that she could see better through the hole in the wall and caught sight of two figures standing beside the flowerbed. One was the detective inspector, the other a young woman with bleached blonde hair and the kind of figure that would have been described as "buxom" in the old days. Their voices carried clearly across the quiet of the garden and Poppy realised that Suzanne was questioning the young woman.

"...an' he said he'd be out late so not to wait up for him, so I said all right, but I'd leave a sandwich in the fridge, so he could have that if he came home an' felt peckish. An' that's the last time I spoke to Pete." The woman sniffed loudly and Poppy saw the flash of red nail varnish as she dabbed a tissue to her eyes.

"Did he seem normal when you spoke to him, Mrs Sykes?"

"How d'you mean?"

"Well, did he sound agitated or angry or upset about anything?"

Jenny Sykes shook her head. "No, he was jus' like always."

"Did he say why he was going to be late?"

She shrugged. "Jus' said he had some stuff to finish up at the cottage."

"But Mary Lancaster is dead and, as far as I understand, the nursery has been shut for months now, ever since she'd taken ill, so what could he have been doing here?" Suzanne cast a disparaging glance at the overgrown landscape around her. "I doubt he was doing any garden maintenance."

"Um... he used to meet people here sometimes."

Suzanne raised her eyebrows. "People?"

Jenny Sykes shifted uncomfortably. "Yeah, you know, like customers."

"You mean, people coming to buy plants?" asked Suzanne incredulously.

"No, not plants. For other stuff. You know, like... like tobacco and cigarettes and mobile phones and things..."

Suzanne's face hardened. "Ah... you mean, stolen goods and contraband."

"Pete didn't steal them!" said Jenny. "He told me he jus' had the chance to get things for cheap sometimes, an' he liked to pass the saving on to locals who deserved it."

Suzanne's expression made it clear what she thought of this story, but she didn't comment. Instead, she said, "So do you know who Pete was meeting the night before last?"

Jenny shook her head. "No, he never told me much 'bout his customers."

Suzanne asked casually, "And you, Mrs Sykes, where were you that night?"

Jenny stiffened. "I... I was at home, watching the telly."

"The entire night? You didn't go out?"

"Yeah. I mean, no, I didn't."

"Is there anyone who can confirm that?"

Jenny shifted her weight. "Uh... not really. I was jus' at home, by myself."

Suzanne considered her in silence for a moment, then said, "It's strange that you didn't raise the alarm when Pete didn't come home yesterday morning. Even if you'd gone to bed first, you must have noticed in the morning that the sandwich you'd left him was untouched. Weren't you worried?"

Jenny shrugged. "He's done it before: gone out all night an' not come home till suppertime the next day. Sometimes he crashes here at the cottage instead of bothering to come home, especially if he'd had a pint or two at the pub... I jus' thought he was doing the same thing again. It wasn't till last night, when he didn't come home again—an' I hadn't heard from him all day—that I started to wonder..."

"And yet you still didn't call the police," Suzanne said.

"I... I wasn't sure if... I mean, maybe Pete was jus' tied up with something an' he wouldn't have been happy if I made a fuss... you know, bothered the police an' all that..."

"In other words, he might have been involved in a shady deal and wouldn't have thanked you for bringing him onto the police radar."

Jenny just shrugged again and said nothing. There was a long silence, then Suzanne said at last, her voice brisk and business-like:

"Well, thank you for coming to ID the body, Mrs Sykes. I may have some more questions for you... You're not planning to leave the area, are you? Good. I'll be in touch. Now, one of my constables will see you home. Perhaps while he's there, he can go in and have a look at Pete's..."

Suzanne's voice faded as the two women turned and retreated into the cottage. Poppy leaned through the gap, trying to catch the last of Suzanne's words, then froze as she heard the crunch of footsteps in the undergrowth behind her.

A quavering voice growled: "Who are you? What are you doing here?"

CHAPTER THIRTEEN

Poppy whirled around. She found herself facing the old man she'd seen earlier. She gasped as she saw the sinister-looking black rifle he held in his hands.

"I... I... my name's Poppy... I just... I'm sorry, I didn't mean to trespass... I happened to see... um... and I wondered how you... anyway, don't worry, I won't tell the police that you were sneaking in... not that I'm suggesting you were doing anything underhand... *ah-hahaha*—" she babbled, "—right, I'm sure you've got things you want to get back to so... um... I'll just go back the way I came..." She started to edge sideways but jerked to a stop again as the old man waved the rifle.

"Don't move!" he cried.

"Okay! Okay!" gasped Poppy, flinging her hands

up in the traditional gesture of surrender. "Just don't shoot me!"

"Eh?" The old man looked at her quizzically, then his gaze dropped to his hands and his face brightened. "Ohhh... This isn't a gun—it's my Loo Blaster!"

"Your Loo *what?*"

"Loo Blaster. I was just testing it out..." said the old man, thrusting the rifle towards her. Poppy flinched, then slowly relaxed as she eyed the gun. On closer inspection, she realised that the barrel was wider than normal and there was a bushy toilet brush protruding from the muzzle.

"It's my latest invention," said the old man proudly. "It's a rifle with ejectable toilet brush heads—see? So you can dispose of the brush each time, after you clean the loo, and load a fresh one for next time." He leaned forwards earnestly. "Do you know how much bacteria resides in the average toilet brush? It's absolutely filthy! All those bristles, clogged up with urine and faecal matter... just the perfect breeding ground for bacteria and other nasties!" He waved the rifle wildly. "Aha... but never fear, now we have a new weapon in the lavatorial battle! This will revolutionise toilet hygiene—look, I designed all the details myself. It has a telescopic sight for precision aim in the toilet bowl and a one-piece trigger lock mechanism—finely tuned, of course, so that the pull will fit a variety of hand sizes—and an easy way to clamp in the toilet brush.

You can even do it one-handed," he said, beaming.

Poppy stared at him, wondering if she was having a hallucination.

"Um... right..." she said. "Er... well, if you're not going to shoot me, why did you tell me not to move?"

"Oh! Because you were going to step right into some stinging nettles," said the old man, pointing to the ground next to her.

Poppy looked down and realised that he was right: she was standing next to a big clump of leafy stalks, each covered in prickly hairs. Hastily, she took a step back and gratefully accepted the old man's hand as he helped her out of the overgrown tangle beside the stone wall.

"Nasty things, those plants—although I have to say, they can have their uses. They've been used since ancient times, for medicine and food, did you know that? And their fibre can be spun to make clothes—hmm, I've been thinking about experimenting with that..." He held up his forefinger excitedly. "Maybe a fabric where the stinging needles haven't been removed! It would make a marvellous protective bodysuit, don't you think?"

Poppy looked at the strange old man beside her, with his twinkling eyes and infectious grin, and couldn't help liking him. He seemed completely mad, but harmless with it, and when he invited her back to his house for a cup of tea, she found herself accepting.

The inside of the house was in shambles, with strange contraptions in every corner and laboratory equipment littered all over the kitchen counter, dining table, and every other available surface. The little terrier rushed over to meet them as soon as they stepped in, his suspicious growl and raised hackles transforming into excited whines and a wagging tail as he recognised Poppy. He jumped up and danced around on his hind legs, waving his front paws in the air and making her laugh.

"That's enough, Einstein... You show the nice young lady your manners now," said the old man.

"*Ruff!*" the dog replied and trotted over to Poppy, sitting obediently in front of her.

"I think I met Einstein yesterday morning," said Poppy with a smile as she crouched down to pat the terrier. "He was in the cottage garden next door, having an argument with a big ginger tom. He disappeared all of a sudden and I couldn't work out where he had gone to. Now I know—he must have used that gap in the wall as his personal doggie door to come back here."

"Ah yes, Einstein can be very naughty like that. Always running off and getting into places he shouldn't." He looked vaguely around. "Now... where did I put the teapot...?"

Poppy glanced up and spotted a teapot balanced precariously on top of a test tube rack, next to a glass flask in which some bright pink liquid was bubbling ominously. "Er... is that it?"

The old man turned to look and smiled in delight. "Oh yes, that's right—I was using it this morning to brew some explosive washing-up liquid. It's a special blend I'm developing. Don't worry..." he said at Poppy's look of alarm. "I'll rinse it out thoroughly. Now, what would you like to have, dear? I have English breakfast tea, peppermint tea, curry leaf tea, broccoli tea... and there's still a bit of mushroom tea left, I think—"

"Just normal English breakfast tea would be great," said Poppy hastily.

She watched askance as he boiled the kettle and filled the teapot. When she finally accepted her cup, she sipped it with some trepidation. After a few swallows, she paused to see if her stomach would erupt in a soapy explosion, and when it didn't, she relaxed slightly.

"Do you live here alone?" she asked.

"Yes, yes, it's just Einstein and me," said the old man, leaning down to give the terrier an affectionate pat. "But don't worry, we keep busy... very busy... Haven't even popped into the village yet... We're not lonely, are we?" he said to the little dog.

Poppy looked at the old man thoughtfully. If he was scurrying around at odd hours, gathering things for his strange experiments, and hadn't introduced himself properly to the villagers, it wasn't surprising that they viewed him with suspicion. In fact, she was pretty sure now that he was the "tramp" that Charles Mannering had said was seen lurking about.

"Did you hear about the body found next door?" she asked.

"Eh? Body?" He looked bemused.

"Yes, a man's been murdered—Pete Sykes, the gardener who used to work here. Did you know him?"

He shook his head. "No, I'm afraid I haven't had the pleasure. I only moved here a few weeks ago... Dear me, murdered, you say? But why?"

"I think that's what the police are trying to find out. Have they been round to speak to you yet?"

The old man frowned. "Hmm... now that you mention it, the doorbell did ring earlier... but I was in the middle of a fungus replicator experiment, you see, and I didn't want to take my eyes off the medium to answer the door..."

"Oh well, I'm sure they'll be back." Poppy looked at him enquiringly. "I don't suppose you noticed anything unusual or out of the ordinary the night before last?"

He furrowed his brow, deep in thought for several minutes, then sat up excitedly and said: "I got up after midnight to go to the loo and happened to look out of the window... and I spotted a DSO!"

Poppy frowned. "What's a DSO?"

"Deep Space Object. They are normally only visible using telescopes but there are a few that can be seen with the naked eye—you know, star clusters, nebulae and such—and I'm positive that I saw the fifth-magnitude Phi from the NGC 457 cluster in Cassiopeia. That's a constellation, in case you didn't know, dear," he added kindly. "It was a most exciting moment! I think I saw the whole cluster—which is an amazing feat using just averted vision." He beamed at her.

Poppy stared at the old man. *Oh boy. The police are going to have great fun questioning him.* Thoughts of the police reminded her that Suzanne was still waiting for her return and she stood up.

"Thanks very much for the tea but I'm afraid I have to go now. I need to speak to Inspector Whittaker—"

"Oh, what a shame, but do come again, dear... any time you like," he said, jumping up as well. "Oh, bless me! We haven't been properly introduced!" He held a gnarled hand out and said, with charming old-fashioned formality, "My name is Dr Bertram Noble—but you can call me Bertie. How do you do?"

Poppy smiled, putting her hand in his. "And I'm Poppy—Poppy Lancaster. It's lovely to meet you."

"You *will* come back, won't you?" he said, sounding slightly forlorn. In spite of his protests, Bertie looked suddenly very much like a lonely old man. "I haven't had a chance to show you my ultrasonic rat repeller yet," he said with a shy smile.

CHAPTER FOURTEEN

Suzanne Whittaker was deep in conversation with the young constable when Poppy got back to the cottage gate.

"Ah, you're back..." Suzanne smiled at her. "I've got a moment free now, so I can take you over to Nick's place, if you like?"

As they walked together, Poppy thought of the gossip she'd overheard in the village pub and wondered how she could tell Suzanne about Jenny Sykes's affair without revealing that she'd eavesdropped on their conversation.

"Um... so has Pete's wife come to identify the body?" she asked casually.

Suzanne gave her a sharp look. "Yes, she just left actually. Why do you ask?"

"Oh, nothing... I just wondered if she might have

told you anything useful."

"She gave me a bit of background," said Suzanne noncommittally.

Poppy hesitated, then blurted: "Did you know that Jenny Sykes had wanted a divorce and Pete wouldn't give it to her?"

Suzanne raised her eyebrows. "Where did you hear that?"

"I heard the villagers talking about them when I was having lunch at the pub just now. They think she killed him because she was having an affair."

"I'm not sure we can rely on village gossip as evidence of a murder motive," said Suzanne dryly. Then she smiled and added, "But it's certainly worth knowing that the Sykes' marriage may have been under strain. Thank you for passing it on. I will check up on that."

"If it wasn't her, do you think it could have been someone he was meeting that night? A 'customer'?"

"It's too early for me to think anything, really. It's certainly suggestive... The forensic reports should give us more information."

Her tone suggested that she wasn't willing to speculate further about the investigation and Poppy let the subject drop. As they approached the front steps of Nick's house, Poppy heard a familiar cry:

"N-ow... N-ow!"

There was a rustle in the neatly clipped hedge lining the path and, a minute later, a ginger tomcat stepped out in front of them. Suzanne paused to give him a scratch behind the ears, saying, "Looks like Oren has come to welcome you."

"Oren? That's an unusual name."

"It means 'orange' in Welsh, I believe. Nick's family were originally from Wales."

"Oh. I thought a writer's cat would have a more literary name—you know, like a character from Shakespeare or a Charles Dickens novel or something," said Poppy.

Suzanne laughed. "Well, Oren was called Dorito when Nick adopted him from the shelter, so almost any name would have been literary in comparison. Actually, I think most of the time, Nick calls him 'you bloody cat!'. They have a funny relationship. They're two peas in a pod, really—Nick likes getting his own way and Oren does too, and both can be as stubborn as the other. It makes for some fireworks sometimes! I used to tease Nick that they're like two grumpy old men living together."

Poppy looked curiously at the woman next to her. Suzanne spoke so warmly and easily of Nick, you could almost believe that they were still together. Was it normal to be so friendly with your ex? Poppy wished that she dared ask about the nature of their relationship. Instead, she asked:

"Do you live in the village as well? I was surprised when Nick called you instead of the police... and you arrived so quickly too."

"No, I live on the outskirts of Oxford, but it's only about twenty minutes away by car. Actually less...

probably fifteen, when there's no traffic in the early hours." She smiled. "And Nick knew that I would probably be notified anyway if there was a suspicious death discovered in this area. He was just cutting to the chase, instead of wasting time going through Emergency services. That's typical Nick... he can be very impatient."

The door of the house was suddenly flung open and the man they had been talking about loomed in the doorway. He looked very different from the last time Poppy had seen him: in a black dinner jacket and bow tie, he looked more suave British spy than reclusive author. His hair, though, was as unruly as ever and he ran a hand distractedly through it, messing it up even more, as he surveyed them on the doorstep.

"Oh, it's you," he said without much enthusiasm. "Well, come in. I'm just about to leave for Oxford." He stepped aside to let them pass but Suzanne held back.

"I'll leave Poppy with you, Nick—I've got to get back to the crime scene." She turned to Poppy with a smile. "In fact, you're doing me a favour: Nick had asked me to feed Oren while he was away and I was going to pop in every day, but things are going to be crazy now, with the extra work from this new murder, so it'll be a relief if I don't have to worry about Oren as well. Here—" She handed over the spare keys to the house. "You can have these. I'll catch you both later!"

With a wave, she was gone, leaving them standing on the doorstep. There was an awkward silence, then Poppy cleared her throat and said stiffly:

"Thanks again for letting me stay... um... I know it must be very disruptive when you're trying to write..."

Nick made an impatient noise. "It's fine. The house is more than big enough for two and I needed someone to feed Oren anyway. Just as long as you don't expect me to entertain you—I don't talk to anyone when I'm writing."

Poppy flushed and started to reply, but he had already turned and was striding away down the hall, calling over his shoulder:

"Come on—I'll show you to your room."

The guest bedroom was nicer than anywhere Poppy had ever stayed before. Decorated in soothing earth tones, with Scandinavian furniture and quality fabrics, it exuded style and class. She set her few belongings on the bed, then followed Nick back downstairs to the large modern kitchen.

"Glasses and cups in here... cutlery... plates..." Nick stopped in the act of pointing around the kitchen and made that impatient sound again. "Well, you can just find things for yourself." He nodded at the fridge in the corner. "And help yourself to any food and drink. I haven't got anything prepared for dinner but I'm sure you can rustle up something—"

Poppy flushed again. "Oh, I wasn't expecting—I mean, it's very kind of you already to let me stay. I wouldn't want to impose by eating your food as well."

He raked her with an amused glance. "You're only a slip of a thing. I doubt you'd eat me out of house and home. Anyway, I wouldn't want Suzanne accusing me of starving her prime witness."

He turned and led the way out of the kitchen, leaving Poppy no choice but to follow. They went on a brief tour of the house, finishing up in the spacious sitting room which featured a sleek marble fireplace and large French doors overlooking a manicured lawn.

Gesturing to the bookcases lining the walls, Nick said: "If you're a TV addict, you're out of luck—I don't have a television—but there's plenty to read. Oh, that reminds me..."

He walked over to one of the bookcases and withdrew three large hardback volumes, then brought them over to where Poppy was standing.

"These belonged to your grandmother. She lent them to me and I never had a chance to give them back after she became ill... I suppose they're yours now. You might like to take them back to the cottage."

"Oh... thanks..." Poppy staggered slightly as she took the heavy volumes in her arms. Hastily, she set them down on a nearby console table. There was an enormous tome of over seven hundred pages—a plant encyclopaedia, listing hundreds of flowers, bushes, trees, shrubs, vegetables, and herbs in alphabetical order—as well as two slimmer volumes: one on British wildflowers and one on exotic blooms, like hibiscus, amaryllis, and orchids. The books were all filled with beautiful colour photography and Poppy almost wanted to curl up right then and there, and start reading them from cover to cover.

"I didn't realise you were so into flowers," she said, looking at Nick with some surprise.

"I'm not really—well, no more than the next man," he said, grinning suddenly. "It was actually for book research. The novel I'm currently working on features a lot of flowers."

Poppy raised her eyebrows even more. "I thought you wrote dark crime thrillers."

He chuckled. "I do. But even flowers can have a dark criminal side. You don't believe me? Haven't you heard of 'tulip mania'? Or 'orchidelirium'?"

Poppy shook her head.

"They're both times in history when people became so gripped with a particular flower that they would do anything to get it: pay crazy sums of money, give up their livelihoods, engage in theft... maybe even commit murder." Nick laughed again as he saw Poppy's expression. "Okay, I might have made the last one up. But it's certainly true that there have been crazes for finding and owning a particular flower. The *Semper Augustus tulip*, for example, was once worth ten thousand guilders for a single bulb. That was enough to feed, clothe, and house a whole Dutch family for half a lifetime. And of course, any time the value of something skyrockets like that, crime follows soon after," he added cynically.

"Wow…" said Poppy, thinking of all the times she had wistfully eyed a bunch of tulips in the shops. "I've never been able to afford fresh cut flowers, but I never realised tulips could be *that* expensive!"

"Well, not today, but this was back in seventeenth-century Netherlands, when 'tulip mania' was gripping the country. It was the same here in England with the Victorians: they became completely obsessed with orchids, and wealthy collectors would send expeditions around the world to find new varieties. Things were so secretive and competitive, they would spread false information and sabotage each other. Even today, orchid smuggling is big business, especially since collecting from the wild is now banned by CITES."

"Is this what your new book is about? The black market in flowers?" asked Poppy, intrigued in spite of herself.

"No, although that *would* be a fascinating theme for a novel, wouldn't it?" said Nick enthusiastically. "It would be a refreshing take on the old 'organised crime' trope."

"But you don't think of flowers when you think of illegal trade," Poppy said. "You think of drugs and guns, or exotic animal parts—"

"Ah, but the illegal plant trade is worth hundreds of millions of pounds. There are organised gangs now who specialise in 'plant heists'. In fact, there have been some pretty high-profile thefts from botanical gardens and horticultural shows, to the point that some plants have to be given police protection."

"You're not serious," said Poppy, rolling her eyes.

"I am. When there's a lucrative black market for something, criminals start to move in. Take snowdrops, for instance—"

"Snowdrops?" said Poppy disbelievingly. "What— the little white flowers that pop up everywhere in winter?"

Nick nodded. "They've become very popular, and valuable specimens have been targeted by professional thieves."

"But... but they'd have to dig them up in clumps or something—"

"They do. The national gardens are having to use CCTV cameras and high-tech alarms and even security tags to try and stop the gangs."

"That's ridiculous! For snowdrops? You see them all over the British countryside!"

"Ah, but when a single bulb can fetch over a thousand pounds—yes, there was one which was sold for that much online—then people want to get their hands on them, by any means. And there are always fanatical collectors willing to pay."

Poppy frowned. "But if you get a plant illegally, you can't show it off or tell anyone about it. You have to keep it a secret. So why would collectors want them?"

"Why collect anything?" said Nick with a shrug. "There's the kudos in owning something rare or even better, something unique. The only one of its kind. It's the same mentality that art collectors have. Most art theft is funded by private collectors, you know. And even if it means that they can only admire a painting by themselves, in secret... well, I guess they still feel superior to everyone else." He rubbed his chin and mused, "It's an odd thing about human nature, isn't it? It would be interesting to explore it in a story..."

Poppy cast a surreptitious glance at the man next to her. Ever since he'd started talking about his book research, Nick had seemed like a different person, his face alive with interest and humour, that rich, mesmerising voice full of warmth and excitement. When he wasn't being brusque and moody, he could be incredibly charming, and Poppy was surprised to find that she was enjoying his company more than she'd expected.

"Are you sure your current book isn't about this?" she asked with a smile. "You seem to be so passionate about it and know so much about it already."

Nick laughed a bit sheepishly. "It's one of the perils of book research. You stumble on something fascinating and end up going down rabbit holes that have no connection to the novel you're currently writing. No, my current novel has nothing about the illegal trade in plants. It actually features a serial killer who leaves a different flower bloom behind with each victim, as a sort of 'calling card'. My detective has to work out the messages that are being sent to him—"

"Oh, you mean like 'the language of flowers'?" said Poppy, suddenly remembering the charity volunteer who had given her the heather flower pin.

"Yes," said Nick, looking impressed. "Yes, that's right. Every flower has a meaning associated with it and they can be used to send coded messages. I wanted to go beyond the boring, predictable options like roses and carnations—and the flowers needed to be of certain sizes and colours too—so your grandmother lent me the books to look through and pick the best ones."

"So how do you—" Poppy broke off as they were interrupted by a plaintive *"N-ow! N-ow!"* coming from just outside the French doors. She turned and saw Oren sitting on the other side of the tall glass pane, staring at them reproachfully.

"Oh—does he want to come in?" asked Poppy.

Nick muttered something under his breath. "He has his own cat flap. It's only a few more yards around the side of the house. He's just being lazy— he wants us to open the window for him."

"N-ow!" added the ginger tom, scowling at his

owner.

Nick scowled back. "Use your own bloody door!" he yelled.

Poppy hid a smile, suddenly remembering Suzanne's comment about two grumpy old men. She could really begin to see it!

Nick pointedly turned his back to the French doors, then glanced at his watch and said, "Blast! I'm going to be late. No need to be polite and wait up for me or anything. Just suit yourself. I'll probably see you in the morning."

He started to leave the room, then turned back and added with a growl: "And don't open the window for that cat!"

CHAPTER FIFTEEN

Left alone in the house, Poppy made herself a cup of tea, then carried the mug back to the sitting room, looking forward to a couple of hours curled up with her grandmother's books. But she had barely stepped back into the room when she met a pair of unblinking yellow eyes staring at her from outside the French doors.

"Well, don't look at me," she said to the ginger tom. "I'm under strict instructions not to let you in."

The cat raised a paw and tapped the glass.

"You've got your own entrance—why don't you use that?"

"*N-ow?*" Oren tilted his head to one side.

"Yes, now," Poppy said. Then she shook her head and laughed. She couldn't believe she was having a conversation with a cat.

"*N-ow… n-ow…!*" Oren said indignantly, pawing the glass.

Poppy bit her lip. There was no way she'd be able to sit in here and read with the cat wailing outside. She hesitated a moment, then walked over to the French doors. *Nick will never know anyway*, she thought as she reached out and turned the latch. A minute later, the ginger tom was in the room, strutting around in a self-satisfied manner.

"Don't get too smug," Poppy warned him. "That is just a one-off, because I'm feeling in a charitable mood. It doesn't mean I'm a pushover—just so you know."

"*N-ow…*" Oren said with a feline smirk.

Poppy picked up the huge plant encyclopaedia and was just about to sit down when she remembered guiltily that she hadn't called Nell yet. She had sent her old friend a quick text before bed last night, but that was before she had discovered Pete Sykes's body. It was hard to believe that that was only this morning—so much had happened since then! She hurriedly found her phone and dialled Nell's number, smiling as she heard the familiar motherly voice.

"Are you still in Oxfordshire? I thought you'd be on your way back by now," Nell said in surprise.

"Actually, I'm going to have to stay a few more days…" Quickly, Poppy told Nell about the situation.

"Oh my lordy Lord—a dead body? Murder?" Nell

gasped. "But what about the cottage? Are you still staying there?"

"No, they're still processing the crime scene so I'm staying with the neighbour next door."

"Oh, that's nice of them, dear. Are they friends of your grandmother's then?"

"Er... well, he *was* friendly with her—"

"He?" said Nell suspiciously.

"Yes, the house next door belongs to the author, Nick Forrest—have you heard of him?"

"Don't know him from Adam. Does he live alone?" asked Nell, still in that suspicious tone.

"Yes... well, except for his cat. He's got this ginger tom who—"

"How old is he?"

"Nick? Uh... I don't know... late thirties, I guess?"

"Are you sure it's safe, dear, staying alone with a single man?"

"Don't be silly. Of course it's safe."

"But you don't know anything about him!"

"Well, he's... he's a well-known author. And his ex-girlfriend is the detective in charge of the investigation," Poppy added. "It was actually she who suggested that I stay with him."

"Hmm..." Nell sounded slightly mollified. "So why aren't they together anymore?"

"*I* don't know! That's their private affair."

"Oh, Poppy, I don't like it... Make sure you lock your bedroom door at night, dear. These older men... they might think you're a naïve young thing and try to take advantage—"

"NELL!" Poppy gave an exasperated laugh. "For goodness' sake, this isn't a Gothic romance novel with some old lech preying on a virginal heroine in a tower! Nick isn't interested in me in the least. He's just letting me use his spare room until I can go back to the cottage, and in return I'm looking after his cat. He'll be away from tomorrow morning, anyway—he's going on a book tour—so I'll be alone in the house. And in fact, he's gone out this evening to Oxford to give a talk at one of the colleges, so I probably won't even see him again before he leaves."

"Hmm... well, the sooner you're back in the cottage, the better. Now—" Nell's voice changed and she said briskly, "—is the cottage clean? Have you given the kitchen and the toilet a good scrub before using them?"

"Er..." Poppy thought guiltily of her half-hearted efforts. She hadn't even bothered to really clean the kettle—just giving it a quick rinse before filling it with water. "It's not too bad, actually. Most things seem fairly clean." Then quickly, to distract Nell, she added, "My clothes are filthy, though, from falling in the garden, and I only brought a change of things for one day. Although I don't really want to spend money buying new clothes right now..." she added with a groan.

"How about charity shops? Have they got any of those in the village? You could maybe pick up some second-hand items for cheap."

"I don't know... I didn't see any today. Most of the shops seem to sell knick-knacks for tourists. But I can ask in the tourist information centre tomorrow. That's a great idea—thanks Nell."

Poppy had barely hung up and settled back down on the sofa with the book when her mobile rang again. It was a number she didn't know but, when she answered, Poppy recognised the voice instantly. It was Charles Mannering.

"My dear, Inspector Whittaker has just been to interview me... this dreadful business about Pete Sykes! And to think that you found the body—you must be terribly shocked—"

"Yes, it *was* a bit horrible to think of his body just lying out there the whole night when I was asleep," said Poppy with a shudder.

"Quite so... quite so... most distressing..." said the lawyer, making a tutting sound. "And Inspector Whittaker informs me that you're staying in Bunnington for a few more days? Have you any friends in the vicinity?"

"No, I don't know anyone in Oxfordshire."

"Well, I hope you won't mind an old man's fussing, but I was thinking it must be quite unpleasant for you to be alone, especially on the first night after finding the body, so I was wondering if you'd like to come over for dinner and spend the evening at my house?"

"Oh, that's really kind of you," said Poppy, touched.

"It'll just be me, I'm afraid, so it won't be very glamorous company," said Mannering, coughing apologetically. "I'm a bachelor, you see. But my housekeeper is a very good cook and she makes the most wonderful beef casserole. I'd be delighted if you'd join me," he said with old-fashioned courtesy.

"Thank you. I'd like that very much," said Poppy, smiling. Then she thought of something: "But I don't have a car and it'll take me an hour to get the bus back to Oxford, assuming there's one at this time—"

"Oh, I don't live in Oxford, my dear. My office is there but my house is actually on the outskirts of Bunnington. It's the reason I'm the executor for your grandmother's estate: I used to visit her nursery for plants and, over time, we became friendly. When she heard that I was a solicitor, she asked me to look after her legal affairs. Anyway, so it should just be a twenty-minute walk from the cottage, at the most."

"That sounds great. It'll be nice to get some exercise. Okay, I'll see you soon!"

CHAPTER SIXTEEN

Charles Mannering's home was an elegant house set in well-kept gardens, with a magnificent Victorian conservatory attached—an enormous yet airy framework of steel and glass, with arching ceilings, chequered floor tiles, and wrought-iron embellishments. It was obviously the lawyer's pride and joy, for he wasted no time in taking Poppy through and showing her proudly around as soon as she arrived.

The interior of the conservatory was a lush green oasis filled with ferns, palms, and a host of flowers and plants that Poppy didn't recognise, all in a vivid rainbow of colours. There was a marble fountain in one corner, its soft tinkling adding to the peaceful ambience of the place, and the air was warm and steamy, with condensation fogging up the glass panes as twilight fell and the air cooled outside.

Mannering led her around, pointing out various plants and reeling off a string of Latin names that went straight over Poppy's head.

"...and this here is a *Bergenia crassifolia*, also known as Elephant's Ears because of these wonderful big leaves. Of course, they're considered a bit common nowadays—and you don't really need to grow them in a greenhouse; they're fully hardy, you know—but I think their foliage works marvellously with the other exotics. Very underrated plant..."

He crouched down next to a bushy plant in a pot. It was covered in big, showy red blooms which reminded Poppy of the flowers that island girls put behind their ears.

"This little beauty is *Hibiscus rosa-sinensis*. They can get as big as a tree, you know, in the tropics, but sadly in Britain they're a bit more delicate. Oh drat...!" One of the large, trumpet-like flowers caught in Mannering's cufflinks and, despite his careful efforts, it broke off from the plant. He removed the bloom caught on his sleeve and placed it at the base of the bush, as if returning a baby to its mother. Then he fussed over the plant tenderly, saying to Poppy, "She likes to be misted on a regular basis during the warmer months, otherwise she wilts a bit."

"Oh... um, right," said Poppy.

Mannering stood up and indicated a lush green

vine climbing up a trellis against the side of the conservatory. "And this is *Pandorea jasminoides*, the Bower Vine. Isn't she just ravishing? Hails from the east coast of Australia. She *can* be a bit of a diva as well: she will defoliate if she gets too cold, even here in the conservatory, and I need to pamper her with a bit of fleece in the winter—but she's well worth it. Just look at those flowers! Perfect trumpet shape and with those deep pink throats!"

"Er... yes, she's lovely," said Poppy, thinking that she was beginning to understand why Charles Mannering was a bachelor. Which woman could hope to compete with "ravishing" *Pandorea* and all his other pampered botanical darlings?

She started to walk around the climbing vine to get a closer look, but Mannering grabbed her arm and said eagerly, "Do you like her colour? Then you must have a look at my *Bougainvillea!*" He practically dragged her to the other side of the conservatory where another vine was climbing, this time around an iron pillar that was part of the conservatory framework. The stems of this vine were brown and gnarled, and there were vicious thorns poking out from between the leaves, but its flowers more than made up for it. There was a cascade of them all along the branches—ruffled, papery blooms in the most amazing shade of magenta.

"Wow..." said Poppy, suitably impressed.

Charles Mannering beamed. "Magnificent, isn't

he? He's a hybrid between *Bougainvillea glabra* and *Bougainvillea peruviana*. He needs to be kept warm—but otherwise, he flowers his heart out every summer."

"These are all very different from the sort of flowers you usually see, aren't they?" said Poppy.

"Yes, I do love the exotics," said Mannering with an embarrassed smile. "I know many people prefer a traditional English garden, but I must confess, my weakness is for plants from more tropical climes."

"I'm surprised you went to my grandmother's nursery, then. Didn't she just sell cottage-garden plants?"

"Oh no. English cottage-garden plants were her speciality, of course—especially the traditional favourites, like foxgloves and hollyhocks, but she also offered a range of other plants, especially flowering ones. It may seem strange for such a stern woman, but your grandmother loved flowers, you see, in all their shapes and sizes—"

"That must be where I inherited it from," said Poppy with a laugh. "Although, sadly, I don't think I've inherited her green fingers as well."

"You never know, my dear," said the lawyer complacently. "You may yet find that you have more skill with plants than you thought. It's all about practice and experience, really. Have you ever gardened?"

"No, not really," Poppy admitted. "We—my mother and I—could never afford to stay anywhere large enough for a garden. We mostly lived in flats—very small flats! And we never stayed anywhere for long either."

"Well, now is your chance... if you decide to stay on at the cottage, that is." He gave her a searching look. "Or are you still determined to sell the property, my dear?"

Poppy hesitated, then said, "Oh yes, I'm sticking with my original plan. I don't suppose you've had any interest?"

"Well, as a matter of fact... I was intending to call you tomorrow to let you know that a property agent in Oxford has contacted me and said that a development company might be interested in the site. The challenges of renovation and restructuring would not be such an issue, since they would simply raze the cottage to the ground and pull up most of the trees and shrubs—"

"What?" said Poppy, horrified. "But... that would destroy the garden and everything!"

"Well, yes," Mannering admitted. "But they would build a new house in its place—several houses, in fact. The site is so large, it could be subdivided into several townhouses, each with a small courtyard garden and—"

"Can you put them off?"

"I... I'm sorry?"

"The property agent. Can you stall them for a bit?"

"Well, certainly, but I'm afraid I don't

understand, my dear... If we want a quick sale, the sooner we start negotiations, the better."

"Yes, well... um... what if... er... what if we just put things off for a few weeks?"

He gave her a surprised look. "Are you thinking of changing your mind about selling the cottage, my dear?"

"No... yes... I mean... no, no, of course not. It's just..." Poppy trailed off, not knowing how to voice the turmoil of feelings inside her. She couldn't bear the thought of the garden being destroyed... but at the same time, she needed the money from the sale of the property. "I... I just need a bit of time, okay?"

The lawyer looked nonplussed. "Well... er... certainly. Your grandmother's will doesn't stipulate a time frame so I see no reason why we can't take things slowly." Then he frowned slightly. "I shall have to think of a way of dealing with the property agent. He has been very persistent, calling me several times a day." He sighed. "Things are a bit awkward, you see, because he is family of a sort and so he has a vested interest—"

"Family?" Poppy said in surprise.

Before Mannering could answer, they were startled by the sound of the doorbell ringing.

"Who on earth can that be?" muttered Mannering, leading the way out of the conservatory and back into the house.

Poppy followed, and they were joined by his housekeeper, who hurried out of the kitchen, wiping her hands on her apron.

"It's all right, Mrs Graham—I'll get it," said Mannering, waving a hand and going up to the front door.

It swung open to reveal a portly, middle-aged man with a balding head and a bushy handlebar moustache. He was dressed in a cheap suit and held a folder in his hands.

"Ah! Charles—caught you at last, you old bugger! I've been leaving messages at your office all day, you know. Blasted secretary of yours is more protective than a Rottweiler! Anyway, I had the evening free so I thought I'd bring you the documents and save you the bother of—"

"Hubert, I really don't like conducting business from home," said Mannering testily. "I must ask you to make an appointment with my secretary and we can discuss things in my office."

"But there's nothing to discuss, really! I told you, I've negotiated a marvellous deal for you and all your client has to do is sign on the dotted line. Have you had a chance to speak to her again yet? I wish you'd tell me where she is in London—I could pop down and have a chat with her. I'm sure once she hears what she stands to gain..." He trailed off as he noticed Poppy for the first time. He gave Mannering a lascivious grin. "You old fox! Didn't realise I was interrupting a hot date." He leaned sideways and elbowed the elderly lawyer in an exaggerated manner, saying in a loud whisper,

"She's a pretty little thing but a bit young for you, eh, Charles?"

Charles Mannering went very red in the face. "*Ahem!* This is Poppy Lancaster—Mary Lancaster's granddaughter."

"Mary Lancaster's..." Hubert's eyes bulged as the words sunk in. An ugly look flashed across his face, then it was quickly wiped clean, to be replaced by a greasy smile.

"Cousin Poppy!" he cried, reaching out to grab her hand.

Poppy stared at him. *Cousin?*

Hubert pumped her hand up and down. "I'm delighted to meet you at last! Have you come to see Charles about the sale? Perfect timing, eh?"

Mannering said irritably, "No, Miss Lancaster is not here on business. I've invited her over for dinner and we're just about to sit down, so if you don't mind—"

"Ooh, what are you having?"

Mannering looked taken aback. "A beef casserole, as a matter of fact, but I—"

"Beef casserole! My favourite!" Hubert smacked his lips. "You don't mind if I join you, do you? I haven't had anything to eat since lunch and I'm starving!"

Poppy was shocked by the man's brazen manner and she could see that Mannering was at a loss over how to respond. It was ridiculous—Hubert was the one being boorish and presumptuous, and yet somehow, he made them feel rude and petty if they excluded him.

Hubert saw the elderly lawyer wavering and added in a wheedling voice: "It's a trek back to Oxford—you wouldn't make me come all the way out here and deprive me of the chance to talk with my long-lost cousin, would you?" Then, before Mannering could answer, he stepped past him and walked boldly into the foyer.

Sniffing the air in an exaggerated fashion, Hubert said: "Mm-mm... that smells good! Which way to the dining room?"

Mannering compressed his lips, then took a deep breath and said, "If you'll follow me..."

Pivoting on his heel, he walked stiffly out of the foyer. Hubert started to follow, then turned to Poppy and made a sweeping bow.

"Ladies first."

CHAPTER SEVENTEEN

Poppy half expected Hubert to start giving her a sales pitch as soon as they sat down at the table, but to her relief, the man seemed to be telling the truth when he said that he was starving. He focused most of his attention on the food, and he wasn't shy about asking for second helpings, or badgering Mannering to open one of his best bottles of wine. Poppy could see the elderly lawyer struggling to maintain a civil demeanour.

"Mm... mmm..." said Hubert, guzzling the glass noisily. "This is fantastic plonk, Charles! Never realised you kept such a good cellar. Should pop by more often, eh?" He laughed and raised his glass in a mock toast.

Feeling sorry for Mannering and hoping to give him a bit of respite from Hubert's attentions, Poppy said: "So you live in Oxford, Mr... sorry, I don't know your last name?"

"It's Leach, but you can call me Hubert. After all, we're second cousins, did you know that?" He grinned and gave her a lewd wink. "Close enough to be kissing cousins but far enough for the kissing to be legal, eh?"

Poppy recoiled in distaste. "I didn't realise I had other family here."

"My mother and your grandmother were first cousins. So I'm her cousin once removed. And to answer your question, yes, I live in Oxford. Got an office there too. Real estate. Specialising in new housing projects and developments."

Charles Mannering cleared his throat. "It was Hubert who first approached me and told me that Hollyhock Cottage would be a prime site for redevelopment. In fact, I believe he may have been a bit rash and already negotiated a deal with the developer months ago, on the assumption that he would have the property to sell," he added tartly.

The other man flushed. "Yes, well... it was a fair assumption, considering that I thought I was going to inherit the estate." He shot Poppy a sour look and added bitterly, "I *was* Mary Lancaster's only living relative and her previous will left everything to me. How was I to know that there would suddenly be a new will leaving everything to her 'long-lost grandchild'?"

Poppy looked down, feeling guilty even though

she knew she had no reason to.

"I suppose you've checked her credentials and everything?" Hubert said to Mannering, only half joking.

The lawyer looked outraged. "I beg your pardon!" he said icily.

Hubert laughed, unabashed, and put his hands up in a defensive gesture. "Hey, no harm in asking. I mean, when a new will suddenly appears out of nowhere, you've gotta wonder, eh? How do I know it's legitimate?"

"I assure you, the new will was thoroughly vetted and is completely legitimate," said Mannering through gritted teeth. "It was signed by Mary Lancaster, in the presence of two witnesses."

"Yeah, and one of those was Pete Sykes. We all know how trustworthy *he* was," said Hubert sarcastically.

Poppy's ears pricked up. Her grandmother's last will had been witnessed by Pete Sykes, the man who had been murdered... was that a coincidence?

Mannering looked like he had reached the end of his tether. Raising his voice, he said curtly, "Mr Leach, if you have any issue with Mary Lancaster's final will, I suggest that you take it up formally in a court of law. But I warn you, it can be a lengthy and expensive process to contest a will, so you would be well advised to ensure that you have the grounds to do so first."

Hubert scowled. A long, strained silence

descended on the dining table. At last, trying to ease the tension, Poppy asked:

"Um... do you garden, Hubert?"

"Oh yeah, when I have the time."

"What sort of plants do you grow?"

"Oh, the usual stuff—and bulbs. Really into bulbs."

"Bulbs?" Poppy looked confused.

"Yeah, you know—daffodils, tulips, freesias, crocuses, anemones... and snowdrops. Especially snowdrops. Love 'em."

"Hmm... I tried some snowdrops in a pot last year, but I must say, they were quite disappointing," said Mannering, thawing enough to join in the conversation again.

"Yeah, they don't like pots, snowdrops," said Hubert with authority. "Prefer to naturalise in the ground proper. But you can dig 'em up 'in the green' and move 'em around after they've finished flowering, so they're actually a lot easier to manage than other bulbs."

"You seem to know a fair bit about them," Mannering commented, looking at the other man with new respect. "You must grow a lot of them?"

Hubert grinned. "Yeah, every variety I can find. There's very little I won't do to get my hands on some of the small white stuff."

"Small white stuff?" said Poppy, startled.

"Good God, you're not one of those galanthophiles, are you?" said Mannering.

Hubert gave a sheepish laugh. "Yeah, guilty as charged. Bank manager was gobsmacked last time he called to check an unusually large withdrawal and I told him it was to buy a *Galanthus plicatus*."

Mannering turned to Poppy, who was still looking blank, and explained, "'Galanthophile' is the name given to people who are fanatical snowdrop collectors." He shook his head. "Although I have to say, even as a keen gardener myself, I really cannot understand the hobby. They charge up and down the country in freezing winter every January and February, hunting for new varieties and paying hundreds of pounds to get their hands on something that looks, frankly, just like any other snowdrop."

"Hey, that's not true," protested Hubert. "There are important subtle differences—you just can't see 'em. Besides, I'll bet you spent a fair whack on that conservatory of yours," he added with a knowing wink.

Mannering gave a dry laugh. "Well, yes, you're right... guilty as charged as well. It *is* wonderful to have somewhere to grow the nonhardy varieties, though, and not have to worry about moving plants when the temperatures drop..."

The two men plunged into a discussion about different methods of overwintering plants and, as she watched, Poppy was amazed to see how the topic of gardening seemed to have acted as a neutraliser and even a sort of bridge between them.

By the time the meal ended, Hubert and Mannering were back on friendly terms. Still, Poppy was glad when her cousin took his leave at last. She herself didn't stay much longer afterwards either. It had been a long day and she was suddenly keen to get to bed. Charles Mannering offered to walk her back, but Poppy waved him off, saying that it was only a short stroll across the village.

As she was stepping out the front door, Poppy thought of Bertie and wondered if she should tell Mannering about him. But for some reason, she felt reluctant to speak. Despite the furtive behaviour she had observed and the mysterious bundle he had been carrying, she didn't believe the old inventor to be dangerous. In fact, he seemed like nothing more than a lonely old man with no one but his little terrier for company, and she didn't want to bring suspicion and trouble on his head. So she simply bade Mannering goodnight and headed out into the night.

The house was still dark and Nick wasn't home yet when Poppy got back. She let herself in and walked down the darkened hallway to her room. When she got there, however, she discovered that while Nell's fears about the crime writer's desire to get into her bed might have been unfounded, the same couldn't be said about his cat. The ginger tom lay sprawled across the pillows and regarded her with lazy yellow eyes as she came into the room.

"Oren—what are you doing here?" said Poppy

with a sigh.

He yawned widely and stretched out his front legs, flexing his claws.

Poppy reached out and gently tried to shift the cat. "Come on...you can't sleep on my bed. You've got to go."

"*N-ow...?*" said Oren.

He rolled onto his back, exposing his white-furred belly, and tilted his head, looking up at her mischievously. Poppy laughed in spite of herself. Like his owner, Oren could switch on the charm when he chose to. Now, he batted her hand playfully with one velvety paw and purred in a persuasive manner.

"Oh... all right, you can stay for a bit," said Poppy. "Just until I get undressed and clean my teeth."

But when she was ready to climb into bed a few minutes later, she couldn't bring herself to push him off. He looked so comfortable stretched out on the blankets.

He can stay a bit longer, just while I'm reading, she told herself, curling up against the pillows with one of her grandmother's plant books. *But that's it. After that, I'm picking him up and chucking him out...*

The next thing she knew, it was morning. Poppy sat up, yawning, then frowned as she felt a heavy weight across her ankles. She rubbed her eyes and gave a groan as she saw who was draped over her legs: a sleek ginger tom, fast asleep with a self-satisfied look on his face. She looked around and found the heavy hardback plant encyclopaedia open on the bed next to her, and the bedside lamp still on. In fact, her pillows were still propped up against the headboard and she had a slight crick in her neck from sleeping in a funny position. She must have nodded off while reading, she realised. Yawning again, she struggled to free her legs from the tangle of cat and blankets, and get out of bed.

Oren meowed indignantly as he was jostled awake. He stood up and arched his back in a perfect cat stretch, then jumped off the bed and stalked to the bedroom door, where he sat down and looked expectantly back at her.

"Uh-uh... first you take over my bed and now you expect me to be your personal butler?" said Poppy.

"*N-ow...*" said Oren, pawing the door.

Aarrgghh. She was beginning to sympathise with Nick's exasperation with the demanding feline. Still, she did need the bathroom so she might as well let the cat out too. Opening the door, she peeked out into the hallway. All seemed clear. Poppy scooted to the bathroom and re-emerged a few minutes later feeling more awake, having splashed some water on her face. But she hesitated as she was about to return to the bedroom and paused, listening, instead. The house seemed quiet. Nick must have got back very late last night and was probably still asleep. She was dying for a cup of coffee and it would probably be safe to slip to the kitchen to make a mug and bring it back to bed.

It took her a few minutes to explore the gleaming kitchen and she tiptoed around, opening cupboard doors and drawers as quietly as she could. There was a monster of a coffee machine in one corner—fancy enough to rival anything in a professional espresso bar—but she eschewed that, fearful that it would make too much noise. Instead, she hunted around until she found a jar of instant coffee, some milk, and a mug, and set about making herself a hot drink. She was just tiptoeing across the kitchen, intent on filling the kettle at the sink, when a deep voice sounded behind her:

"Good morning."

CHAPTER EIGHTEEN

Poppy yelped and whirled around, to find Nick Forrest leaning against the doorjamb, regarding her with amusement. He had a steaming mug in one hand and a whiteboard marker in the other, and Poppy noticed ink marks all over his fingers.

"Oh, you're up!" said Poppy.

She was irritated to find that he looked bright-eyed and cheery, with his jaw freshly shaven and even his normally unruly hair seemingly tamed. In contrast, she was very conscious of how she must look, with sleepy eyes, serious "bed hair" and bare feet, and dressed in nothing but an oversized sleep T-shirt. It made her feel vulnerable and at a disadvantage, and she didn't like it.

"I thought you'd still be asleep after the late night out," she said, almost accusingly.

He didn't react to her tone, saying mildly, "No, I went to bed, but then I suddenly thought of a possible solution for my plot hole, so I went back to my study. I've been at it for a few hours but I think I may have finally worked it out."

"You mean... you've been up all night writing?" she said incredulously.

"Yes, just about. I stopped about an hour ago and thought about going back to bed, but the sun was already coming up so I just had a shower instead."

It's no wonder he's always so crabby, if he stays up half the night writing, thought Poppy. She'd be in a bad mood all the time too if she was always sleep-deprived. Writers were odd creatures. She couldn't imagine giving up a night of sleep, just to finish writing a story.

"So you figured your whole plot out?"

"Not completely—I still have to work out some details—but the general concept should work." He smiled, looking pleased, and again Poppy was struck by how his saturnine features changed when they were alight with good humour.

Nick indicated the coffee machine. "Fancy a cup?"

"Oh, no, don't bother—I'm more than happy to have instant—"

"It's no bother, otherwise I wouldn't ask. I'm making another cup for myself as well."

"Oh... in that case..."

A short while later, Poppy followed Nick out of the kitchen, carrying a steaming mug of her own. The aroma of fresh coffee was wonderful and all she wanted to do was go back to her room and curl up in bed with her flower book again. But after Nick's pleasant manner and efforts in making her the coffee, she felt rude just abandoning him. So she followed him politely as he led her to a room at the end of the hallway, overlooking the back of the property.

She stopped short as she stepped in and looked around with a mixture of incredulity and awe. She had never seen any place in such a mess. Books were stacked haphazardly in every available space—strewn across the desk, teetering atop cabinets, ranked along the windowsill, and even piled high in the single armchair which faced the desk. Any place not occupied by books seemed to be filled with papers: Post-it Notes and scribbled scraps of paper, newspaper cuttings and torn magazine pages, brochures, leaflets, cards, napkins with doodles... and along one wall was an enormous whiteboard on which Poppy could see a diagram that looked a bit like a spider's web, with names and places all connected by various arrows.

"Uh... have a seat..." said Nick, looking distractedly around and running a hand through his hair.

Poppy wanted to say "Where?" but bit her tongue and instead perched on the arm of the armchair.

Nick climbed over a large antique globe, tripped over a tangle of computer cables, and finally rounded the side of his desk, to sink into a large leather chair behind it. Poppy noticed for the first time that there was a laptop open on the desk, half buried under mountains of books.

"Do you do all your writing in here?" she asked, glancing at the chaos around them.

"Most of it. Sometimes I go out on the terrace for a change of scene... but if I stay here, at least I only have to search one room when I'm looking for my research notes and other material." He made a face. "Blasted things—never there when you need them."

"You know.... It would probably be easier to find things if you cleared the floor a bit and sorted out all these papers and put books back onto the shelves. I'd be happy to help you," Poppy offered. "It would be a small thank you in return for letting me stay here."

Nick scowled. "You sound like my housekeeper. She's always trying to clear this room out. No, don't touch anything—I know where everything is. I have a system."

Poppy glanced around once more. *Some system.* She saw Nick scowl again, as if reading her thoughts, and hastily pointed to the diagram on the whiteboard, saying:

"What's that?"

Nick leaned back to look at the far wall. "Oh, that's my character map. The relationships between the characters in my novels can be quite complex sometimes and this helps me keep everything straight, as well as work out their flaws, needs, and motivations."

Poppy got up for a closer look. "Do all authors use character maps like this?"

He shrugged. "Maybe. I don't know. I started doing it, actually, as a relic from my CID days of putting information up in link charts in the incident room, and I guess it's stuck."

Poppy swung around in surprise. "CID? You were in the Force?"

He grinned. "For my sins. Got to the rank of Detective Sergeant before I landed my first book deal and the rest, as they say, is history."

Poppy wondered if that was where he had met Suzanne Whittaker. "I suppose your background and experience comes in really useful in your writing," she commented.

"Yeah, they do say 'write what you know' and it helps when you've had first-hand experience of murder investigations and criminals."

"Don't you miss doing it for real, though, as opposed to writing about it?"

"Sometimes. But the thing is, fictional detective work is much more fun... sadly." At Poppy's puzzled expression, he explained, "What I mean is, investigating a case in real life is often just a boring slog of paperwork, tedious interviews, lack of leads, missing murder weapons, and barely half a decent suspect... whereas in books, you can have all the brilliant deductions, the convenient clues that tell you exactly who the murderer is—and the case is all wrapped up in just a few days, even by amateur sleuths!

"Plus you can use all sorts of unorthodox methods to investigate suspects too," he added. "Suzanne is always reading my manuscripts and shaking her head at the things my detective gets up to. She keeps insisting that he'd never be able to do those things in real life, but the point is, in my books, I am God and rules can be easily broken."

"What sort of things?" asked Poppy, intrigued.

"Oh, things like searching a house without a warrant, 'borrowing' evidence from Forensics to show witnesses, taping an interview without informing the suspect..."

"But... that's all unethical," said Poppy, slightly appalled.

Nick shrugged. "It gets results, though. Sometimes the ends justify the means."

"I'm surprised Suzanne lets you near any investigation now," said Poppy. "Who knows what you might do, just because you want to research something for your latest novel."

Nick chuckled. "Funny you should say that." He reached across his desk and pulled out a piece of paper from the mess, which he handed to Poppy.

It was a photograph which—from the grainy quality—looked like it had been taken on his phone and then downloaded to his computer and printed out on normal paper. It showed the body of a man, slumped facedown in a flowerbed, with various flower blooms strewn around him. Poppy caught her breath as she realised that the dead man was Pete Sykes. Nick must have somehow taken a photo of the crime scene!

"Does Suzanne know you took this?" asked Poppy, giving him a stern look.

"No. I went over while she was questioning you and snapped the picture when nobody was looking." He gave her a wicked grin. "Don't look so horrified, Miss Prim. I'm not planning to sell it to the press or share it with anyone, so I'm not jeopardising the investigation."

"But... why did you take it?"

"Oh, I had some vague idea that it might help me with my plot problem. See, the killer in my story does something similar: leaves the body with flower blossoms strewn all around it. In his case, of course, they aren't random—they're one particular type of flower, chosen to send a message... but the similarities were striking. I thought having an image of it might help me figure out my plot hole... and it worked!" said Nick with elation. "It's what got me up at 2 a.m.—I'm sure of it. I came back from Oxford and had a late-night drink in my study, and I was staring at the photo just before I went off to bed... and the next thing I knew, I was wide awake in bed with the whole solution laid out beautifully in front of me."

Poppy looked doubtfully down at the grainy photo. She didn't see how staring at it could produce so much creative inspiration, but she wasn't a writer. Their minds obviously worked in very strange ways. Then she had a sudden—creative—idea of her own.

"Um... I don't suppose that this could be the work of a random serial killer too?" she asked.

Nick shook his head. "I doubt it. In fact, my money is on the murderer being somebody that Pete Sykes knew."

"Why do you say that?"

"Didn't you notice the body? There were no signs of a struggle; it looks like Pete Sykes was hit on the head from behind and just crumpled where he stood. So he must have known his attacker well enough to trust them and turn his back on them."

"Or he never heard them creeping up behind him," Poppy pointed out.

"Yes, true," Nick admitted. "Although the property is empty and it's quiet in the garden next door—it's hard to imagine how anyone could have approached him without him knowing."

Poppy thought of when she found the body, when Nick himself had come up soundlessly behind her and scared her half to death. For a crazy moment, she wondered if the crime writer could have something to do with Pete Sykes's death—he was certainly perfectly placed for it, being right next door to the cottage. He would have known that the garden was empty and neglected, the perfect place to hide a body. Perhaps he had been returning to the scene of the crime and had been shocked to discover her there—

No, that wouldn't work. He had already known that she was staying at the cottage. She'd taken Oren back to him the night before. In any case, it was ludicrous to think that Nick Forrest could be the murderer. The man was an ex-cop, for goodness' sake!

Aloud, she said: "The garden is so overgrown, it would be easy for someone to sneak up to him under cover, particularly if they came from the other side of the cottage."

The thought made her suddenly remember Bertie, who had secret access to the cottage garden through the gap in the wall. Again, she wondered if she should mention him, but she just couldn't believe that the old inventor could be involved with the murder.

"What is it?" asked Nick, watching her closely. "You're deep in thought about something."

Poppy hesitated, then shook her head and pinned a bright smile on her face. "Oh... er... nothing, really. My mind was just wandering." She drained her mug and walked to the door of the study. "Anyway... thanks so much for the coffee. I'd better let you get ready. You're leaving soon for your book tour, aren't you? Well, I'll see you when you get back. And thanks so much again for letting me stay."

Nick looked at her silently for a moment, then he said, all traces of humour wiped from his face, "Sykes's murderer may not have been a serial killer but that doesn't mean that he isn't dangerous. If you know something which may be relevant to the investigation, you shouldn't withhold the information."

Poppy swallowed, hoping her expression hadn't changed. "Uh... thanks, I'll keep that in mind." Then, as nonchalantly as she could, she turned and walked out of his office.

CHAPTER NINETEEN

"I hear you're Mary Lancaster's granddaughter." Tammy, the plump middle-aged receptionist at the tourist information centre, leaned over the counter and eyed Poppy with avid curiosity. "So are you coming to live at Hollyhock Cottage?"

"I... I'm not sure yet."

"Oh, I hope you do and that you'll reopen the nursery—it will be wonderful for the village! People used to come from miles around just to see the cottage garden, you know. In fact, I still get tourists stopping in, asking me the way to Hollyhock Cottage gardens, because they'd read about it somewhere or heard a friend recommend it. They're always so disappointed when they hear that it's closed."

"They'd be even more disappointed if they

actually saw the garden—it's a bit of a jungle at the moment," said Poppy ruefully.

Tammy waved a dismissive hand. "That's because it's been neglected for months, while Mary was ill—but it just needs a bit of weeding and trimming, and it'll be looking beautiful again in no time." She lowered her voice and added, "It shouldn't really be so bad, you know; Pete Sykes was supposed to look after it while your grandmother was ill—she paid him well enough!—but that fellow was a lazy sod, if you'll excuse the language. If your grandmother had known how he was neglecting the place, it would have broken her heart! It was a mercy in the end, really, that she ended her days at the hospice and couldn't see the state that her beautiful garden had fallen into."

Poppy was surprised to feel a strong rush of anger and indignation, as if Pete Sykes had wronged her personally. "That's... that's terrible!"

The woman nodded in agreement. "I know you're not meant to speak ill of the dead but that's the truth. Pete never did an honest day's work in his life, if he could help it. Always gallivanting off organising his dodgy deals instead." She glanced around and lowered her voice. "It's awful to say this but I'm not that surprised that he's been murdered. I always thought he'd come to no good."

Poppy remembered the other villagers in the pub expressing similar sentiments. Obviously, Pete Sykes was the main subject of village gossip at the moment! Then, as Tammy shot her a coy look, Poppy discovered something else that was the subject of village gossip:

"I hear that they've roped off the cottage as a crime scene and that you're staying with that author chap next door?" Tammy raised her eyebrows in a suggestive way. "Nice of him to offer you a room... Handsome fellow, isn't he?"

"Er... I hadn't really noticed," said Poppy stiffly. "And he didn't offer—I mean, it was Inspector Whittaker who suggested it. It was just because Nick—I mean, Mr Forrest—happens to be next door and has a spare room."

"Mm... yes, *very* convenient," said Tammy in a tone that brought colour to Poppy's cheeks. Before she could reply, however, the other woman continued: "It's strange seeing a lady inspector, isn't it? Always feels like a detective ought to be a man, like in the shows on telly. And she's such a pretty lady too. Don't seem right to think of her as a detective... They seem very friendly, don't they? Her and this author chap. Used to see her coming and going in the village a fair bit... She isn't his girlfriend, is she?"

Bloody hell, is there anything this woman doesn't know?

Poppy hastily tried to change the subject. "Um... by the way, do you know if there's anywhere in the village which might sell second-hand clothes?"

"Hmm... you mean, like charity shops? No, the

best thing would be to pop up to Oxford. There should be several shops there. In fact, come to think of it, I walked past a really nice one in St Michael's Street, when I was up in Oxford a few nights ago. 'Preloved Rags', I think it's called. Next to the Indian restaurant. It was closed, but I noticed they had some nice stuff in the window display." Tammy lowered her voice suddenly and added in a conspiratorial manner: "Do you know who I saw sitting in a cosy corner of the Indian restaurant? Jenny Sykes, that's who!"

Poppy frowned. "Pete Sykes's wife?"

The other woman nodded excitedly. "Yes, and it wasn't Pete she was with, I can tell you. Some other chap in a fancy jacket and tie. Had his hands all over her, he did, and Jenny wasn't doing much to stop him."

"I heard some of the other villagers say that she might have been having an affair?" said Poppy, thinking again of the gossip she had heard at the pub.

"Oooh, yes, there's no question about that. Some fellow who works in an office in Oxford, no doubt—you could see that from his fancy suit. Jenny must have met him through work." Tammy waggled her eyebrows.

"What do you mean?" asked Poppy, puzzled by the woman's expression.

"Well, Jenny works as a cleaner—she goes into offices in the evenings, after they're shut. Her fella was probably working late and they got chatting..." Tammy trailed off suggestively.

"Oh, I see." Then suddenly, Poppy had a thought: "Hang on—when did you say you saw her out having dinner?"

"Three nights ago—"

"The night that Pete got murdered?"

Tammy's eyes widened. "Oh my goodness, I think it was!"

"And Jenny told the police that she was home all evening," said Poppy, remembering the interview she'd overheard.

Tammy looked at her suspiciously. "How d'you know that?"

"Er... never mind. Look, Tammy—you need to tell the police what you saw."

The receptionist shifted uncomfortably. "Well... It's not as if I saw Jenny at the cottage, though."

"Yes, but Jenny lied to the police about her alibi and that may be significant."

"But this just means she has a stronger alibi," Tammy argued. "'Cos I can say I saw her in Oxford on the night of the murder, not in Bunnington."

"Yes, but we don't know when Pete was killed. She could have gone to the cottage later that night and killed him then. The point is, she lied when she told the police that she was home all night."

The other woman still looked unconvinced. "I wouldn't like to get her in trouble—"

"If she murdered her husband—"

"Jenny wouldn't murder anyone!" said Tammy, waving a hand scornfully. "She might be having a bit of a 'slap 'n' tickle' on the side but that's her private affair. No, I'm not snitching on her and don't you go telling the police anything either!" she added, giving Poppy a fierce look. "If you do, I'll deny everything."

"But—"

"Anyway, if you want someone who's likely to have killed Pete, you're better looking at his chum, Boyo."

"Boyo?"

"That's what he calls himself. Real name's Bart Simms. Went to school with Pete. Two of 'em as thick as thieves—literally, if you ask me," she added with a dark look. "Always up to dodgy deals together."

"If they're mates, why would you think—er—Boyo would have murdered Pete?"

"Well, even mates fall out with each other, don't they? Especially when there's money involved. Pete was always good at promising things and then not delivering—including his partner's half of the money from a deal."

Poppy frowned. "How do you know all this?"

The woman gave her a look and Poppy shook her head ruefully. It had been a stupid question. Of course, the village grapevine. Ten times more powerful than the best police intel.

Still, she was doubtful. "If they've been friends

since childhood, I can't see Boyo planning the cold-blooded murder of his—"

"Who said anything about cold-blooded murder?" said Tammy. "Likely as not, it was an accident. The two of 'em got into an argument about the money, Boyo lost his temper—and I've seen him do that a few times down at the pub, I can tell you—and he grabs a spade or whatever and whacks Pete on the head. Then, when he realises what he's done, he panics and runs away."

"The body was buried," Poppy pointed out.

"Only shallowly," said Tammy, surprising Poppy again with the extent of her knowledge.

"Well, you *really* need to tell *this* to Inspector Whittaker. At least let the police investigate him. If Boyo is innocent, then it won't matter—but it's your duty to pass on this information."

Tammy shifted uncomfortably. "Well, I... oh, all right... but it's just rumours, mind. It's not like I have any facts." Then she glanced at the timetable pinned to the wall behind her and said quickly, "You'd better run, miss, if you're going to catch the next bus for Oxford."

Poppy knew the woman was just trying to get rid of her and put an end to the subject. Still, there was probably no point in her staying and trying to persuade Tammy further—the receptionist would either decide to tell the police or she wouldn't. *In any case, I'll tell Suzanne myself when I next see her*, thought Poppy. She didn't care if Tammy denied everything. At least the police could start investigating "Boyo" Simms.

She spent most of the trip to Oxford mulling over the mystery of Pete Sykes's murder. She was so engrossed in her thoughts that she missed the stop in the centre of town and instead rode the bus to the end of its route, pulling into the bus station at Gloucester Green on the west side of the city. Still, Oxford was a fairly small city so it was only a short walk back to the main shopping area in the centre.

She had barely come out of the bus station forecourt and crossed the street, when she noticed a sign saying "LEACH PROPERTIES LTD" above a retail unit with large windows that displayed a series of photographs of flats and houses. The unit was the last one in the row and beyond it was a small area which was being used to store the communal rubbish bins and recycling containers for the whole block. A man was standing by the bins, his shoulders hunched, speaking into his phone.

"...of course not, of course not... that's why they call it 'you scratch my back and I'll scratch yours'... Yes, absolutely...it's just a small thing—all you have to do is express your concerns if they ask... and naturally, I'd make it more than worth your while, Dr Goh... no, no, no one else will know about this..."

The man turned slightly sideways and she caught sight of the jowly face and handlebar moustache. Poppy stopped short: it was her cousin, Hubert Leach. He hadn't seen her yet and the last thing she wanted was to speak to him. Hastily, she turned around and retraced her steps, giving the block a wide berth and taking an alternative route into the town centre instead.

She found St Michael's Street fairly easily—a narrow lane leading off the main shopping boulevard that ran through the centre of Oxford— and saw the sign for "Preloved Rags" almost immediately. But it wasn't the second-hand clothing shop that caught her interest—it was the Indian restaurant next door. Poppy walked slowly over and hovered outside the darkened windows. The place was not open yet and anyway, even if it had been, what could she have done? She could hardly walk in and start questioning the waiters about Jenny Sykes—she didn't even have a photo of the woman to show them!

Then, as Poppy turned away from the closed restaurant door, her eyes widened as she looked down the lane and saw a woman coming out of a doorway.

It was Jenny Sykes herself.

CHAPTER TWENTY

Pete Sykes's wife was with another man: a rather short man in his thirties, with a big nose and a thin, almost weasel-like face. He was dressed in a navy suit, with a loud shirt and tie, and was gesticulating and talking in a brash, cocksure manner, obviously enjoying the way the woman next to him was hanging on his every word. They turned away from Poppy and walked arm in arm up the lane, disappearing around the corner at the end, where it joined the main boulevard.

Poppy hesitated for a fraction of a second, then hurried after them. She reached the corner just in time to see them merging with the crowds which were milling down the wide pedestrianised street that was Oxford's main shopping strip. She followed quickly and trailed them into the Covered Market, one of university city's most popular tourist attractions. It would have been easy to lose them in the labyrinth of alleyways, but luckily the crowds seemed to be thinner in here, so that it was fairly easy to keep them within sight.

As Poppy followed the couple at a discreet distance, she found herself enjoying the historic feel of the place and the bustling market atmosphere. Used as she was to slick, modern supermarkets, with their plastic-wrapped, manufactured goods, it was almost a novelty to see an old-fashioned butcher, fishmonger, and greengrocer, as well as other traditional shops, like a cobbler and a milliner, all trading as they had done for over two hundred years.

She wondered if Jenny Sykes and her companion were heading for a particular shop but it looked like they were just browsing aimlessly and flirting, as lovers do. At last, they stopped in front of a shop window and stood with their heads together. As surreptitiously as she could, Poppy sauntered over and stood next to them, pretending to admire the items displayed as well.

It was a boutique selling handmade leather creations by local artisans and craftsmen, with several pretty embroidered wallets arranged in a semicircle at the front of the window. Each wallet had a design of dainty, pendulous white flowers on thin stalks, surrounded by long green leaves.

"...aren't they gorgeous?" Jenny was saying,

pointing at the wallets. She looked meaningfully at her companion. "And it's my favourite flower too: snowdrops—"

"Snowdrops?" The man pulled a face. "You don't want to carry something with them on... My nan always told me that snowdrops are bad luck. Mum said she used to pick them every February when she was a little girl, but my nan would never let her bring them into the house. Said they were an omen of death."

"Oh, rubbish! That's just an old superstition," said Jenny, wrinkling her nose. "Come on, darling... they're gorgeous and I'd been looking for a new wallet... and it's nearly my birthday..." she wheedled.

The man sighed and glanced at the display again, then did a double take. "Bloody hell—is that the price?"

Jenny pouted. "Are you going to be like Pete was and only ever get me cheap gifts?"

"No, but I'm not paying two hundred quid for that scrap of leather there either," said the man firmly. Then he put his arm around a still-pouting Jenny and said, his voice softening, "Listen, I'll take you out to dinner on Thursday—we'll go to the most expensive restaurant in Oxford... how about that? We'll hire a punt and go on the river first—maybe get some strawberries and champagne—then go to dinner after that—"

"Oh, Tom..." Jenny looked at him reproachfully.

"You know Thursday nights I clean that lawyer's office—I won't be finished until well after eight."

"All right, we'll skip the punt then. I'll come and pick you up straight from work—"

"Straight from work!" Jenny squealed indignantly. "A girl's got to have time to put her glad rags on!"

The man put his hands up defensively. "Okay, okay... how about the night after, then? You got a late job then as well?"

Jenny gave a coy little smile. "No, but if it's a Friday, then I would expect a lot more than a dinner date... I'd expect a weekend somewhere nice..."

The man grinned at her and started to say something, then his gaze slid over Jenny's shoulder, to look Poppy straight in the face.

His eyes turned suspicious. "Eh! What are you staring at, then?"

Poppy jumped guiltily. She didn't realise that she had become so engrossed in eavesdropping, she had completely forgotten to maintain her act of looking in the shop window and had simply been staring at the couple next to her. Mumbling an excuse, she hurried away before Jenny could turn around and see her properly. Not that Pete Sykes's wife had met her before or would recognise her, but still, Jenny did go into Bunnington from time to time and Poppy didn't want any awkward scenes.

She stepped panting out of the Covered Market a few minutes later and paused beside a street sign to catch her breath. *Some detective I turned out to be*, she thought. And she wasn't even sure if her attempt at sleuthing had been worth it. Had she actually overheard anything that might be meaningful to the murder investigation? She frowned as she replayed the couple's conversation in her head. Nothing really... other than the fact that Jenny Sykes seemed to be shockingly blasé about her husband's recent death. Here she was out with another man, laughing and flirting, and her husband had only been dead a few days. There had been no sign of grief, no horror... Poppy felt quite repelled by the woman's careless indifference.

She walked slowly back to the bus station at Gloucester Green, passing the block of units that held Hubert Leach's property agency. She wondered if she might see her cousin again. There was no sign of him—however, something else caught her eye: the logo on the sign next to "LEACH PROPERTIES LTD.". She hadn't noticed it before but now she realised that the logo depicted a dainty white flower with three petals, drooping over shyly. It looked very similar to the designs embroidered on those leather wallets in the Covered Market. It was a snowdrop!

It seemed an odd choice for a property company logo. Then Poppy remembered her cousin talking about his love of bulbs, especially snowdrops. What was it that Charles Mannering had called him? A "galanthophile"...? Yes, that was it. *It's funny*, Poppy mused as she continued walking to the station concourse—*you almost expect a big, brash man like Hubert Leach to prefer big, gaudy blooms like gerberas or giant lilies, not an unassuming milky-white flower that could barely hold its head up!*

The trip to Bunnington seemed a lot quicker than on the day she had first arrived, perhaps because the route was more familiar now, and Poppy almost felt a strange sense of homecoming as she walked down the lane to Hollyhock Cottage. As she approached, she was surprised to see a large crowd milling around outside the garden gate. The air was filled by the hubbub of excited conversation.

"What's happened?" she asked one of the villagers in the crowd.

The woman turned a glowing face to her. "They've found the murder weapon!"

CHAPTER TWENTY-ONE

Poppy looked at her in surprise. "In the cottage?" she asked.

The woman jerked her head towards Bertie's house. "No, in the garden next door! Can you believe it?"

Poppy felt her heart give a lurch of dismay. She pushed through the crowd and hurried down the lane to Bertie's front gate, where the young police constable was now standing guard. She was pleased to see that he was dealing with a particularly persistent journalist and she used the opportunity to slip past him.

"Hey! Wait, you can't go in—" he shouted after her.

"Uh... Inspector Whittaker asked for me," said Poppy quickly. "I'm the girl who found the body.

She wants to ask me some more questions."

"But she's not—"

"Don't worry! I know where I'm going."

Before he could reply, she gave him a breezy smile and stepped into the garden, shutting the gate behind her. Once inside, she followed the sound of voices around the side of the house and soon came upon a small crowd of people standing by the stone wall that separated this property from her grandmother's. It was not far from the gap where she had met Bertie yesterday and she saw him now, looking very old and defenceless, surrounded by several police officers. She was surprised to see that Suzanne was nowhere in sight—no wonder the constable at the gate had been confused when she claimed to be meeting the detective inspector!

Einstein stood beside his master, glaring at the men around them, all his hackles raised. The terrier looked as if he would have liked to fling himself at one of the officers and it was only the taut leash in Bertie's hands that restrained him.

"...but I don't know how that came to be on my property. I assure you, I'd never seen it before," Bertie was protesting.

"Well, of course you'd say that," a man said scornfully. He was the only one dressed in civilian clothes amidst the group of uniformed constables and Poppy guessed that he was a detective— although he looked the very opposite of a "cool, professional investigator". His tie was askew, his protruding belly hanging over his trouser belt, and his face was drawn back in an unpleasant sneer. Poppy recalled seeing him with Suzanne yesterday—she'd heard him being addressed as "sergeant"—and it was obvious that he was enjoying being "top dog" while his boss was not around.

"You might be able to lie to others but you can't lie to me, old man," said the sergeant. "I've got the knack of reading people, see? And I can tell that you're lying."

"But you just said I can't lie to you so how can I be lying?" said Bertie, looking confused.

The sergeant flushed. "Don't mix up my words!" he snapped. "Now, I'm asking you again—how does a bloodstained spade end up in your garden?"

Bertie frowned thoughtfully. "Well, I don't know... It could have arrived here in any manner. There are an infinite number of possibilities, you know, if you really want to calculate all the potential pathways—and then if you believe in the Multiverse Theory, there are all the parallel universes to consider too and—"

"Shut up! I didn't ask you about sodding parallel universes—I asked you about here! Now!" The sergeant jabbed a finger at the ground beneath his feet. "You'd better have a good explanation for why the murder weapon was found in your garden—"

"Sir..." one of the uniformed constables interrupted, looking uncomfortable. "Sir, we're not sure yet that it's the murder weapon. Forensics haven't tested—

"Of course it's the bloody murder weapon!" he snarled. "It's got blood stains on it, hasn't it?" He turned back to Bertie and wagged a finger in the old man's face. "I know you did it and I don't need some stupid tests to prove it." He smirked. "Can't wait to see the guv'nor's face when she gets back and I tell her I've nicked the murderer already—

"Wait—you've got it all wrong!" Poppy cried, darting forwards.

The sergeant swung around. "Who are you?" he demanded.

"I'm... I'm the girl who found the body," she said. "And I think you're making a terrible mistake. I mean, anyone could have tossed the spade over the wall, from the cottage garden. It has nothing to do with Bertie— with Dr Noble, I mean."

The sergeant scowled at her. "The weapon was found in his garden, there is a gaping hole in the wall between the two properties, and he has no alibi for the night of the murder... don't tell me that doesn't look suspicious?"

"Well, yes, it does, but... but it could just be circumstantial evidence. Honestly, he isn't the murderer. He's just a normal resident of the village—" Poppy glanced at Bertie and noticed for the first time that the old man was wearing a white lab coat over a cooking apron, and had swimming goggles on his head. She cleared her throat, "—

um... who has an unusual wardrobe. But he wouldn't hurt anyone, much less murder them. Look—if he had really murdered Pete Sykes, surely he wouldn't have been stupid enough to leave a bloodstained spade lying around in his own garden?" she pointed out.

The sergeant flushed angrily. "That's... that's just random speculation," he blustered. "I deal in facts and the facts point to Dr Noble being the murderer."

"But they don't! They don't have to point to anything!" Poppy burst out, losing her patience. "Where is Inspector Whittaker? Have you spoken to her since finding the spade?"

"She's been called to another case. I'm Detective Sergeant Lee—I'm in charge here now," he said, jutting his chin out. "And I don't need you sticking your nose in and questioning my judgement!" Pointedly, he turned his back on her and said to Bertie, "Come on—you're coming down to the station with me."

"Oh!" Bertie jerked back, looking alarmed. "I must get back—" He turned and started trotting towards the house.

"The suspect is getting away!" yelled the sergeant, obviously thinking he was in an American cop show. "Quick! Stop him!"

Two officers hesitated for a moment, then hurried after Bertie, trying to reach out and grab the old man. It was hard to do, though, with Einstein running in circles around his master, barking and growling and his leash tangling in everyone's legs. One constable tripped and fell on his bottom, whilst the other hopped from foot to foot, trying to avoid the terrier's teeth on his ankles.

The whole thing looked more like a comic farce than a dangerous arrest and Poppy saw Sergeant Lee scowling furiously. He stalked over himself and grabbed Bertie's elbow roughly. Poppy gasped as she saw him aim a kick at Einstein—although thankfully, the little terrier's reflexes were quick and he easily dodged the vicious foot.

Bertie struggled to pull his elbow free. "Let me go! I must get back in the house—"

"Hah! You think I don't realise your ploy to escape?" said Lee. "Think you can sneak out of a window on the other side of the house and go on the run?"

Bertie looked at him in astonishment. "On the run? Why would I want to go on the run? No, no, I need to get back in the house because I've left the rice pudding in the oven and if I don't take it out before we go to the police station, it will burn terribly. It's so hard to achieve that perfect caramelised skin on top of the rice, don't you think?"

"Wh-what? Rice pudding?" spluttered Lee, going very red in the face. "Are you trying to take the piss?"

Bertie looked affronted. "Certainly not. I would never urinate here in the garden—how uncouth. I always use the indoors lavatory." Then he brightened. "Oh! Would you or one of the other officers like to use the toilet? I'm looking for some test subjects for my new Loo Blaster." At the looks of bewilderment from the other police officers, he added proudly, "It's a new toilet brush gun I've invented, with ejectable heads."

Sergeant Lee's chest heaved and veins stood out on his forehead. He spluttered ineffectually, looking totally at loss for words. Finally, he took a deep breath and said through gritted teeth, "Just... go and sort out your bloody rice pudding... and get back here."

Bertie trotted off, Einstein at his heels, and returned a few moments later, minus his goggles but now carrying a battered leather suitcase and an umbrella.

"Always be prepared—you never know when it's going to rain in England," he told Poppy cheerfully. Then he handed her the leash. "Would you do me a favour, my dear, and look after Einstein for me? I don't think they allow dogs at the police station and I wouldn't like to leave him tied up outside on the street."

"Oh, of course, but Bertie, listen..." Poppy put an urgent hand on his arm. "You know you don't have to answer any questions until you've spoken to your lawyer? You do *have* a lawyer, don't you?"

Sergeant Lee made an angry movement. "You keep out of it!" he snarled at Poppy. "Don't go giving him any ideas!"

Bertie patted her hand. "Don't worry, my dear. I'm sure it's just a mix-up, that's all. And in fact, this is a marvellous opportunity to test my new Laughing Gas Air Freshener! It not only freshens the air, you see, but also injects some much-needed cheer and humour into the workplace." He patted his suitcase. "I've got the cannisters here and I just need a group of men and women in an enclosed space... so the police station should be perfect!"

"Er... Bertie, maybe that's not such a great idea..."

Before she would say more, Sergeant Lee grabbed the old man's arm and began stalking towards the front gate, hauling Bertie after him. The other police officers, looking a bit shamefaced, trooped after the sergeant. Einstein gave a forlorn whine as he watched his master disappear from sight.

Poppy reached down to give the little terrier a reassuring pat. "It's all right... he'll be back soon," she said, with more conviction than she felt. Giving the leash a gentle tug, she started to lead the dog out of the garden as well. He resisted for a moment, then trotted uncertainly after her.

The police cars had left and the crowd was thinning out now. Poppy led the terrier up the lane, past the cottage garden, and back to Nick's place. She hesitated on the threshold—this wasn't really her house and she hadn't got Nick's permission to bring a strange dog into his home—but the only other option was to tie the terrier up outside and she didn't have the heart to do that.

Anyway, it's just for a few hours, she thought. *I'm sure Bertie will be released soon. And even if they keep him overnight, surely he'll be released tomorrow? Whatever Sergeant Lee says, they have no concrete evidence showing him to be the murderer, so surely they can't keep detaining him?* And Nick was away for a few more days still, she remembered. By the time he returned, Einstein would be back in his own home, so Nick need never know.

So salving her conscience, she unlocked the front door and led the terrier into the house, releasing him from his leash. They hadn't gone two steps down the hallway, however, when she heard a ferocious hiss followed by an outraged yowl. *Uh-oh.* Nick might have been gone, but she'd forgotten that there was another resident here—one who *did* mind the presence of a strange dog in the house very much.

"*H-OW? H-OOOW?*" demanded Oren, stalking forwards, his eyes narrowed to slits and all his fur standing on end.

Einstein stiffened on seeing his old enemy and lifted his lips to show his teeth. He let out a loud growl which was undoubtedly the canine equivalent of "*Go stuff yourself!*"

Oren hissed at the insult and spat furiously,

sending back a few choice words of his own. The terrier bristled and returned with a volley of barking, which had the cat puffing up even more.

"N-now, now... there's no need for this," said Poppy, putting out her hands. "Why don't we just... uh... calm down and try to make friends, eh?"

Oren shot her a contemptuous look which clearly told her what he thought of that idea, whilst Einstein kicked back with his hind legs a few times, his head lowered, looking as if he planned to charge the cat. Poppy grabbed his collar and, holding on tightly, she dragged him sideways into the first doorway she could see, slamming the door shut after them. In the hallway outside, she heard Oren give another furious yowl—obviously making sure that a cat always got the last word—then subside into silence.

She straightened with a sigh and realised that they were in the sitting room. Well, Einstein could simply stay here until his owner got back to claim him. It was a large comfortable room, with direct access to the garden through the French doors, and soft carpet for the terrier to lie on. She glanced at the bookcases lining the walls and decided she would keep Einstein company by spending the afternoon here—it was a great excuse to curl up and read.

Her growling stomach reminded her, though, that she hadn't had any lunch yet and it was already mid-afternoon. Slipping back out into the hallway, she found Oren sitting outside, twitching his tail and staring fixedly at the closed sitting room door. He gave her a reproachful look as she bent to pat him, and she said:

"Don't worry, Oren—Einstein's not staying. He'll be going back to his own home."

"*N-ow!*"

She laughed. "No, I can't take him back now. He's got to stay here until his owner gets back, but it should just be for a few hours, okay?"

The ginger tom got up and stalked away with offended dignity. Poppy made her way to the kitchen, where she collected a bowl of water for Einstein, a mug of tea for herself, and several biscuits from the tin on the counter. Then she returned to the sitting room, picked up her grandmother's plant encyclopaedia, and made herself comfortable on the sofa for the rare luxury of an afternoon reading.

CHAPTER TWENTY-TWO

The rest of the day passed in relative calm. Poppy made sure to keep the dog and cat apart, and aside from one heated argument through the sitting room door (in which Oren still got the last word), the two animals maintained a frosty stalemate. Poppy ploughed her way through her grandmother's books, delighting in learning the names and habits of many flowers and plants she had previously only vaguely recognised or heard about.

As the light faded and the evening began to draw in, however, she began to worry. Where was Bertie? Were the police going to keep him overnight? A phone call to the police station didn't help much— all the duty sergeant would tell her was that Dr Noble was "still helping the police with enquiries". As darkness fell outside and she went around drawing the curtains in the house, Poppy resigned herself to keeping Einstein with her overnight. She took the terrier out into the garden for a little walk, then brought him back into the house, cautiously keeping an eye out for the ginger tom. Thankfully, though, Oren seemed to have gone off on patrol at dusk and so she had the house to herself. She let the terrier loose and he rushed around, his nose to the floor, sniffing everything excitedly. Calling him after her, she walked to the kitchen, then realised her mistake when he dived instantly on the bowl of dried cat food in the corner and began gobbling the contents.

"Hey! No, Einstein—stop that!" Poppy cried, rushing over to grab the bowl.

Too late. Most of the little fish-shaped biscuits were gone, and Einstein was busily hoovering up any pieces which had fallen to the floor. Poppy was just looking around the cupboards for a box of cat food to refill the bowl when the sound of noisy slurping made her whirl around in dismay. Einstein was now attacking Oren's water bowl with gusto, sloshing water and dog drool all over the kitchen floor.

"Nooo..." Poppy groaned.

It took her several minutes to clean up after the dog, but the kitchen was restored to order at last, this time with the cat bowls safely out of reach on the counter. Then she opened the fridge and pondered its contents. She didn't really want to cook—the less mess she made in the kitchen, the better—so she settled for some cheese and fruit, accompanied by some fancy oat crackers she found in the pantry. As she prepared the simple meal, she glanced down and saw Einstein sitting at her feet, looking up hopefully.

"You've already had a whole bowl of cat food and several of my biscuits this afternoon," she told him severely. "Surely you can't still be hungry?"

The terrier jumped up on his hind legs and danced around, waving his front paws and wagging his tail. *"Ruff! Ruff-ruff!"*

Poppy laughed in spite of herself. Suddenly, she was glad the little dog was here. It made the big house seem less empty. Then, for some reason, she thought of Nell and felt a pang of guilt. Her old friend would be wondering what was happening—she should really give her a ring. As soon as Poppy finished her dinner and had washed up and tidied the kitchen, she put the call through to London.

"Poppy! Oh, my lordy Lord, I'm so glad you rang—I was beginning to get worried, especially after that thing on the news about South Oxfordshire Police Station—"

"What thing?"

"Haven't you seen it, dear? It was on all the news channels and everyone's talking about it."

"No, Nick hasn't got a TV. What is it? What happened?"

"Well, actually, no one is sure what happened

exactly but... it seems like everyone at the police station suddenly got an attack of the giggles!"

"Attack of the giggles?" said Poppy, perplexed.

"Yes, apparently all the officers started giggling uncontrollably. Even the suspects in custody were laughing their heads off. And anyone who entered the station to see what was going on would fall about laughing as well. They had to evacuate the station in the end and several national security experts are now trying to work out what happened. They think it might have been some kind of gas released in the station... er... I can't remember the name now... nitrogen something—"

"Nitrous oxide? Laughing gas?" said Poppy, suddenly having an inkling what could have happened.

"Yes, that's exactly right! Laughing gas... although no one knows how so much could have got into the station to affect everyone like that. There's even talk that it might have been some form of terrorist attack. But, really, why on earth would a small provincial police station be a target—"

"I doubt it's a terrorist attack—more likely a 'mad scientist attack'," said Poppy, chuckling and thinking of an old man carrying a battered leather suitcase containing his latest invention.

"Eh? Mad scientist? What are you talking about?"

"Never mind. Don't worry—it's definitely not a terrorist attack or anything really dangerous."

"Well, it all sounds very odd to me," said Nell, tutting in disapproval. "And now there's this murder as well! It sounds like all sorts of strange things are going on in Oxfordshire. Where are you now? Are you coming back soon, dear?"

"I'm still in Bunnington—"

"At the cottage?'"

"No, in Nick's house. The police haven't released the crime scene yet."

"Hmm..."

Poppy could almost see Nell pursing her lips and, to forestall another anxious lecture, she said quickly, "And he's not trying to have his wicked way with me—in fact, he's not even here. He's gone away on a book tour, remember? There's only his cat here with me."

"Hmm... And what about the murder? Have the police solved the case yet?"

"Nell...!" Poppy gave a slightly exasperated laugh. "This isn't a crime drama on TV—they can't just solve the case in an hour! The body was only found yesterday. I don't think the police even have any suspects yet—or at least, not any correct ones," she added sourly, thinking of poor Bertie.

"What do you mean?"

She told Nell about meeting Bertie and the discovery of the bloodstained spade in his garden, followed by Sergeant Lee's high-handed treatment of the old inventor.

"Well, that's a shame, but I'm sure the police

know what they're doing, dear."

"But I don't think they do! It was terrible how Sergeant Lee was treating Bertie," Poppy protested. "It was practically bullying! I couldn't believe it. And he didn't even let poor Bertie get a word in edgewise to defend himself. He should really have a lawyer before speaking to the police—Bertie, I mean. I tried to tell him that, but Sergeant Lee snapped my head off and told me to mind my own business."

"Well, he's right," said Nell primly. "You shouldn't interfere with a murder investigation."

"I'm not! I'm just trying to make sure that Bertie is treated well. You know, I've been thinking... maybe I should ring the police station again and ask if he's okay, see if he needs help finding a lawyer—"

"I'm sure the police will advise him of his rights and contact his family."

"But what if he doesn't have any family? He seemed so old and alone—"

"Poppy, dear..." Nell's voice was gentle. "Bertie isn't your father, you know."

Poppy flushed. "I know that! I never thought of him that way."

Nell didn't answer but her silence spoke volumes.

Poppy continued doggedly, "Sergeant Lee is just fixated on poor Bertie and is determined to prove him guilty, instead of considering any other possible suspect. I mean, what about Pete's wife? Jenny

Sykes lied about her alibi—she was seen out having dinner with another man on the night of the murder, when she said she was at home the whole evening. In fact, I saw them together myself in Oxford earlier today. Jenny was flirting and laughing, and didn't look remotely upset about her husband's death."

"Maybe it wasn't a happy marriage."

"Well, that's exactly it! The villagers said that Jenny wanted a divorce and Pete wouldn't give it to her. That would be a good reason—"

"People don't commit murder just because they want a divorce," said Nell.

"Aww, come on, Nell—you're the one who's always reading those romance novels. Don't people do things in the heat of passion?"

"Well, they don't do *those* sort of things, dear," said Nell. "My romances never have things like dead bodies." Her voice turned dreamy. "Mmm... what would happen is that Jenny's lover would be her true soul mate and he would be six foot tall, with rippling abs and eyes the colour of a stormy night... and he would fight Pete for her honour—oh, not kill Pete, but maybe just punch him in the face—and then he'd take Jenny away to a romantic little cottage with a four-poster bed and a roaring fire, and make love to her until she—"

"NELL!" Poppy cried, not knowing whether to groan in disgust at the image conjured up or to laugh in exasperated disbelief. The latter urge won.

"Honestly, you have no idea how far the reality is from what you're imagining," she said, thinking of the short, weaselly man that she had seen with Jenny. "Anyway, my point is, there are so many far more likely suspects than Bertie—like Jenny... or... or even Hubert Leach—"

"Who's Hubert Leach?"

"Oh, sorry... I never told you about him," said Poppy, recalling that she'd only met her cousin the night before, after she'd spoken to Nell. "You know the lawyer Charles Mannering? Well, he invited me over to his house for dinner last night, so that I wouldn't have to spend the evening alone."

"That was nice of him," said Nell, sounding impressed.

Poppy smiled. "Yes, Mr Mannering is so nice. I mean, I know he's sort of my lawyer—but I feel like he's really trying to take care of me. Anyway, Hubert Leach turned up on the doorstep just as we were about to start dinner. He's the son of Mary Lancaster's first cousin, you know, which makes us second cousins, I think."

Nell gasped in delight. "I never knew that you had a cousin! Why, that's lovely, Poppy; some family for you to get to know at last—"

"Yes, except... I'm not sure he's that thrilled about my existence. I mean, he acted super-friendly—smarmy, even—but I got the impression..."

"What?"

"Well, he made a comment suggesting that the final will might not have been valid—you know, like I might be an imposter or something."

"Oh, I'm sure he was joking, dear—"

"Maybe. He did try to pass it off as a joke—but I got the impression that inside, he was being serious. Mr Mannering got quite offended, actually."

"Was there a previous will where Hubert got everything?"

"Yes, actually, there was," said Poppy. "How did you know?"

"Then I'm not surprised that he's bitter. The sale of the cottage and land would bring in a lot of money, and it would all have been his if you hadn't turned up. He probably resents you, but that's not your fault, dear, and you mustn't feel guilty about it."

"I'm not, really. At least... I *did* feel guilty at first for not liking him more—because he is my cousin, after all—but to be honest, Nell, he... well, he's a bit of an obnoxious git. He practically invited himself to dinner and really took advantage of Mr Mannering's hospitality; I'd never seen anyone with so much *chutzpah!*"

Nell sighed. "Well, people who are loud and demanding often get what they want, so they continue behaving that way." She paused, then added: "But I don't see what this has to do with the murder?"

"Oh... well, I had this thought... See, during

dinner, Hubert started talking about how much he's into bulbs—"

"Bulbs? What, like light bulbs?"

"No, silly!" Poppy laughed. "Flower bulbs. You know, like tulips and daffodils and things like that. Both he and Mr Mannering are really into gardening, and they started talking about their plants and... and then this morning, when I was in Oxford, I happened to walk past Hubert's property agency and I noticed that his company logo is a snowdrop."

Nell sounded puzzled. "So what, dear? I don't understand—lots of people like flowers and put them in designs and things."

"Yes, but Mr Mannering said there's a name for people who are into snowdrops—they're called 'galanthophiles' and they do crazy things, just to get a plant they want."

Nell began to laugh. "You're not telling me that you think your cousin murdered Pete Sykes for some snowdrops?"

Poppy laughed sheepishly. "Well... when you put it like that, it does sound a bit stupid. But... but I still think there's something dodgy about Hubert. I don't know what it is—it's just a feeling I've got."

"If you have any suspicions, you should tell them to the police," said Nell.

Poppy made a face at the thought of having to speak to Sergeant Lee. If her own friend had laughed at her "snowdrop theory", what would the sneering detective sergeant do?

"I don't know... I haven't got all the details worked out yet. Maybe I need to find some more supporting evidence first before I go to the authorities—"

"Poppy..." Nell's voice was stern. "Investigating a murder is the police's job. Don't get involved."

"But, Nell, you don't understand," Poppy protested. "Sergeant Lee—the sergeant in charge of the case—is such a pompous arse! I know he won't listen to me... not unless I've got something very convincing to show him."

"I thought you said there was a lady inspector in charge of the case? She seemed quite nice, from what you said."

"She is—but she's been called away to another case, and in the meantime her sergeant's in charge and he's an absolute prat."

"Whatever he may be, he's the detective in charge of the investigation. Now..." Nell's voice turned brisk as she moved on to a subject that she considered far more important than mere murder. "Did you wash the pillows on the bed before using them, dear? Or at least take them out in the sun and give them a good beating? Most pillows are absolutely filthy, you know—full of dead skin and dust mite faeces—and Lord only knows how long those pillows have been sitting in that cottage..."

CHAPTER TWENTY-THREE

Poppy was woken up the next morning by a cold, wet nose snuffling in her face and, when she opened her eyes, she saw a small bundle of shaggy black fur jump off the bed, stretch, then trot to the door.

"*Ruff!*" Einstein said, looking back at Poppy and wagging his tail.

Poppy groaned and sat up, rubbing her eyes blearily. With Bertie not returning last night, she'd had no choice but to keep Einstein with her and this meant keeping the terrier shut up in her bedroom during the night. The dog had instantly jumped up and made himself comfortable on the bed, and she hadn't had the heart to remove him. He had been sad and subdued all evening, obviously missing his master, and sleeping near her seemed to have given him some comfort.

Now, though, she winced as she saw the dog hairs on the bedspread. Not only had she not got permission from Nick to bring a strange dog into his house, but she had let the uninvited guest sleep on the bed! *I'll make sure to wash and replace all the linen and bedding before I leave so no one can tell*, she thought as she hurriedly dressed and opened the door to the hallway. Then she stopped in her tracks.

Oren sat outside the bedroom door, his tail twitching up and down, like someone impatiently tapping their feet. He had been staring fixedly at the door and, as she opened it, his yellow eyes gleamed with triumph as he spied his nemesis in the room behind her. The ginger tom had been outraged last night when he had finally returned from his evening sojourn to discover that not only was the canine intruder still in his home, but had slobbered all over his cat food and water bowl too!

He had been furious and let Poppy know it, walking up and down the kitchen, yelling *"N-ow! N-OW!"* as he demanded the dog be removed. It was only after she had found some fillet steak in the fridge, and supplied him with several large helpings, that Oren had finally been mollified and stalked off to wash himself in Nick's study. Still, Poppy wondered if the ginger tom had been waiting outside the door all night, plotting his revenge.

She stepped into the hallway and slammed the

door behind her before Einstein could follow. She heard the terrier whine in protest and scratch at the door, and saw the cat's hackles rise in response to the sounds.

"Er... hello, Oren! Looking for your breakfast?" she said brightly, scooping the cat up in her arms and hurrying away from her bedroom door. She bundled him into the kitchen and placated him with some fresh cat food in his bowl, then—as he was busy eating—she sneaked back to her bedroom. Making sure that Einstein was securely clipped to his leash, she took him the other way and breathed a sigh of relief as they stepped out of the front door without being intercepted.

Once in the garden, Poppy released the terrier to do his business, then put a call through to Charles Mannering. In spite of what Nell had said last night, Poppy had been unable to stop worrying about Bertie. She didn't know if the old inventor had called his own legal advisor but it wouldn't hurt to get another lawyer on his side. And Mannering *had* invited her to call him whenever she needed help— she was sure his offer had been genuine.

She smiled as she thought of the lawyer's kindly, fatherly manner. He would be the perfect person to confide in, someone who would listen and advise and reassure her with his wisdom. The kind of figure she'd always wished she had, growing up...

"Miss Lancaster—how lovely to hear from you... No, no, it's not too early... I tend to arrive at the office quite early—I like to get here before the rush starts, you see... I was simply enjoying a cup of tea and perusing the morning papers..." He made a loud tutting sound. "Terrible goings-on in the House of Commons... I really don't know what the Conservatives are thinking... Anyway, was there something in particular that you wanted to speak to me about, my dear?"

"Um, well, first I wanted to say thank you again for dinner—"

"Oh, not at all. It was my pleasure, it was my pleasure." He cleared his throat and added, "*Ahem*... I... er... I'm sorry about your cousin intruding like that. I hope you didn't find the evening too much of an ordeal."

"No, no, it was fine... and I picked up a lot of gardening tips!" said Poppy, chuckling. Then she sobered and said, "Actually... speaking of Hubert, I was wondering—do you know if he and Pete Sykes were friendly?"

"Well, they certainly knew each other, if that's what you're asking—whether they were close friends, I'm afraid I have no idea. Why do you ask?"

She hesitated, then plunged in: "I think Hubert might be involved in Pete's murder."

"Goodness me, *Hubert*? But why—"

"I... I have this theory. I know it might sound a bit crazy but... well, I was thinking... what if... what if Hubert had been doing a deal with Pete Sykes and something went wrong?"

"Doing a deal? I'm sorry, I don't follow," said Mannering, sounding completely befuddled.

Poppy took a deep breath. "Sorry, I should have started from the other end. You know I'm staying at Nick Forrest's house? He's the crime author who lives next door to Hollyhock Cottage."

"Yes, I believe I've met him once and I have certainly read his books. They are remarkably good."

"Well, I was talking to Nick yesterday, before he left on his book tour, and he told me about some research he's doing for his latest book. Apparently, there's a black market trade in rare and exotic plants—you know, people smuggling plants into the country or stealing them from other gardens, and then selling them to collectors, who will pay ridiculous prices just to get their hands on a variety they want."

She heard Mannering make a sound of surprise and continued hurriedly, "And Pete is known for getting things from dodgy sources and selling them privately. You know, like mobile phones and things. His wife admitted it to the police."

"Did she indeed? But how could you know that, my dear?"

Poppy hesitated. She didn't feel ready to admit that she had been eavesdropping on a police interview. Mannering was a lawyer, after all, and no matter how friendly and supportive he was, she didn't think he would approve.

"I... uh... happened to overhear something. Anyway, the point is, smuggling rare and illegal plants is exactly the sort of thing that Pete would get involved in, right? Especially if he was working at my grandmother's nursery. It would have provided him with the perfect cover! He would have access to plant shipments and he could hide things amongst the legitimate plants."

"What... what an extraordinary idea!" said Mannering.

"Yes, and so I was thinking: Hubert probably got Pete to source illegal plants for him—like a rare snowdrop variety or something... You said he was a 'galanthophile', didn't you? And they're known for being a bit obsessive, aren't they?" Warming to her subject, she continued earnestly, "Suppose Hubert and Pete arranged to meet at the cottage for the exchange, but suppose something went wrong—like maybe Pete asked for more money and Hubert wouldn't give it to him, or something like that... And suppose they had an argument, and somehow Hubert ended up whacking Pete on the head with a nearby spade. Then he panicked, buried the body in the flowerbed and ran home."

There was silence for a long moment on the other end of the line. Now that she had voiced her theory aloud, Poppy realised how outlandish it sounded. Somehow, everything seemed a lot more plausible in her head.

"Um... I... I realise it sounds a bit far-fetched,"

she said defensively. "But it could all fit, honestly! We just need to find out a bit more about Pete's illicit activities—whether he really was using the nursery as a cover for smuggling illegal plants and who some of his clients were—"

"Have you told the police about this?"

"No... not yet. I wasn't sure they would believe me—I mean, I thought it might look better if I went to them with some kind of proof. That's why I think we need to do some more digging and—"

"My dear, I fear you may be right about your cousin."

Poppy stopped. The lawyer's ominous tone chilled her. "What do you mean?"

He hesitated, then said, "I hadn't wanted to mention it as I didn't want to distress you unnecessarily... and it may all still come to nothing... but... well, I heard a disturbing rumour from some colleagues yesterday. It seems that your cousin may be planning to contest your grandmother's will."

"But... but how can he do that? I mean, the will has been executed, hasn't it? I've already inherited the estate."

"Ah... well, claims can still be made within six months of the date the Grant of Probate was obtained. And in your case, the situation is even more complicated," said Mannering awkwardly. "You see, because of the unusual clause in the will—the one stating that you have to keep the nursery going, if you wish to remain at Hollyhock Cottage—and because you have opted not to continue the family business, things are in a sort of limbo state until the property is sold. In a sense, the current situation makes you especially vulnerable."

"But... but I still don't see how Hubert can challenge things when the will clearly states that I'm the beneficiary!"

"Ah, well, you see, that was not the only will that Mary Lancaster made. It *was* her final will and testament, but she had made a prior will in which she had left the estate to her closest living relative: Hubert Leach. Now, under British law, it is possible to challenge a will if one feels that one has been unfairly disinherited; there are various grounds for this, such as showing that the will was forged or that it was not executed in the proper manner—for example, not being signed in the presence of two witnesses."

"But it was, wasn't it?" asked Poppy quickly.

"Yes, yes, there are no issues in that quarter."

"So then—"

"Well, a will can also be invalidated if you can prove that the person making the will was not of sound mind, and therefore unaware of their actions—such as someone suffering from mental illness or under the influence of medication." Mannering paused, then said sombrely, "I fear that your cousin may try to claim that your grandmother lacked testamentary capacity—that is, she wasn't mentally capable of making a new will. If he can prove that, then he may be able to claim that the estate should be discharged as per her prior will— the one that named *him* as the sole beneficiary."

Poppy felt a cold flash of fear. "Are you saying that he could succeed? That I could be disinherited, and the estate revert to him?"

The lawyer hesitated. "As I said, I don't want to alarm you, my dear, but... yes, essentially, it could happen. You could lose everything."

CHAPTER TWENTY-FOUR

A wave of despair, stronger than anything she had felt before, engulfed Poppy. Lose the estate? Lose Hollyhock Cottage? The thought made her sick. She didn't want to admit it, but a part of her had begun to think of the place as "home". Which she knew was silly, of course. She wasn't staying here. She was selling the cottage...

She gasped as a second thought struck her: the money! The money from the sale of the cottage was going to be her freedom, her chance to leave her old life of constant poverty, worry, and drudgery behind. Even more than that, it was going to give her the chance to follow a dream, to find her father and completely transform her dull, meaningless life into one filled with glamour and excitement.

And now it was being snatched away... If Hubert

succeeded in contesting the will, she would have nothing. She would be back to boring, dreary Poppy with her mundane, dreary life, her dead-end job and her bullying boss—

Wait.

Her heart lurched as reality hit her. No, she didn't even have that dead-end job now. Without the inheritance from her grandmother, she really had nothing: no job, no prospects, no place to live...

"He can't!" she said fiercely. "He can't win! We have to do something. We... we have to fight him in court and—"

"My dear, until Hubert makes an official complaint, it is best if we don't do anything. The first rule of engagement is always to let your opponent show his cards first, then we can respond accordingly."

"Oh... yes... of course," said Poppy, calming down and reminding herself that a lawyer would know best how to handle such legal challenges. She felt incredibly grateful again to have Mannering on her side. She took a deep breath, feeling her mind clear as the rush of panic left her. Hubert hadn't won yet, she reminded herself. And she wasn't going to let him. She was going to find a way.

A thought occurred to her and she asked: "You said there were two witnesses to the will—wouldn't they be able to testify that my grandmother was fine?"

"Yes... well... that's just the point. One of the

witnesses was your grandmother's GP and the other was Pete Sykes." The lawyer sounded uncomfortable. "That's why I brought this up—I mean, it had never occurred to me that Hubert might be involved in the murder. But when you mentioned your... er... 'interesting' theory just now, it struck me that with Sykes gone, there is only one witness left to dispute Hubert's claims, and if that witness can be persuaded to testify that your grandmother lacked full mental capacity..."

He trailed off but Poppy understood his meaning immediately.

She drew her breath in sharply. "You're saying that Hubert could have murdered Pete Sykes to get rid of one witness, so as to smooth his way to contest the will."

"This is all pure speculation, of course," said the lawyer, sounding even more uncomfortable. "I must remind you that we have no proof—"

"No, no, it all fits!" cried Poppy excitedly. "In fact, it fits even better than my silly snowdrops theory. Murdering someone for an illegal plant probably belongs more to the pages of Nick's novels," she admitted. "But killing them to silence them is a *real* reason. People will do anything when there are large sums of money involved—"

The lawyer interrupted anxiously. "But my dear, I must remind you again—there has been no official challenge to the will yet. It was merely a rumour and I urge you to proceed with caution. You could lay yourself open to a lot of unpleasantness, not to mention a defamation suit, if you accuse Hubert of a serious crime, of which you have no evidence..."

But Poppy was barely listening. She was thinking furiously back to the dinner at Mannering's house and trying to remember what Hubert had said. He had definitely questioned the validity of the will—she wondered now if he had been "testing the waters" and seeing what the reaction would be. Because he must have already had his plan in place by then. He must have arranged to meet Sykes at the cottage the night before she'd arrived—although perhaps not with the initial plan to kill him. Perhaps Hubert had tried at first to persuade Sykes to support his claim regarding Mary Lancaster's mental state, and when the gardener had refused, for whatever reason, Hubert had decided to silence him permanently instead.

Yes, it all fits! I've got *to find a way to prove Hubert's the murderer*, thought Poppy.

Not only would it be bringing a criminal to justice—and releasing Bertie from suspicion—but also, if her cousin was arrested, then there would be no danger of him contesting the will. Her inheritance would be safe. The estate, the cottage, everything would be hers to do with as she wished...

She came back to the present and became aware again of what Charles Mannering was saying:

"...am afraid I have a meeting with a client in a

few minutes. I'm sorry to have to cut this short—"

"No, no, that's no problem," said Poppy quickly. "It was kind of you to listen."

"Not at all... and I urge you to bear in mind what I said regarding the dangers of defamation. Until your cousin makes an official claim, the best course of action is simply to wait and see, and in the meantime, I'm sure the police are continuing with the investigation—"

"Oh! I nearly forgot!" Poppy exclaimed. "The police have someone in custody at the moment. His name is Dr Bertram Noble; he lives on the other side of Hollyhock Cottage. Sergeant Lee jumped on him and took him in for questioning, but Bertie has nothing to do with the murder! I'm not sure if he has any legal support of his own, so I was wondering—would you be able to help him?"

"But, my dear, are you *sure* he has nothing to do with the murder?" Mannering asked doubtfully. "I mean, if the sergeant feels that he is worthy of investigation—"

"No, no, Bertie is innocent. Trust me! The sergeant is just a total ars—I mean, he's just got the wrong end of the stick."

"But why would the police have taken him into custody? There must be some reason," insisted Mannering.

"Well, okay, the murder weapon *was* found on his property," said Poppy reluctantly.

"Ah..."

"And... and Bertie doesn't have an alibi for the night of the murder," Poppy continued. She knew that if Mannering was to help Bertie at all, she had to tell the lawyer everything. "Plus, there's a gap in the wall between his garden and that of Hollyhock Cottage—a gap big enough for a man to get through."

She didn't add that she herself had seen Bertie climbing furtively through the hole in the wall. As long as she kept quiet, no one had to know about that.

"I see."

Poppy winced at the lawyer's tone of voice and hurriedly added: "But that could all just be 'circumstantial evidence' or whatever you call it. For example, anyone could have tossed that spade over the wall into Bertie's garden."

"True... but you have to see it from the police's point of view as well, my dear," said Mannering gently. "These are all strong coincidences which cannot be ignored."

He paused, then asked, his voice changing, becoming much more detached and lawyer-like, "And how well do you actually know Dr Noble? Do you know anything about his background? What he does? Where he came from?"

"No, not really," admitted Poppy. "I only met him the day before yesterday, actually. I think he's some kind of inventor or something. The inside of his house looks like a school lab. He's a bit eccentric.

Okay, a *lot* eccentric," she amended with a laugh. "He's something of a mad scientist, but he's harmless, really, and rather sweet. And I'm sure he would never murder anyone."

"But if you've only met him recently, how can you know? I'm sorry, my dear, I don't mean to criticise your judgement, but as a lawyer, I feel compelled to point out that it is dangerous to draw conclusions when you do not have all the facts. Your friendship with Dr Noble could be making you biased. When we like someone, we automatically want to believe them to be *good*."

The lawyer's words made Poppy uneasy and defensive, especially as she knew, deep down, that he was right. She felt a bit like a schoolgirl who had been chastised by a kindly headmaster. Mannering must have sensed her feelings because he added, in a more conciliatory tone:

"I can certainly recommend one of my colleagues, who would have more experience in the area of criminal defence, to represent Dr Noble. That is no problem, and I would be happy to help. But I would urge you to not get involved and let the police complete their investigations as they see fit."

CHAPTER TWENTY-FIVE

Poppy had barely returned Einstein to the sitting room and was just thinking about making breakfast for herself when the sound of a car outside in the lane made her hurry to the front door. Her eyes widened as she opened it and saw a police car through the iron bars of the front gate. It had come to a stop and an old man with unkempt grey hair got out of the passenger seat. *Bertie!*

She rushed out and into the lane, arriving just as the elderly inventor was giving the driver a jaunty wave. He turned and began toddling towards his house, swinging a battered leather suitcase in one hand and an ancient umbrella in the other.

"Bertie, I'm so glad the police released you," Poppy cried, hurrying after him. "Are you all right?"

"Oh yes, never better, never better!" The old man

beamed at her. "It was a most enlightening visit. Wonderful to have human test subjects like that. I shall have to adjust the formulation of my Laughing Gas Air Freshener slightly—it's a bit too potent at the moment. Not much use in offices if the staff keep falling about in giggles, you know..."

"Bertie, what about the murder? How come the police released you? Was the spade not the murder weapon after all?"

"Oh, indeed it was—the blood matched that of the poor fellow who had been killed."

"So how come—"

"Well, they tried to find my prints on the handle but there was nothing there. No prints of any sort."

"How can there be no prin—oh, it must have been wiped," Poppy realised. "Or the murderer used gloves..."

"Yes, I imagine there would be several pairs of gardening gloves lying about in that greenhouse at the back of Hollyhock Cottage. That's where the spade came from, you see," said Bertie.

She looked at him, surprised. "The police told you that?"

"Well, the detective sergeant kept asking me how I had got into the cottage. He said that since the spade was from the greenhouse, I must have had a means of entry in order to access it. Well, he didn't quite use those words," Bertie added, giving her a slightly disapproving look. "But I couldn't repeat his words in front of a young lady. I'm afraid he wasn't a very well-spoken young man."

"And there were no signs of a break-in when I arrived... which means that the murderer must have had keys to the cottage in order to have been able to get the spade from the greenhouse!" said Poppy, working it through out loud.

"Yes, apparently, there is an empty space, where a tool has gone missing. And the brand and style of the spade matches several other tools in the greenhouse. Not proof, of course, but very suggestive."

"Oh Bertie—you know what? The main set of keys for the cottage has gone missing from Charles Mannering's office! That means whoever took those keys is likely to be the murderer." Poppy frowned, thinking hard. Who could have had access to the keys? Mannering's secretary had insisted that she was at her desk almost all the time so anyone who tried to get to the cabinet where the keys were kept would have been seen by her.

Unless it was the secretary...?

Poppy laughed at that absurd suggestion and pushed the thought away. If she was going to start suspecting *her*, then she might as well suspect Charles Mannering or Tammy, the woman at the tourist information office, or those women at the pub...

No, it had to be someone else who had come in from the outside—someone who had managed to slip in and nick the keys from that cabinet while the secretary wasn't at her desk. Perhaps she had gone into Mannering's office for a moment to hand him some messages or even gone to the toilet (as she had admitted herself), but that would have meant that the person knew the exact moment when the secretary would be away from her desk, and how could they have managed that? Not without hidden cameras and spy equipment... and that really *was* getting ridiculous! Poppy laughed at herself again. *This isn't a James Bond movie!*

Then it hit her. Why hadn't she thought of it before? There *was* another person who would have had access to the key cupboard when nobody was around: the after-hours cleaner! Of course! When the office was closed and Mannering and the secretary had gone home, the cleaner would have vast amounts of time at her leisure to explore the office and search for the keys...

And Poppy had a strong idea she knew who Mannering's office cleaner was. She recalled overhearing Jenny Sykes and her lover in the Covered Market. Jenny's lover had suggested a dinner date and Jenny had told him she was working late that night: *"You know Thursday nights I clean that lawyer's office—I won't be finished until well after eight."*

Of course, it could have been any lawyer in Oxford, but Poppy was willing to bet that it was Charles Mannering. And that would mean that Jenny had had ample chance to steal the keys the day before Pete was murdered. Perhaps she had lured her husband to the cottage and then hit him on the head with the spade when he had turned his back to her? Poppy thought of Jenny's carefree attitude only a few days after her husband's death. That could be an explanation for her callous indifference. After all, if she had killed him, she would hardly be grieving for him, would she?

Poppy came out of her thoughts to realise that Bertie was looking at her quizzically. She gave him an apologetic smile. "Sorry, Bertie... so have the police cleared you for the murder?"

"Eh? Oh yes, of course. Just a mix-up, like I said. Explained the hole in the wall and the *Acanthus mollis*—"

"The what?"

"*Acanthus mollis*. That's why I was going through the gap—to gather it from the cottage garden next door. Look, I'll show you..."

He led the way into his house, taking her to the kitchen. From the back of the pantry, he dragged out a laundry basket containing something wrapped in burlap. Poppy recognised it as the item he had been furtively carrying when she saw him climbing through the hole in the wall. He peeled back the heavy fabric to reveal an enormous clump of leaves, stems, and damp soil.

It was a plant that had been dug up from the ground. It had large, lobed leaves, fanned out and curled at the edges, like feather plumes, and there were even a few flower spikes sticking out of the clump. The individual purplish-white flowers themselves weren't particularly pretty, but there were so many of them arranged up and down the long spikes that the overall effect was quite dramatic. The plant itself must have been nearly four feet tall and wide when it was in the ground and would have been an impressive sight.

"What is it?" she asked.

"*Acanthus mollis*, otherwise known as Bear's Breeches or the Oyster Plant," said Bertie. "Marvellous plant—been around since Roman and Greek times. Look at those beautiful big leaves!" He crouched down next to the clump and fingered one broad, dark-green lobe. "They were the inspiration for the carvings on the famous Corinthian pillars in Athens, you know. It's even said that Helen of Troy wore a dress embroidered with acanthus leaves." He shook his head sadly. "Of course, many people think of them as weeds, nowadays. Well, they *do* self-seed everywhere and they *can* regrow into a whole new plant from the tiniest piece of root left behind, so I suppose it *is* very hard to get rid of them if you no longer want them in your garden."

He looked earnestly at Poppy. "That's why I didn't think anyone would mind me digging one up. I was careful to only take a plant from the back of the clump, though. There's a whole swathe of them growing at the very bottom of the garden next door."

"Are you going to plant it in your own garden?"

asked Poppy.

"Oh, no, no... it's the roots I want. The Romans used them to cure all sorts of things, like burns and sprains and even gout, you know, but I've discovered a fabulous new use for them," he said excitedly. "To combat smelly armpits!"

"Sm-smelly armpits?" said Poppy.

"Yes, yes! *Acanthus* roots are very high in tannins, you see, which is a strong astringent, and I discovered—quite by chance—that it is remarkably effective, when combined with a formulation of citrus oil, bicarbonate of soda, and beeswax gel, to form a barrier to odour-causing bacteria. In fact, I have been testing it on myself and I'm delighted with the results!"

He sprang to his feet and came towards Poppy eagerly. "Smell my armpits!"

"*What?*"

Bertie raised one arm above his head and leaned towards her. "Go on, smell them! Smell them!"

"I... I don't want to smell your armpits!" cried Poppy, rearing back as far as possible.

"Oh, don't worry, my dear, you won't be repulsed. Trust me!"

Poppy stared at him. She couldn't believe she was considering smelling a weird old man's armpits, but Bertie was so full of innocent enthusiasm—like a little child proudly showing off the drawing they had done on the first day at school—that somehow, she just couldn't refuse him. She hesitated, then leaned slowly forwards and gave a cautious sniff. Then another. And another. Then she looked at him in amazement.

"There's no smell!" she said.

The old man beamed at her. "You see? Isn't it marvellous stuff? A revolutionary new all-natural deodorant that will work all day! Well, thirty-two hours and fifty-three minutes, to be precise. I haven't trialled it beyond that... But I imagine it should hold good for at least forty-eight hours and perhaps more. Hmm... I wonder if the effectiveness could be improved by subjecting the ingredients to a high-pressure environment before combining..."

Muttering to himself, he turned away and started rummaging through the various test tubes and beakers on the kitchen counter. Then he paused as if remembering something and turned back to her, asking:

"Where's Einstein?"

"Oh, he's still at Nick's house—you know, Nick Forrest the crime author, who lives in the house on my other side. I'm staying there until the police release the crime scene. I'll go and fetch Einstein now..." She started to turn away, then paused and asked, "Or actually, would you like to come over for some tea? I'm sure Nick wouldn't mind, and anyway, he isn't around at the moment..." Poppy broke off as she noticed the expression on the old man's face. It was the strangest combination of guilt, dread, and sadness. "Bertie? Is something the matter?"

He blinked. "Oh... no, nothing, my dear. You said Nick isn't there?"

"No, he's away on a book tour. His cat's there—but I'm sure Oren won't mind." *Especially if you're coming to take his nemesis away*, thought Poppy with a smile to herself.

Bertie hesitated, then drew himself up to his full height and said very formally: "I would love to come and have tea with you at Nick Forrest's house."

CHAPTER TWENTY-SIX

Einstein bounded out of the sitting room as soon as the door was opened and engulfed Bertie in an ecstasy of tail-wagging and face-licking. Poppy watched them for a moment with a smile on her face, then belatedly remembered Oren and looked up to see the ginger tom skulking in the hallway behind her, peering through her legs to watch the reunion. He actually seemed to be more curious than hostile, although when he caught Poppy's eyes on him, he hastily assumed a disgusted expression and turned to stalk off, his nose in the air.

Poppy tried to get Bertie to wait in the sitting room while she went to the kitchen to make tea, but the old inventor seemed keen to explore the house. In fact, he was like a child in a toy store—poking things, opening drawers, peering into cupboards—

whilst his eyes eagerly soaked up all the details.

"Hey! Bertie... I don't think... I'm not sure Nick would like that... Bertie! Stop... you shouldn't look in people's—Bertie!"

Poppy followed him around, snatching things out of the old man's hands or shutting cupboards and drawers after him. She felt like she was babysitting a toddler or something... it was a surprise how hungry Bertie seemed for any kind of information about Nick Forrest: what books the author read and what music he listened to, what cereal he ate for breakfast, what detergent he used in the laundry... She wondered if Bertie was a big fan of Nick's books—after all, most people were avidly curious about celebrities and public personalities that they admired, and most wouldn't be able to resist the chance to snoop around in their private homes. Still, it was more the sort of behaviour she expected from a star-struck teenager, not a learned old man—although she had to admit that Bertie was almost childlike sometimes...

She came out of her thoughts to see that the old inventor was at the end of the hall. In fact, he was wandering into Nick's study. Poppy gasped and charged after him.

"No, no—Bertie, you mustn't go in there!"

She caught up with the old man just inside the door and glanced around. If possible, the room looked even more chaotic than when she had last seen it, with even more books, folders, and loose papers strewn everywhere. She shook her head in disbelief. She wondered how Nick managed to write a coherent sentence in this place, never mind a whole book!

"Is this where he writes his books?" asked Bertie, his eyes shining.

"Y-yes, this is Nick's study. But I really don't think we should be in here..." said Poppy uncomfortably. "Bertie, come on... Let's go back to the sitting room—"

But Bertie wasn't listening. He was picking his way gingerly across the room to Nick's desk.

"Oh God—" Poppy swallowed another gasp. She remembered Nick's scowl and his protective attitude towards his ramshackle "system".

"Bertie! Don't touch *anything* on that desk!"

To her relief, the old man seemed to listen to her for once. He peered at the mess piled on the desk but didn't touch anything. Then something pinned to the wall next to the desk caught his eye. Poppy had managed to negotiate the room and reach Bertie's side just as he plucked the item off the wall.

It was the photograph Nick had furtively taken of Pete Sykes's body at the crime scene—the one he was using as inspiration for his current novel. Poppy shuddered. She didn't think she would ever forget that image: the man's body slumped facedown in the middle of the flowerbed, his arms splayed out and his legs twisted beneath him... and scattered all around him—like a gruesome parody of confetti—were flowers in all shapes and colours. They were obviously blooms that had dropped or been torn off the surrounding plants, as the murderer had dragged Pete's body roughly into the flowerbed and then hastily covered it with some soil.

"Flowers..." said Bertie, staring down at the grainy photo.

Poppy followed the direction of his gaze, and this time she found, to her surprise, that she was able to focus on the flowers themselves and ignore the body in the picture. She stared at them, wishing—like she always did—that she could recognise the different blooms. She loved flowers but, to her shame, she could only name a few common, popular varieties, like roses, daffodils, tulips...

Then, as she continued to stare down at the photo held in Bertie's hands, Poppy's eyes widened and a delighted smile began to spread across her face. She *did* recognise them! That big white daisy-like flower... that was *cosmos*... and the long purple spikes were from a *salvia* bush... the big cupcake blooms were her namesake—*Papaver nudicaule*, to be precise, otherwise known as the Icelandic poppy... and those clusters of colourful, tubular-shaped flowers? Of course... they were snapdragons!

There were a few she didn't recognise, although she could guess at their names—that dainty blue flower with the circle of thin petals was probably a

Michaelmas daisy and those sprays of airy white florets—she was sure they were *gypsophila*... and that cheerful little flower which looked so much like a carnation—that was probably *dianthus*, also known as Sweet William or garden pinks...

Poppy found herself grinning from ear to ear. She hadn't realised how much she had absorbed in those hours she'd spent poring over her grandmother's plant encyclopaedia. It might have been silly, but she felt a wonderful sense of achievement—like she had suddenly deciphered a new language and could make sense of things that had previously been so obscure to her.

She glanced at Bertie, keen to share her excitement, and noticed that the old inventor was still staring at the picture and frowning.

"Bertie... is something wrong?" She reached out to touch his arm gently.

He started in surprise, then he muttered, still looking intently at the photo, *"A Voyage to Laputa, Balnibarbi, Luggnagg, Glubbdubdrib, and Japan."*

Poppy frowned at him. "Bertie? What on earth are you talking about?"

He didn't answer, just muttered the same words once more. Puzzled, Poppy took the photo from him and he let it go without demur. Then he seemed to completely forget about the photograph.

"Shall we have tea now?" he asked brightly.

"Er..." She looked at him quizzically, then decided that maybe she should stop questioning things and just be thankful for small mercies. "Yes, come on."

Back in the kitchen, Poppy made tea, then they sat together, sipping from their mugs and nibbling biscuits, whilst Einstein danced on his hind legs around them and begged for crumbs—and Oren sat on the windowsill, shooting dirty looks in their direction. To her surprise, Bertie sat quietly, with none of his earlier hyperactive inquisitiveness. She wondered if—having sated his curiosity about his favourite author—the old inventor had burned out, like a child who had been on a sugar high and was now drained of energy.

He's such a strange mass of contradictions, Poppy thought, and realised again how little she knew Dr Bertram Noble. She was still thinking this as she walked him and Einstein to the door and stood watching as they made their way through the iron gate and down the lane towards his house. She waited until they were out of sight, before closing the door with a sigh and heading back to the kitchen to tidy up.

She found Oren hovering around the table, close to where Einstein had been sitting. The ginger tom was sniffing the table legs and floor with great disgust, his nostrils flaring and his whiskers quivering indignantly. He looked up as Poppy came back into the room and gave her a reproachful look.

"Yes, Oren, I know the whole place stinks of dog," she said with a rueful smile. "I'll get a mop and give the floor a wipe later, okay?"

"*N-ow!*" Oren said, twitching his tail. "*N-oow!*"

Poppy sighed. "Oren, you can't—" She broke off as she spied something on the floor beneath the chair that Bertie had been sitting in. She bent down to retrieve it: it was a scrunched-up piece of paper. She didn't remember seeing it on the floor before— aside from his study, Nick's home was spotless—so she guessed that it must have fallen out of Bertie's pocket.

Absent-mindedly, Poppy unfolded the paper and spread out the creases. Then her heart skipped a beat as the scrawled words jumped out at her:

Bertie ~

Thanks for the book—it'll be a great help to know what to avoid. And don't worry, your secret is safe with me!

Pete S

A wave of unease washed over her. She distinctly remembered Bertie telling her that he had never met Pete Sykes and didn't even know that the man had been murdered. And she had believed him—it had seemed completely plausible that an absent-minded "mad scientist" would be so caught up in his own world that he wouldn't even notice the police presence in the property next door.

And yet here, now, was a note to Bertie, written from Pete Sykes himself. Did that mean that the old inventor had lied to her? But why?

Unbidden, Charles Mannering's words from that morning came back to her: *"How well do you actually know Dr Noble? Do you know anything about his background? What he does? Where he came from? ...When we like someone, we automatically want to believe them to be good."*

Poppy swallowed uneasily. Could she have been wrong about Bertie? Could he have had something to do with the murder after all?

CHAPTER TWENTY-SEVEN

The morning seemed to drag. Poppy found that she was unable to stop thinking about the murder, constantly comparing one suspect against the other and going around and around in circles until her head ached. She just couldn't bring herself to believe that Bertie could be involved—in spite of the mystery surrounding him and that incriminating note she had found—and so she put all her energies into the other two suspects: Hubert Leach and Jenny Sykes. One of them had to be the murderer.

Alibis, she thought suddenly. Wasn't that what police always focused on? Because no matter how guilty someone looked, they simply couldn't be committing a murder if they were proven to be somewhere else at the same time. She knew that Jenny had lied about her alibi... what about

Hubert? Would the police have questioned him? Would he even be on their radar as a suspect? Well, if he wasn't, she could easily change that by speaking to Suzanne Whittaker. Oh, not about the "snowdrop theory"—no, she had to admit that that did sound a bit far-fetched and ridiculous—but the other suspicion regarding Hubert's attempts to invalidate her grandmother's final will by getting rid of one of the witnesses—yes, that was a very good motive and a realistic possibility.

And yet she hesitated as Charles Mannering's cautionary words echoed in her mind. The lawyer was right: her cousin hadn't actually made any official challenge to the will yet. If she went to the police with her accusations now—without any proof—it would be tantamount to slander and could lay her open to a defamation suit. She couldn't afford that!

But perhaps she could go halfway? If she could just find out what Hubert's alibi was for the night of the murder—if he even had one—then she could decide whether to reveal more to the police. Seizing on the decision, Poppy put a call through to the police station and asked for Suzanne, but was disappointed when she was informed that "Detective Inspector Whittaker was out on a case". She left a message asking Suzanne to call her, although she didn't hold out much hope of any reply for a long time. She was pleasantly surprised, though, when her phone rang barely twenty minutes later.

"Poppy—Suzanne Whittaker here. I had a message that you wanted to speak to me?" said Suzanne in a harassed voice.

"Oh! Yes, I... thanks for ringing back... There's... there's something important... about the Pete Sykes murder."

"Yes?" asked Suzanne impatiently.

"Um... well..." The other woman's brusque tone made Poppy nervous, and suddenly she wondered how she had thought that she could call up the police and grandly say: *I think I know who the murderer is. Can you tell me if he had an alibi?* So instead, she started rambling about "possible suspects" and "people Sykes may have known, who should be questioned" until Suzanne cut her short.

"Poppy, look, I'm sorry, but I really don't have time for a long discussion right now. I'm on a double homicide case and things are really crazy here. Why don't you speak to Sergeant Lee? He's handling the Sykes case and I'm sure he'll be happy to talk things over with you."

"But—"

"Is everything else all right otherwise? Are you comfortable in Nick's house? Managing okay with Oren?"

"Yes, he's fine and the house is great, but I—"

"Good. Look, I need to go now. Take care of yourself and I'll catch you soon!"

Poppy stared at the darkened screen, then

sighed and put her phone away. What should she do now? Well, she couldn't just sit in Nick's house any longer—she would go crazy! She checked Oren's food and water bowl, grabbed her handbag, then—pausing only to give the ginger tom a scratch on the chin—she headed out.

***

Poppy stepped off the bus, then paused uncertainly, looking around her. She had jumped on the bus for Oxford on an impulse and with only a vague idea of what she wanted to achieve. Now that she was here, she wasn't quite sure what to do. Slowly, she wandered out of the station forecourt and into the large, piazza-like square of Gloucester Green. This had been empty the last time Poppy arrived, but today she was surprised to see the wide expanse filled by row upon row of temporary stalls. It looked like some kind of farmers' market, with local growers and farmers, bakeries and cheesemakers, and a whole host of other artisans, selling their produce and creations. The stalls and stands were bulging with fresh fruit and vegetables, cheeses, bread, cakes, herbal soaps, candles... as well as the inevitable hotchpotch of mobile phone accessories, cheap toys and souvenirs, second-hand books, handmade jewellery, pottery and more.

Glad of a distraction, Poppy began wandering between the stalls, admiring all the things on display. Despite her worries, she soon found herself genuinely caught up in the vibrant market atmosphere—in fact, it was hard to resist buying things on impulse! She was just sniffing some wonderfully perfumed soy candles, wondering if she could justify the expense, when she saw a stall selling fresh flowers and potted plants. Poppy watched enviously as a woman filled her arms with bunches of ruffled pink sweet peas, their fragrance heady in the morning air.

Suddenly, she flashed back to another time when she had stood beside a flower stall and enviously watched another woman buy a bouquet of fresh flowers. That had been in London, on her way to work one morning—before she'd quit her job, before she'd come to Hollyhock Cottage, before she had discovered Pete Sykes's body... Had it really only been a week ago? It felt now almost like a lifetime away.

Poppy drifted over to the flower stall and gazed longingly at the buckets filled with colourful blooms. She reached out and touched one of the flowers, admiring the blend of colours—magenta and salmon pink and orange, with darker flecks that looked almost like tiger stripes long the inside of the petals. Then she smiled in sudden delight as she recognised the bright, lily-like flower.

"It's an alstroemeria!" she exclaimed. She looked up to see the flower seller giving her an odd look and she laughed sheepishly. "Sorry.... I never knew the names of many flowers before and I've been reading a plant encyclopaedia and it's exciting to recognise things in real life."

The woman gave her an *"O-kay... customers are weird but humour them..."* kind of look and said: "Alstros are great value. Last for ages in a vase— weeks and weeks, if you change the water. An' I got a special going—if you buy two bunches, you get a third free." She indicated the label on the side of the bucket

Poppy glanced at the price on the label and gulped. It seemed an exorbitant amount of money, even for flowers that would last several weeks. It was an extravagance that she really couldn't afford. And yet her hand was already creeping towards her pocket as she stared at the beautiful blooms.

"Or... if you want even better value, I'm selling a couple of 'em in pots, for the same price, with the pot thrown in. If I were you, that's what I'd buy, " said the woman, bending down and lifting something up from underneath the bench.

Poppy looked at the terracota pot askance: the dark-brown compost was bulging with fleshy stems and whorls of green leaves, and looked nothing like the bunches of bright flowers. The flower seller must have caught her expression because she said hurriedly:

"They don't look like much now—the buds haven't opened, see?" She parted some of the leaves to show a stem ending in a cluster of tightly shut oval buds, just beginning to show a hint of red. "But they'll open in a couple of days an' then they'll knock your socks off! Gorgeous cherry-red, this one is, with dark flecks an' gold streaks in the throat. They're also known as the Peruvian Lily or—"

"Lily of the Incas," said Poppy excitedly. "Yes, I read that last night in my book. They came originally from South America and they symbolise friendship in the meaning of flowers." She saw the woman give her an odd look again and tried to explain, "I've got this... er... friend who's a writer and he's researching the meaning of flowers for his latest novel. I saw that he'd made a note about alstroemerias."

"Er... right. So d'you want one? They really are fantastic value," said the woman, obviously not caring about the meaning of flowers as long as she made a sale. She added persuasively as she saw Poppy hesitate: "You just have to water 'em an' they'll keep giving you new blooms, right up until the first frosts."

"Can I keep it in the pot?"

"Well, you could for a couple of months... but they really like to be in the ground. You can put 'em in a nice spot in your garden, mulch 'em well over the winter to protect 'em, an' they'll bounce back in the spring. Then you'll be able to enjoy 'em for years, eh?"

Poppy was about reply that she didn't have a garden, when an image of the cottage garden flashed in her mind. *The alstroemeria would look lovely planted right by the path, near the front door*, she thought. *Then I can enjoy seeing the flowers every time I go in and out of the house*—she pulled herself up short. What was she thinking? Hollyhock Cottage was going to be sold! It wasn't her garden and she wasn't going to be walking up to the front door.

Poppy gave the woman a regretful smile. "Thank you, they look lovely but I really can't afford it..."

She started to turn away, then she stopped, hesitated, and whirled back to the startled woman.

"Actually, I'll... I'll take one," she said breathlessly.

A few minutes later, Poppy walked away from the stall, wondering if she was a bit mad. She had just spent much-needed money on a potted plant that didn't even have a flower on it; a potted plant that she had nowhere to plant and couldn't even lug overseas with her when she left England.

It was such a silly extravagance, such an irresponsible act, unlike anything she'd ever done, that she felt slightly giddy with exhilaration. She looked down and caught a whiff of fresh compost, mingled with the smell of the green leaves, and couldn't help smiling to herself. It might have been a crazy thing to do... but it felt good.

Clutching the pot, she began making her way out of the market, but she hadn't gone a few steps when loud voices nearby caught her attention. She glanced over curiously: the commotion was coming from a stall at the end of the row. It looked much more makeshift than the rest—almost as if someone had stacked a board on some milk cartons, and just hijacked a space—and unlike the rest of the displays which were lovingly decorated with tablecloths, banners, and pretty homemade signs, this one looked cheap and rough, with most of the items stacked in careless piles. Also, unlike most stalls which specialised in one type of item, these were a strange hotchpotch: from the large pile of mobile phones and accessories to another pile of cosmetics—all bearing the logos of famous designer brands—as well as handbags and T-shirts (again with ostentatious designer logos); there were also cheap plastic toys, stacks of computer games, and even some packs of cigarettes.

A young man stood behind the stall, wearing a hoodie despite the heat of the summer's day, the hood pulled up to partially shield his face. He was facing an older man—a market trader, by the look of things—who was standing on the other side of his display, yelling and gesticulating wildly.

"...won't have the likes of your sort! We're all good, honest traders, selling quality items we've grown or made ourselves—we don't deal in junk and fakes!"

"Who said they're fake?" the younger man sneered. "Just because *you* can't recognise a designer brand, old man, doesn't mean that they're no good. People like my stuff. You're just jealous 'cos no one's buying your stupid trains!" He looked with contempt at a stand across from him, filled with beautifully carved wooden trains in local Cotswolds timber.

The trader narrowed his eyes. "I'll bet you haven't applied to the local council for a trader's licence, have you? You've got no right to be here!" He glanced at the other side of the square, where two police constables could be seen chatting under a street lamp, and jabbed a finger. "You'd better pack up right now or I'm going to call the police!"

The young man cast a furtive glance over his shoulder at the police officers, then turned back to stare defiantly at the trader for a minute longer, before cursing and beginning to pack up his display. He grabbed items at random and shoved them into a large canvas holdall, his angry, violent movements making his hood fall back to reveal his face.

Poppy stared at him. He looked familiar...

Then she realised where she had seen him before: he was the man she had caught trying to break into Hollyhock Cottage, on the first day she had arrived in Oxfordshire.

CHAPTER TWENTY-EIGHT

Poppy found herself walking over to the young man before she realised what she was doing and stood in front of his stall, watching him pack. He paused and looked up, eyeing her suspiciously.

"What?" he demanded.

Poppy glanced at the pile of suspiciously cheap mobile phones, at the obviously counterfeit designer goods, and had a sudden hunch who this man might be. Taking a punt, she said:

"Boyo? Boyo Simms?"

He narrowed his eyes at her and said belligerently, "Yeah, that's me. Who're you?"

Poppy hesitated, then she felt a rush of daring and said, looking him straight in the eye: "I'm the person who saw you trying to break into Hollyhock Cottage."

He paled and took a step back. "I... I don't know what you're talkin' about."

Poppy glanced meaningfully at the police constables in the distance and took another step forwards, leaning over the table. "Maybe when the police question you about it, it'll help to jog your memory."

He blanched even more and licked his lips. "No... no need to bring the fuzz into this. What d'you want?"

"Why were you trying to break in that day? Were you doing something to cover up for Pete's murder?"

He recoiled, yelping: "*What?* No way! I had nothin' to do with Pete's murder!" He realised several people were staring and hurriedly lowered his voice. "I didn't even know that he were dead, okay? It wasn't until the next day when the fuzz came round an' questioned me..." He swallowed and looked away.

Poppy felt a pang of doubt as she watched him. Maybe she was wrong to think that Boyo could be involved? He looked genuinely shocked and upset at the mention of his friend's death. Then she reminded herself that people could be good actors.

"I heard that you and Pete fell out?" she challenged him.

He swung back to her, his eyes blazing. "Yeah, so what? That don't mean that I murdered him! We disagreed 'bout stuff an' had bust-ups all the time... and then we'd have a pint an' make up. Wouldn't be the first time." His voice cracked. "Pete was my mate... we'd gone to school together, you know... we did everythin' together..."

Poppy shifted uncomfortably. Boyo might have been a brilliant actor, but she could have sworn that those were real tears in his eyes. She cleared her throat and said, her voice softening:

"So... do you have any ideas who might have wanted to kill Pete?"

He shrugged. "The fuzz asked me that—over and over again. Like I told 'em, I dunno! I mean... Pete didn't have that many friends. I was his only mate, really. But he didn't have any enemies either..." His face turned ugly. "Unless you count Jenny. She's a right slapper. I wouldn't be surprised if she was the one who killed him."

"His own wife?"

"She were only his wife in name," Boyo sneered. "Never cooked for him, house was a tip, always askin' him for money an' then goin' off shoppin' and stuff... an' she was playin' around behind his back too!"

"If she's so awful, why were they still married? I heard that she wanted a divorce."

Boyo shrugged again. "Pete didn't believe in divorce. He was Catholic an' a bit old-fashioned like that."

Poppy thought of the gossip she'd heard the day she'd had lunch in the Bunnington village pub. "Are you suggesting that Jenny killed Pete just so she could leave him? It's... it's so absurd!"

"Well, I dunno about that," Boyo admitted. "Maybe she had some other reason. All I'm sayin' is, wouldn't surprise me if it was Jenny who did it."

He started packing his things again and Poppy watched him for a moment, then she said: "You never told me why you were trying to break into the cottage."

He stopped and looked shifty. "Look, it weren't anythin' really bad, okay? I promise you it were nothin' to do with Pete's murder."

"If it was nothing bad, then why can't you tell me?"

He looked down and said sullenly, "I was just lookin' for a place to store my stuff."

"Your stuff?"

He gestured to the pile of items on the table. "This. Other things. I've got them stashed in a mate's garage at the moment but they're getting twitchy, so I need to find a better hidin—I mean, storage place for the stuff." He threw a glance over his shoulder at the police constables again, then gave her a pleading look. "You don't need to go reportin' that, do you? I mean, it's nothing to do with Pete's murder. I just knew the cottage was empty 'cos Pete mentioned it a while back. He said it was deserted and didn't look like anyone was coming to live there soon."

"Well, the police know about the attempted break-in already—I put that in my statement when I was questioned after Pete's body was found."

"But they don't know it was me, right?" said Boyo quickly.

"No, they don't," Poppy admitted.

"And you won't tell them, will you? Please?"

Poppy hesitated. "I... all right. But if I ever see you skulking around the cottage again—"

He raised a hand, palm out. "Won't come near the place again. I promise."

A few minutes later, Poppy watched him walk away, a bulging canvas bag slung over his shoulder, and wondered if she had done the right thing. Boyo was pretty much a petty criminal, and what was his word worth? Still, she didn't feel comfortable about going to the police to snitch on him and if he really had nothing to do with the murder...

With a sigh, Poppy turned away and began cutting through the market, intending to come out on the other side of the square. She tried not to look at the stalls as she walked past, knowing that it would be so easy to get sucked in again, but just as she was about to reach the edge of the market area, she spotted a second-hand bookseller. His table was filled with teetering towers of books—well-thumbed paperbacks, faded hardbacks, children's colouring books, and even some vintage magazines.

Poppy couldn't resist. She was missing her regular visits to the bookshop near her old London office, and now she felt that familiar thrill of anticipation as she approached the stacks of novels.

Just as she was reaching towards the first book, however, she noticed the box of old magazines. She felt another familiar—but different—spurt of excitement and she pulled a few issues out eagerly, scanning the celebrity faces on the covers. Then she opened them and flipped through the pages, whilst her eyes skimmed the headlines: a rock star caught coming out of rehab... a Hollywood actress after her divorce... another looking several pounds thinner on her new diet... a director and actor having coffee on set... a pop star performing on tour...

They were all "old" celebrities, of course—many no longer seen or heard of anymore—but that was exactly what Poppy wanted. She was interested in any male rock stars from around the time she was born and she pored over the pictures, looking hopefully at the faces...

Then she paused, her eyes widening as the magazine fell open on the centrefold: an article about the suspicious death of an Oxford research student who had been working late in the university laboratories one evening. A name in the text jumped out at her and she felt the breath catch in her throat as she read the sentence: *"Dr Bertram Noble, head of the Department of Experimental Science at Oxford, is being questioned by the police and is currently the prime suspect..."*

Bertie? Poppy gripped the magazine tighter, her eyes devouring the rest of the article. There was not very much more information—just interviews with the tearful parents of the student, begging for justice to be done, and then a rehash of the young man's achievements and his promising future that had been cut short. Poppy put the magazine back in the box and rifled through the rest of the stack but although she pulled out every issue she could find from that time period, there was no other article about the student's death.

"Hey—you buying anything? This isn't a library, you know!"

Poppy looked up to find the irate stall owner glaring at her from the other side of the table.

"Oh... er... sorry..." She shoved the magazines back in the box, retrieved the potted alstroemeria, and walked away.

She paused on the street corner just beyond the square, her thoughts in a tumult. Could she have been wrong about Bertie after all? She still couldn't bring herself to believe that he could hurt anyone on purpose. But Charles Mannering and Nell were both right—how much did she really know about the eccentric scientist? The article she had just found proved that it wasn't very much. She'd had no idea that Bertie had once been a prime suspect in a suspicious death. And now he was a suspect in another—was that too much of a coincidence?

But the police have already questioned him and released him, she reminded herself. They would have had access to his past records and yet they still let him go. Surely that proved that Bertie was innocent? Although she *had* watched enough police dramas to know that suspects were often released if there wasn't enough evidence to charge them with a crime. Still, Poppy recoiled from the idea. She just couldn't believe that that sweet old man could kill anyone! *Blow them up accidentally, yes*—she thought with a wry laugh—*but not murder them in cold blood.*

And yet... she couldn't help suddenly remembering Nell's voice, warning her of her blind affection for the old inventor.

It's not true—I'm not prejudiced, she thought fiercely. *And I'm not trying to find a substitute father figure in Bertie!*

CHAPTER TWENTY-NINE

Poppy stopped outside the window of LEACH PROPERTIES LTD. and looked up at the display of posters, each profiling an available property. She still had no plan, but suddenly that didn't seem to matter. Her impulsive purchase of the potted plant followed by the confrontation with Boyo had filled her with a sense of reckless courage. She opened the door to the agency and marched straight in. The interior was not very big and consisted mostly of more property posters covering the walls, a small conference table in one corner, a door to an inner office, and a reception desk behind which sat a young woman tapping away at a keyboard.

She looked up and smiled as Poppy entered, saying with practised smoothness: "Welcome to Leach Properties. Can I help you? Are you looking for a property?"

"Uh... yes, I am," said Poppy, taking the cue given to her.

The girl lifted a clipboard with a printed form attached and handed it to Poppy. "If you can fill in your information... Are you looking to buy or to rent?"

"Oh... er... to rent."

"Any area in particular?"

"Um... do you cover south Oxfordshire?"

"Yeah, we've got a few properties there."

Poppy glanced at the closed door of the inner office. "Does... er... Mr Leach handle all the properties himself?"

"Oh, he mostly does sales, although he does occasionally show some of the rentals. He's away this afternoon, though—were you hoping to speak to him?"

"Oh no, that's fine," said Poppy, hoping that the relief wasn't too obvious in her voice. In actual fact, she had walked in without considering whether her cousin might be there and had been bracing herself for Hubert to suddenly appear from the inner office.

"You can put the pot down here, if you like, while you fill out the form," the girl said, indicating an empty spot on her desk. She peered at the green stems. "What is it, by the way?"

"It's an alstroemeria," said Poppy, feeling a silly sense of pride. "I just bought it from the farmer's market."

"Oh, I didn't recognise it without the flowers—my nan used to grow alstros!" said the girl. "She was mad about them. Had all sorts of different colours. Said they were the best flowers for cutting—they last ages."

"Yes, that's what the lady in the market said too," said Poppy. She glanced at the closed door of the inner office again and said nonchalantly, "So... um... have you been working here long?"

"Yeah, about a year. I used to work in Didcot before this—Oxford's much nicer." The girl grinned. "Better shops at lunchtime."

Poppy gave the girl a conspiratorial grin of her own and said in a chatty tone, "Ooh, yes, tell me about it. I love having a mooch in the lunch hour. Do you get a decent break?"

The girl made a face. "I'm supposed to get an hour but Hubert is always finding excuses to make me come back earlier."

"I had a boss like that," said Poppy sympathetically. "She was always making me stay late too—but never paid me any overtime."

"Yeah, old Hubert is just like that!" said the girl indignantly. "Like earlier this week—" She broke off as the phone on the desk rang. "Leach Properties—can I help you? ...I'm afraid Mr Leach isn't here this afternoon... I'm not sure if he's returning to the office at all today... Yes, okay, I'll tell him that... Yes, of course... Don't worry, Dr Goh, I'll make sure to tell him it's important and ask him to ring you as soon as he can..."

Dr Goh? Poppy stared at the girl, who had hung up and was busily writing a note on a yellow pad, oblivious to her sudden interest. *Where have I heard that name before?*

Poppy racked her brains. Then it came to her: the first day she'd come to Oxford and had nearly bumped into Hubert outside the agency. He had been talking rather furtively on the phone and she had been so intent on avoiding him that she hadn't paid the conversation much attention. Now, though, his words came back to her with vivid clarity:

"...that's why they call it 'you scratch my back and I'll scratch yours'... all you have to do is express your concerns if they ask... and naturally, I'd make it worth your while, Dr Goh... no, no, no one else will know about this..."

Poppy felt her pulse quickening as the implication suddenly hit her: *"...and naturally, I'd make it worth your while..."* Had Hubert been offering *a bribe?* But for what?

Then the answer hit her as well: what if Dr Goh was her grandmother's GP? Charles Mannering had said that there were two witnesses to the will: Pete Sykes was one and her grandmother's doctor was the other. With Sykes dead, the doctor was the only person who stood in Hubert's way if he decided to contest the will on the grounds of mental incapacity…

Had she overheard Hubert offering a bribe to her grandmother's GP? After all, who better to testify than a doctor, whose professional opinion would be trusted and respected? She had to find out if Dr Goh was her grandmother's GP!

"Are you all right?"

Poppy came out of her thoughts to find the receptionist looking at her oddly. She realised that she had been gripping the edge of the desk and staring into space, her breathing fast and urgent. Now she made a conscious effort to relax her hands and drop them to her side, while forcing a smile to her face.

"Uh… yeah, sorry, my mind wandered for a moment… Um—was that Mr Leach's doctor?" she asked brightly.

"I dunno. Don't think so."

"Um… I hope Mr Leach hasn't got any serious medical issues or anything like that?"

The girl shrugged and eyed her with sudden suspicion. "I dunno. He didn't say. Why are you asking?"

"Oh, no reason… I just thought maybe… it sounded urgent…" Poppy stammered.

The girl gave her another strange look, then she held out a hand. "Have you finished with that form?"

Poppy glanced down at the clipboard. The last thing she wanted to do was to leave something with her name in writing for Hubert to see. She made an exaggerated show of looking at her watch, then gave a loud gasp.

"Oh God—is that the time? I'm sorry, I've got to run. I'll have to pop back another time. Thanks so much for your help!"

Shoving the clipboard back across the counter, Poppy grabbed the potted alstroemeria and hurried out of the agency before the girl could say another word. Outside in the street, she paused several yards down from the agency door and considered what to do.

The key thing was to confirm that Dr Goh was her grandmother's GP. She wondered how she could find him... *There must be a directory somewhere of GPs practising in Oxfordshire.* But even if she did find him, how was she ever going to get a look at his list of patients? Perhaps the clinic where he worked would have a database on a computer that she could somehow sneak a look at? But how would she distract the receptionist and—

Suddenly, she realised the easiest way to check Dr Goh's identity. It was so simple, she wanted to smack her head for not thinking of it earlier. Of course! She could simply ask Charles Mannering! He had a copy of the will with the two named witnesses, and in any case, he would probably know the name of her grandmother's GP anyway. "Goh" was uncommon enough that if her grandmother's GP *did* have that name, the chances were good that it was the same man.

And if she could show that Hubert was bribing one of the witnesses, surely that would scotch his attempt to contest the will? It wasn't proof that he was the murderer but it certainly gave him a very strong motive and would hopefully convince the police to investigate him further. And in the meantime, her inheritance—and the cottage—would be safe...

Shifting the pot into one arm, Poppy pulled her phone out with her other hand and called Mannering's office. Unfortunately, the lawyer was also out at meetings all afternoon and wasn't expected to return to the office that day.

"I can leave him a message to call you first thing tomorrow morning," offered the secretary.

"No, that's all right—don't bother," said Poppy, remembering that Mannering's house was in Bunnington. She didn't have his home number but she could pop over later to see him. She was sure the kindly solicitor wouldn't mind.

***

When Poppy arrived back in Bunnington, she was surprised to see that the young constable was no longer standing outside the gate to Hollyhock Cottage, and when she peered into the garden, it seemed eerily quiet and empty after so many days of seeing men in masks and white overalls coming and going. She noticed that the striped police tape was also no longer around the house... Had the police released the crime scene?

Elated, Poppy stepped into the garden and walked slowly up the path. She felt as if she was looking at the cottage garden with new eyes. Yes, it was still overgrown and crowded with weeds, but it no longer seemed like such an intimidating jungle of green. In fact, she found that she was beginning to recognise some shapes and colours in the jumbled undergrowth. Yes, that was a *phlox* plant! And there, peeking out from under a tangle of brambles, was a *geranium*—a true hardy geranium, not a *pelargonium*, she thought, with a smug smile to herself—and surely that was a *delphinium* over there in that corner? Poppy found that she was grinning like an idiot. It might have sounded silly but, somehow, finding and recognising plants from her grandmother's encyclopaedia—"in real life" here in the garden—felt as thrilling as catching sight of a lion or rhinocerous on safari.

She stopped at last by the front door of the cottage and, with a sense of ceremony, bent and placed the potted alstroemeria down to the right of the doormat. Then she stood back and admired the effect.

"*N-ow? N-oow?*"

Poppy turned around to see Oren strolling down the path towards her. He must have followed her through the open gate into the cottage garden. His tail was up and his expression friendly as he approached—a far cry from earlier when Bertie and Einstein had been at Nick's house for tea. Now that the canine intruder had been removed from his home, it seemed that the ginger tom was ready to forgive her and was coming over to say hello.

Oren walked up to the alstroemeria and rubbed his chin on the rim of the pot. As Poppy watched him, she realised that with the crime scene now released, she could move back into the cottage. She wouldn't have to spend the night at Nick's place. She was surprised to find that she felt a sense of regret—not only at losing the obviously more comfortable sleeping arrangements but also at not having Oren's company. Somehow, the irascible feline seemed to have grown on her.

"Come on, Oren—let's go back and get my things."

"*N-ow?*" said Oren, looking up at her.

Poppy laughed. "I'd better do it before it gets dark. Don't worry—I'll still be coming over to feed you until Nick gets back, and you can spend the evening with me in the cottage, if you like."

The ginger tom flicked his tail in approval, then turned and led the way back up the path, out of the gate and over to Nick's house.

CHAPTER THIRTY

Poppy spent the next hour tidying up Nick's house (minus his study), stripping and remaking the bed in the guest bedroom with fresh linen, and generally making sure that all evidence of Einstein's stay were removed. She had picked some flowers from the cottage garden on her way over and now arranged them in a small vase, which she left on the kitchen counter together with a thank you note. Then, with her few belongings stuffed in a carrier bag slung over one arm, she hefted the thick volumes of her grandmother's plant books in the other and left the house, carefully locking the door behind her.

Dusk was falling as she let herself into Hollyhock Cottage and deposited her things on the wooden table in the kitchen. It had been nice to have the distraction of the domestic chores in the last hour, but now her troubled thoughts returned—in particular, her worries about Bertie's involvement in the murder. For a second Poppy was tempted to go next door and ask the old inventor about the magazine article she'd seen, to find out more about his past and what had really happened with that old case of suspicious death. But she knew she couldn't really do that—for one thing, she didn't know how to bring up the subject without making it sound like an accusation, and for another, it felt too insolent. She had met Bertie barely two days ago and although they seemed to have quickly struck up a warm friendship, she really hadn't known him long enough and certainly didn't know him well enough to justify that kind of presumption.

Thinking of Bertie reminded her of something else that had been nagging at the back of her mind: the strange words the old inventor had muttered as he had looked at the photo of the crime scene. What had he said? It had sounded like complete gibberish... Poppy closed her eyes and dredged up the memory: *Something about a voyage to Laputa... and Barbi? No, Balnibarbi... and Luggnagg... and then something like Glubdub... Glubbub-drib? Oh, and Japan.*

It did sound vaguely familiar, almost as if she had read it somewhere a long time ago, but Poppy couldn't figure out what it meant. She went to find her phone and—relieved to see that the battery was holding up for once—she fired up the internet browser and did a search. She wasn't sure of the exact spelling for some of the words, so it took a bit of detective work, but at last she found the text. She sat back, smiling to herself as she looked down at the screen: *"A Voyage to Laputa, Balnibarbi, Luggnagg, Glubbdubdrib, and Japan."* Of course! That's why it sounded familiar! It was a title from one of the sections in *Gulliver's Travels*, a favourite childhood book of hers.

Poppy frowned. Even though she had found the source, she wasn't sure if she was closer to understanding anything. From her memory of the story, that section had no obvious relevance to the photo of Pete Sykes's body lying in the flowerbed. *Perhaps the reference isn't in the story but in the title itself?* she wondered. It was such an odd title, with its list of strange fictional names—and then "Japan" standing out from the rest as a real-world place. She caught her breath. Perhaps that's what Bertie had been hinting at? That something in the photo didn't belong there—something was the odd one out? But what?

Poppy sighed. Maybe there was no hidden meaning, no cryptic message. Maybe Bertie had just been trying to express—in his eccentric way—that the dead body looked incongruous in its beautiful surroundings, amidst the bed of flower blooms. She put her phone down. She wasn't getting anywhere mulling over Bertie and the host of mysteries surrounding him. What she needed to do was focus on the other suspects in the case.

Hubert, she reminded herself. Yes, she had been planning to ask Charles Mannering about her grandmother's GP. She glanced at her watch and decided that the lawyer had probably come home now. Slipping a cardigan on to combat the night chill, she let herself out of the cottage and set off across the village.

The old lawyer's home looked very attractive in the gathering dusk, especially the conservatory, which was lit from within. Mrs Graham, Mannering's housekeeper, answered the door. She looked surprised to see Poppy but readily invited her in.

"Mr Mannering isn't home from work yet, but he should be back soon," the housekeeper said, glancing at the clock. "Would you like to wait for him? I can bring you a cup of tea or coffee in the sitting room."

"Thanks, I'd love to wait for him—but if you don't mind, I'd rather wait in the conservatory?" Poppy gave a slightly embarrassed chuckle. "I've just learned lots of new plant names and I'm keen to test myself."

"Oh, of course. Mr Mannering normally only allows guests into the conservatory when he accompanies them—he's very particular about his plants, you know, and is always fussing over them." She rolled her eyes and gave an indulgent laugh. "I think he's worried people might step on them or break off a stem and damage his precious darlings. But since he's already shown you around, I'm sure he won't mind."

The housekeeper led the way to the conservatory, then left her to wander through the warm, steamy interior. Poppy walked slowly around, admiring the lush green leaves and bright, tropical colours, and smiling in delight as she found that she was able to name several specimens. Of course, some she remembered from the other day when Mannering had showed her around and told her their names, so that was cheating a bit. Yes... there was the *bergenia*, with those big leaves like elephant ears... and the beautiful red *hibiscus*, with its opulent blooms... and here, the "ravishing" *pandorea* vine from Australia...

She went closer to the vine for a better look at the pale pink flowers and discovered that the trellis it was climbing on was actually attached to a screen, behind which was a beautiful little sheltered area tucked in the corner of the conservatory. You would never have known it was there if you hadn't walked around the vine and looked behind the screen. Poppy stepped into the alcove and smiled in surprised delight as she looked around her.

A bank of ferns grew in long planter boxes, set against the glass wall of the conservatory. They screened out the outside world and ensured that all light which filtered through their heavy fronds was a soft green, giving the area the feel of an enchanted garden or hidden grotto. In the centre was an artfully arranged mountain of rocks and tucked between them were all manner of orchids. Clumps of thick, dark-green leaves nestled in the cracks and crevices, and from each clump rose long stalks on which hung rows of delicate orchid blooms.

Pink, magenta, cream, white... spotted, striped, ruffled, tipped... the petals came in an amazing array of intricate shapes and colours. Poppy had only ever seen the occasional orchid for sale in the supermarket (and she had never even dared look at the prices on their labels). They'd seemed like the ultimate extravagance: an exotic beauty to be pampered in a luxurious home. But those orchids she had seen paled into comparison to these...

There were little plant labels inserted at the base of each clump, bearing the name of the specimen. She smiled as she wondered if there were labels next to every plant in the conservatory—she hadn't noticed them earlier—but it was exactly the sort of thing a pedantic gardener like Charles Mannering might do.

She reached out to touch the velvety petals of one large pink orchid, but her sleeve brushed against a smaller clump growing in a crevice beneath it, and something came loose, fluttering to the ground. Poppy gasped in dismay and quickly crouched down to retrieve it. She picked it up and realised that it was a tiny, dainty bloom. It must have broken off a stalk from the small clump—which, on closer inspection, was not one plant but several plants grouped together. Each had a single hairy leaf at the base and a thin stalk bearing a flower on the end.

As she looked closer, Poppy realised that these were orchids too. She'd thought that orchids only came in shades of pink, orange, and white—but no, this one was blue! Yes, the dainty bloom she'd picked up was the palest cornflower-blue, and unlike the big, rounded petals of most other orchids, the petals on this flower were small and narrow, five of them arranged around the centre, almost like a daisy...

Wait.

Poppy stared at the tiny orchid, her smile slowly changing to a frown. This flower looked familiar. She glanced back at the clump it had come from and saw the label inserted at the back. Tilting her head, she read the neat writing:

Blue Fairy Orchid (Pheladenia deformis)
Western Australia

So it was from overseas; she couldn't have come across it randomly in a garden here in England. And yet... she was sure she had seen it recently... Had it been in one of her grandmother's plant books?

No.

She knew where she had seen it.

A chill of realisation went through her body. It had been in the photo Nick had taken of the crime scene—the picture of Pete Sykes's body lying in the flowerbed, with broken blooms scattered around him. Poppy could see them in her mind's eye now, as vividly as if she was staring at the photograph in front of her: the big, white, daisy-like *cosmos*, the long purple spikes of *salvia*, the poppies and snapdragons, and a dainty blue Michaelmas daisy...

Except that it hadn't been a blue Michaelmas daisy.

She had got it wrong. At a glance—and to the inexperienced eye—they certainly looked similar, and in her eagerness to identify the bloom, she had pounced on the image of the Michaelmas daisy in the encyclopaedia. But she was beginning to realise that the flower in the photo had in fact been a blue fairy orchid. Just like the one she now held in her hand.

Oh my God... and Bertie had known!

That was why the old inventor had uttered that strange line while looking at the photo! The title from *Gulliver's Travels* with one place—Japan—that was the odd one out from the rest of the list. He must have known or recognised, somehow, that the tiny blue flower was a foreign invader. Bertie's mind was brilliant but it didn't work like most normal people's, so he hadn't been able or willing to tell her directly. Or perhaps he hadn't even been sure himself and had simply repeated that title as a way of puzzling things out...

Poppy took a step back, forgetting Bertie and swallowing hard as the real implications began to dawn on her. The blue fairy orchid was from Australia—an exotic import from a foreign land—and it couldn't have been growing in her grandmother's cutting flowerbed, or even in the rest of the cottage garden. Which meant that one way it could have ended up in that photo, as part of the crime scene, was if the murderer had inadvertently dropped it there.

And she had just seen herself how easy it was to do. The tiny orchid blooms snagged on your clothing when you brushed against them. If you were wearing long sleeves—such as a man in a suit—they could get caught in your cuffs and unwittingly carried out of the conservatory. In fact, she remembered something like that happening on the night she had come for dinner and Mannering had been showing her around the conservatory. That time, it had been a big red hibiscus bloom which had snagged against his cufflinks. That had been easily noticeable, but if it had happened with a tiny, pale-blue flower...

The old lawyer obviously hadn't noticed it lodged against his cufflinks, and then, later, the little flower had become dislodged and fallen to the ground during the struggle to bury Pete Sykes's body...

Poppy didn't want to voice it, even in her head, but she couldn't ignore the knowledge bearing down on her. The man that she had trusted—the kindly, fatherly figure she had looked up to—had been lying to her all along.

Charles Mannering was the murderer.

CHAPTER THIRTY-ONE

No... it can't be true.

Poppy stood frozen, her heart sick with denial. She couldn't believe that the lawyer could be the killer. He had been so nice, so kind, so full of fatherly concern... how could he be the murderer?

Perhaps she had got it wrong again. After all, she didn't have Nick's photo in front of her—she couldn't be totally sure that the orchid here in Mannering's conservatory was the same as the blue flower she'd seen in the picture of the crime scene. But even as she ran through the arguments, Poppy knew she was only deluding herself, ignoring the evidence that was staring her in the face.

She thought of the way Mannering had grabbed her arm and led her away from the pandorea vine when she had tried to approach the screen for a closer look the other day. He had made it seem like he was taking her across to show her another plant, but she knew now that he had actually been preventing her from discovering the secret area behind the screen which held his illicit collection of smuggled orchids.

Because she was sure that's what they were. Hadn't Nick talked about "orchidelirium" and said that orchid smuggling was still a big business, especially since collecting wild specimens was now banned? And what could be more desirable to an avid plant collector than something unique, gathered from the wild? She remembered Mannering's glowing face as he talked about his plants, the bizarre way he fussed over them and spoke about them as if they were spoilt children to be indulged. And then she heard Nick's voice again:

"...people became so gripped with a particular flower that they would do anything to get it: pay crazy sums of money, give up their livelihoods, engage in theft... maybe even commit murder."

Nick had laughed at his own words then and said that the last probably only happened in the pages of his novels—but he had been wrong. Pete Sykes had been murdered because of his involvement in the illegal plant trade; she was sure of it. Her original crazy theory had been correct; only Pete Sykes hadn't been dealing with Hubert Leach, as she'd thought—he'd been dealing with Charles Mannering.

And there's one way to confirm that, she thought grimly. Stepping forwards again, she pulled her phone out of her pocket and snapped a couple of photos of the little clump of blue orchids. She checked the screen, making sure that she had a good close-up of one of the blooms—something she could use to compare to Nick's photo.

Then her ears picked up the sound of wheels crunching on the gravel outside. A car pulling in and stopping. Charles Mannering had come home. Panic seized her. He couldn't find her here, in his hidden grotto. She saw now why guests were not allowed to come into the conservatory unaccompanied and why the screen with the lush vine had been erected in this corner—so that no one would discover Mannering's secret. A secret that he was obviously willing to kill for.

Poppy whirled to run out of the grotto, grabbing the side of the screen to swing herself around the corner faster. But her haste was her undoing and she didn't notice the long tendril of the pandorea vine trailing along the ground. It was around her ankle, jerking her feet out from underneath her, before she knew it. She went crashing down, her hands clawing frantically at anything to break her fall and ripping more tendrils from the screen. Broken leaves and stems rained down on her. She lay winded for a moment, then scrambled to her feet. The pandorea vine looked in a sorry state, missing chunks of leaves and half hanging off the screen.

Voices sounded in the house. Poppy felt panic surge through her anew as she heard Charle's Mannering's cultured tones, followed by a female voice. It sounded like he had just come in and his housekeeper was greeting him at the front door. Any minute now, Mrs Graham would tell him about his visitor and he would come hurrying to the conservatory...

Poppy looked desperately around. The conservatory was attached to the house via a double doorway which led into the main hall and the foyer. If she tried to get out that way, she was bound to run straight into Mannering. The only other exit she could see was through the French doors on the other side, fitted into the glass outer walls of the conservatory. There were large ceramic pots filled with tall palms standing in front of the doors and she didn't know if they would open, but she had to try.

She darted across and squeezed her upper body between the pots, shoving the palm fronds out of her face. She yanked at the door handles. Nothing. She tried pushing instead. Nothing again. She gripped the handles harder and shoved frantically, pushing and pulling against the door frame. The hinges protested, emitting a high-pitched squeal that made Poppy wince, then suddenly they gave way and the doors swung outwards.

She clambered over the pots, practically falling

out of the conservatory. Quickly, she shut the French doors behind her and scurried away, ducking low and keeping behind the hedge running around the house. A few minutes later, she had skirted the building and was on the gravel drive. She panted with elation. She'd done it! She'd got away!

Giving the house a last nervous look, she hurried down the driveway and started making her way across the village at a run. She had to tell the police—but first, she had to make sure. She had to compare the photos she'd taken of the blue fairy orchid with the picture that Nick had taken of the crime scene. She was accusing an elderly solicitor, a respectable figure in the community who nobody would expect to be mixed up in crime and murder. Without some kind of proof to back up her accusations, she didn't think even Suzanne Whittaker would believe her.

She arrived back at Nick's house to find it in darkness and cursed herself for not thinking of leaving the porch light on as she fumbled with the lock on the front door. At last, she got it open and flew down the hallway to Nick's study at the back of the house. But when she'd stepped in and flicked on the light, she stopped short.

The photograph wasn't on the wall by his desk. Where was it?

Then she remembered. That morning, after she had taken the photograph from Bertie, she had taken it back to the kitchen with them and absent-mindedly tucked it into the pages of her grandmother's plant encyclopaedia, which had been sitting on the kitchen counter. It must still be sandwiched somewhere in the pages of that huge tome, which she had taken back to Hollyhock Cottage earlier that evening.

Exhaling in frustration, Poppy whirled and dashed out of the room. A minute later, she was running up the path in the cottage garden and letting herself into the house. She rushed into the kitchen—where the plant books were neatly stacked on the kitchen counter—and frantically began flipping through the encyclopaedia. It took her only a few seconds to locate the photograph, wedged in between the chapter on "Herbaceous Perennials" and "Ornamental Grasses".

Poppy leaned panting against the counter as she stared at the photo—and then at the image on her phone screen. Nick's picture had been hastily printed out on normal paper, so the image was grainy, but still, there was no doubt when the pictures were held side by side: that little bloom in the soil, just beside Pete Sykes's left elbow, was a blue fairy orchid.

Poppy took a shuddering breath and dialled Suzanne Whittaker's number. The detective inspector answered on the second ring.

"Poppy? Slow down... what is it? I can't understand you—"

"I know... I know... who... the murderer is..." gasped Poppy, struggling to catch her breath. "I've got proof... I—" She broke off, wheezing. Her mad run through the village and the panic flooding through her veins was catching up with her; she felt as if her lungs were burning, unable to suck in enough oxygen.

"My goodness, Poppy—what have you been doing? Calm down, take a deep breath. There's no rush."

"No, you don't understand..." Poppy gulped. "I must... tell you—"

"Listen, I'm actually in the car, on my way to you. I was coming to tell you that the cottage has been released and also to ask you a few more questions. Are you at Nick's place?"

"No... the cottage—"

"Oh, good. Well, I'm almost there. See you in a minute!"

The line went dead. Poppy sagged into a chair, clutching a hand to her chest. Now that she knew professional help was coming, she felt like something that had been wound tight in her was finally beginning to relax. She leaned back, taking deep, gulping breaths, trying to calm her racing heart. Her legs felt rubbery and her head was spinning slightly.

My God, I'm so unfit, she thought ruefully. A life spent working at an office desk—with a hasty dash for the commuter train as her only exercise—had left her with embarrassingly little cardiac stamina. She vowed to start doing more exercise; perhaps she'd take up jogging or cycling... or even join a gym—

There was a knock on the front door and Poppy sprang up eagerly to let Suzanne in. As she hurried to the door, she heard a familiar plaintive cry from outside:

"No-ow... Noo-ow!"

It sounded like Oren had joined Suzanne at the front door and was demanding to be let in as well.

"All right, all right, I'm coming!" called Poppy, shaking her head and laughing.

She swung the door open and stepped back in surprise as the ginger tom sprang into the room, his eyes dilated and his fur all on end.

"Oren! What's the matt—" She broke off as she saw who was standing on the threshold.

It was Charles Mannering.

CHAPTER THIRTY-TWO

"Hello, my dear." The lawyer gave her a pleasant smile. "I believe you wanted to see me?"

Poppy licked dry lips. Maybe Mannering didn't suspect that she'd found out his little secret. Maybe he just thought that she'd got tired of waiting and left.

"It... it was nothing... I made a mistake... um, I'm sorry to have bothered you—I should have told your housekeeper before I left... There... there was really no need for you to come—"

"Oh, on the contrary, I think there was every need. May I come in?" He stepped over the threshold before she could answer and slammed the front door behind him.

Poppy backed away. "Er... well, it's actually not a good time... um... The... the police are coming!" she said, rather wildly. "Inspector Whittaker is on her way here right now... She's going to arrive any moment—"

"Ah... then I'll have to be quick, won't I?" said Mannering. "You made a dreadful mess in my conservatory, you know—my poor *Pandorea* will take months to recover—and of course, once I saw the broken screen, I knew you'd found out my little secret. Ah... what a shame. I was really growing quite fond of you, Miss Lancaster, and had been looking forward to teaching you more about gardening. It is really such a rewarding pastime..." He advanced towards her.

Poppy whirled and ran. The cottage was tiny and there were not many places to run to. The bedrooms were out of the question—he would easily corner her there—so her only hope was to go through the kitchen to the greenhouse at the rear and escape out of the back door. Then, even if she couldn't double around to the front, she could still use the hole in the wall to get through to Bertie's place! Bertie, with his feisty little terrier and his wonderful inventions—he would come to her rescue.

And there are garden tools in the greenhouse as well, she remembered with sudden elation. A whole array of garden forks with lovely sharp prongs and spades with heavy metal edges. She could grab something on her way out, so that she'd have something to defend herself with. Besides, Suzanne was on her way too. Official help was coming...

Poppy raced into the kitchen, her feet slipping on the worn linoleum flooring, and was dismayed to hear Mannering's footsteps right behind her. He moved much faster than she'd expected for an older man. Her heart lurched with fear as she felt something grab her arm just as she rounded the kitchen counter.

"No—!" she gasped, trying to jerk her arm loose.

But she felt herself being yanked backwards and thrown violently against the wall, the impact knocking all breath from her lungs and smacking her head so hard that she saw stars. She crumpled to the floor and lay still for a moment, gasping and trying to recover.

Then she heard a *click*. She jerked her head up to see Mannering standing by the door that led to the greenhouse. He had just locked it and was now pocketing the key. Her escape was cut off, and also her access to any weapons.

Mannering turned back and faced her, tutting as if she were a naughty child. "Dear me, Miss Lancaster... this is all so unnecessary. I do so abhor having to hurt anyone but you are leaving me no choice—"

"Let me go!" gasped Poppy. "You... you can't hope to get away with it again. The police will figure out it was you who murdered Pete Sykes."

"Oh, I doubt it, my dear. There are so many more worthy suspects."

"Like Hubert Leach, you mean? Oh my God, that

was all a lie, wasn't it?" she said, the truth suddenly dawning on her. "He never said anything about contesting the will. *You* made up that rumour and put it into my head!"

Mannering gave a modest cough. "Yes, rather clever of me, if I do say so myself. Especially as I had to come up with something on the spur of the moment. When you started telling me your theory about Sykes being involved in the illegal plant trade—very astute of you, by the way—I knew I had to do something fast. Even though you thought it was *Hubert* who was Sykes's client and not me, it was still too close for comfort. I didn't want the police investigating Sykes's plant smuggling activities and possibly tracing something back to me. Focusing on the will instead should hopefully send the investigation off in a different direction."

Poppy stared at him, not wanting to believe how easily she had been fooled. All her indignation and anger at Hubert had been unnecessary; her cousin might have been a buffoon but he wasn't a sinister manipulator like she'd thought. No, *this* man was the manipulator—and he had manipulated her so easily. Yes, he had been clever, making sure that he had shown doubt and worry that they were accusing an innocent man; he'd counselled caution like a typical lawyer and reminded her that it was all "speculation"—all while continuing to poison her mind against her cousin.

If he had simply attacked Hubert outright, it

might have looked suspicious, so he had cleverly seeded it, then used reverse psychology to convince her of her cousin's guilt. And she had played right into his hands. Poppy felt ashamed of how easily she had been led, how much she had accepted his words without questioning.

Then she snapped herself out of it. *No time for remorse and recriminations now. There'll be time for that later—if I get out of this alive.*

Her eyes darted frantically around the room as she racked her brains for a way to escape. With the greenhouse door locked, the back door was out of the question now, but perhaps she could retrace her steps through the house and get out of the front door? Except that the door leading to the hallway was on the other side of the kitchen and she didn't know if she could get there fast enough. If her legs had been rubbery earlier, now they felt completely like jelly—jelly that had been sloshed around a lunchbox and then left outside in the sun for a few hours. She would probably only manage three unsteady steps before Mannering caught her again and she winced at the thought of another violent impact against a wall. Her head was still hurting from where she had smacked it when he had hurled her the first time.

Hoping to distract him and keep him talking, Poppy said: "So Sykes *was* smuggling plants into the country for you?"

"Oh yes, Pete Sykes was very helpful... very

helpful," said Mannering, his eyes taking on a distant look. "He had all sorts of contacts, and of course, working in a nursery meant that he had regular shipments of plants to hide things in. It helped that your grandmother herself sold orchids in the nursery—oh, completely legitimate cultivars, which had been hybridised by plant breeders, of course—but it meant that she had regular shipments of orchids from the Far East, and it's so easy to slip a wild specimen in amongst the boring domestic lot." He made a contemptuous sound. "Most Customs officials can't tell the difference between a run-of-the-mill *Phalaenopsis* and the exquisite, rare *Paphiopedlium*."

It was all exactly as I'd thought—except that I'd got the wrong man, Poppy thought grimly. She had been blinded by Mannering's professional reputation and kindly manner and—yes, she had to admit it—his paternal attitude. She had been so flattered and touched by his interest and solicitude, that she had never thought to question the reasons for them.

But now that she was looking at things with new eyes, she realised how odd so much of his behaviour had been. His generous invitation to dinner—surely he didn't invite every new client to his home, just because they were a stranger in the area? It had simply been a ploy to find out more about her discovery of the body and the police investigation, and to gain her trust so that she would confide in him.

Poppy realised that the lawyer was speaking again and dragged her mind back to the present.

"...was a wonderful arrangement and it would have gone on swimmingly, if it hadn't been for Sykes's greed. In our last exchange, he demanded that I not only pay him the agreed fee for the orchid but also another sum for his silence! Yes, can you believe it? He actually tried to blackmail me. Really, it was very cheeky of the boy," said Mannering, shaking his head and tutting, once again sounding like a weary headmaster discussing a naughty child. "Of course, I couldn't have it. Such behaviour had to be nipped in the bud. And when I spotted the spades in the greenhouse, I thought—how simple: one little knock on the head and that's that." He smiled in a benign manner.

"So you buried him in the flowerbed and then planned to move the body later on?"

Mannering nodded. "Yes, that's right. It had been very dark the night before when I killed him, you see, and to be honest, it had been a rather impulsive decision, so I hadn't given any thought as to how to dispose of the body. I assumed that it would be safe enough temporarily buried in the flowerbed, as I knew that Mary Lancaster was dead and the property was deserted." He gave her a reproachful look. "Naturally, I hadn't expected you to come up all of a sudden—you gave me quite a shock, my dear, when I arrived back from London and my secretary told me that you'd taken the keys and were planning to stay at the cottage."

Mention of the keys made Poppy realise something else. "The keys! It wasn't Jenny Sykes who took them... it was *you!*"

He smiled complacently. "Yes, well, I knew that if I took the keys in the outer office, it would push suspicion away from me because everyone would assume that I would just use the keys in the safe in my own office. Taking the main bunch made it look like someone from the outside was involved."

"And it was easy for you because you would have known exactly when your secretary popped to the toilet," said Poppy, marvelling at how it all fitted. "And then... when it was obvious that you couldn't dissuade me from staying, you tried to prevent me from exploring the garden and going into the flowerbeds by concocting scare stories about tramps and thorny brambles and other hazards in the garden."

She strained her ears for the sound of a car in the lane outside. *Where is Suzanne? Why isn't the inspector here yet?*

Poppy glanced at the old lawyer again, desperate to keep him talking. "It was all just a ploy to keep me from discovering the body, wasn't it?"

Mannering nodded but he barely seemed to be listening. He had bowed his head and seemed to be contemplating something, his fingers steepled under his chin. Keeping her eyes on him, Poppy began to edge away. Her legs were feeling a bit stronger now and she felt a flash of renewed hope. Perhaps she could get out through the front door after all...

Mannering raised his head. "Well, I've enjoyed our little chat, my dear, but time is pressing on and I really can't have you sharing your clever theories with the police..." He advanced towards her. "I'm afraid I'm going to have to—"

A loud clatter interrupted him. Mannering turned around. The sound had come from the back of the kitchen. Poppy saw that the door to the pantry was slightly ajar, and a tin of beans rolled out, coming to a stop by Mannering's feet. The lawyer frowned. He glanced at Poppy, then stepped across to fling the pantry door fully open. At the same moment, there came another loud clatter and a mini-avalanche of tins tumbled out of the pantry.

"What the—!" Mannering cried.

He tried to dodge the rolling tins, but instead stepped on one and reeled backwards. Cursing, he toppled over, just as an enormous ginger tom sprang out of the pantry, tail stiff and whiskers bristling.

"N-OW!" yowled Oren.

CHAPTER THIRTY-THREE

Poppy needed no further urging. She lunged for the door to the hallway and ran, tripping and stumbling, through the cottage and towards the front door. It was shut and it took a horribly long moment to wrestle with the doorknob... but then she wrenched it open... she was free!

She staggered out. But someone grabbed her from behind in a body tackle. She screamed as they both went down, crashing to the porch. Rolling over, Poppy found that Charles Mannering had one arm clamped around her legs, the other one reaching for her neck.

"Let me go! Let... me... go!" cried Poppy, trying to kick him.

But he didn't loosen his grip, even an inch, and she felt panic overwhelm her. *How can an old man be so strong?*

She screamed again, thinking of Bertie—only a few hundred yards away next door. Surely he'd hear her? Surely he'd come to help? Or Suzanne... surely she must have arrived by now? Surely she must be in the lane outside?

But no one came and her scream faded away in the night. As the cruel grip on her tightened, Poppy felt a wave of despair. No one was coming to help her, she realised. And Mannering was on top of her now, pinning her down with his body. His hands were moving to her throat, choking off her next scream.

She had to find a way to save herself... or she would die.

She gasped and sobbed, struggling with all her might. Her arms flailed as she groped desperately around for something, anything, that might be a weapon.

Then her fingernails scraped against something coarse and hard. Terracotta. The rim of a pot.

The potted alstroemeria that she had set beside the front door.

Poppy grasped it with the last of her strength, heaved it up, and smashed it down on Charles Mannering's head.

There was a clatter of shattering terracotta.

Clumps of soil and pieces of broken pot fell into her face.

Then she felt Mannering slump onto her, his

body becoming a dead weight.

Poppy lay stunned for a moment, then she wriggled madly, desperate to get out from underneath him. She managed it at last and sat up shakily, her breath coming in shuddering gasps.

"Poppy? What on earth...?"

Poppy turned to the familiar voice. Suzanne Whittaker was just opening the garden gate. She came slowly up the path, staring at the scene in front of her. Oren trotted suddenly out of the cottage and met her halfway down the path, saying reproachfully:

"*N-ow?*"

Poppy caught her breath on a half-sob and fought the urge to laugh hysterically. For once, she totally agreed with the ginger tom's grumbling. *The police arrive now? When it's all over?*

Suzanne gave the cat an absent-minded pat, then came forwards, staring at Mannering, who lay out cold on the ground, with chunks of broken terracotta scattered around his head. She crouched down and reached out to check the lawyer's pulse.

"Poppy—what the hell happened here?"

But Poppy wasn't listening. She was staring at the lump amongst the broken terracotta. Bereft of its pot, the alstroemeria was tipped helplessly on its side, its mass of fleshy white roots exposed, its stems hanging limply, as it lay in the spilled compost.

"Oh!" she cried, scooping the plant up in both

hands and looking frantically around, like somebody holding a gasping goldfish, searching for a bowl of water.

Suddenly, she was terrified that it was going to die—this plant that she had bought on a whim... this plant that had somehow saved her life. Nothing else mattered now, but saving it. Ignoring Suzanne's bewildered gaze, Poppy hurried to the side of the path beside the front door and began digging in the soil. She had no trowel or fork, but she didn't care, scraping with her bare hands until she had made a good-sized hole in the soft earth. Then she lowered the alstroemeria carefully into the depression, scooped the soil back, and tamped it down gently around it.

It was strange—she had never planted anything in the ground in her life, and yet it was as if... as if invisible hands were there, guiding her. She knew instinctively how big a hole to dig, how deeply to place the plant, how to gently firm the soil back around the stems...

"Poppy?" Suzanne rose from Mannering's side, where she had been putting the lawyer in the recovery position, and came over to her. "Was there an accident? Mannering is out cold. What happened?"

"The alstroemeria saved my life," said Poppy, hearing her own voice as if it were coming from far away.

"The what?" Suzanne frowned, then put a gentle

hand on Poppy's arm. "I think you're suffering from shock. Why don't you come into the cottage and I'll make you a hot drink while we wait for the ambulance? I've called for back-up and—"

"I need to give the alstroemeria some water first," said Poppy anxiously. "It needs water."

Suzanne started to say something, then changed her mind. She nodded and helped to find the garden hose, then watched in bemusement as Poppy tenderly watered the plant. Finally, Poppy stood back, satisfied, and saw that the other woman was eyeing her dishevelled state, the bump on her forehead, the bruises on her arms.

"You'd better let the paramedics have a look at you too when they arrive," Suzanne said. "You look like you've been through the wars."

"That's because Charles Mannering tried to kill me," said Poppy bluntly.

Suzanne's eyes widened. "*What?* Mannering? But—"

Poppy nodded. "He had to silence me because I knew the truth—that he was the one who had murdered Pete Sykes."

Suzanne stared at her for a long moment, then sighed and put a gentle hand under Poppy's elbow, steering her towards the cottage. "Come inside while we wait for the ambulance. I'll make you a cup of tea—I have a feeling you have a *lot* to tell me."

CHAPTER THIRTY-FOUR

"Now, are you sure you don't want me to come up? Hospital food is terrible—I can bring some of my homemade chicken soup and—"

"No, no, Nell... there's no need, honestly. They're just keeping me in for observation, because I had a knock to the head; it's a standard precaution... but I'm sure I'll be released this afternoon."

"What about that dreadful man? I hope he's safely locked behind bars! What if he tries to attack you again?"

"Charles Mannering? He's actually here in the hospital too, I think—but don't worry, they've got a police guard on him. Suzanne—Inspector Whittaker—popped by to see me a short while ago and she told me they'll arrest Mannering as soon as he's released by the doctors. In any case, I don't think he'll be attacking anyone for a long time," Poppy said dryly. "He had an even bigger knock on the head than I did, courtesy of a terracotta plant pot." She sighed, then added, "I think the biggest punishment for Mannering will simply be taking him away from his beloved plants. He treats them like his children, you know. He talks to them and puts fleece around them in winter and stuff... I don't know how he's going to cope with being in prison without them."

"You almost sound like you feel sorry for him," said Nell tartly. "Don't forget, dear—the man tried to kill you."

"I know, I know..." Poppy sighed. "I still can't believe it. It's like my mind is struggling to understand it. I mean, he was so nice... it's like he was two different people."

"What *I'm* struggling to understand is why he had those orchids out in the conservatory. If they were illegal, why would he have them where anyone could see them?" asked Nell.

"Well, people would only have found them if they walked behind that screen," Poppy reminded her. "And I suppose he had to keep them *some*where—so in fact, hidden amongst all the plants in the conservatory was probably the best place. Mannering's housekeeper said that he normally only allowed guests to go in the conservatory when he was there. So that means he could always make sure they didn't look behind the screen, like he did with me. But even if they *did* somehow find the grotto, the average person probably wouldn't recognise the orchids and know that they're endangered, smuggled specimens. So there's very little danger of being exposed."

"It still seems a silly risk to me," said Nell.

"Maybe that was part of it—the risk, I mean," said Poppy. "Maybe he got a thrill when he was showing people around, knowing that they were just a few feet away from priceless, illegal plants but they had no clue. Maybe it made him feel smug or something." She sighed. "You know, I keep thinking of that night when Mannering invited me over to dinner and was showing me around the conservatory. I should have picked up then that he was a bit bonkers. I should have realised that he was exactly the kind of fanatical collector who would do anything to get his hands on a particular plant—I don't know how I never saw it."

"Don't blame yourself, dear," said Nell. "People can be very good at putting up a false front."

"Oren saw through him, you know."

"Who?"

"Oren, Nick's cat. I think he saved my life."

"What do you mean?"

"Well, first, I think he tried to warn me about Mannering. He was outside the door when Mannering came, making a terrible racket. I thought he was just crying to get in, but I think now that he was actually trying to warn me not to open the door. And then later on, he distracted Mannering by knocking all those tins down in the pantry. If he hadn't done that, I would never have had the chance to get out of the house." She shuddered at the memory. "I know it sounds silly and it could all have been coincidence but I feel like Oren knew I was in danger."

"I wouldn't be surprised. They do say animals have a sixth sense," said Nell complacently.

"I wonder if he likes catmint," mused Poppy. "Maybe I can plant some in the garden for him, as a sort of thank you. And then when he comes over to visit me—"

"But you're not going to be living in the cottage," Nell pointed out. "You're selling it, remember?"

"Oh..." Poppy drew a breath. "Yes, I forgot..."

Nell gave an incredulous laugh. "Oh my lordy Lord, Poppy, how can you forget something like that? If I had that kind of money coming to me, I wouldn't be able to think about anything else!"

"Yes... I mean, I *have* been thinking about the cottage," mumbled Poppy. "I just..." She hesitated.

"What is it, dear?"

Poppy sighed again. "Nothing."

"Well, I'd best be getting on. If you're sure about not wanting me to come up—"

"Yes, I'm sure, Nell. I'll be back in the cottage this evening and I'll probably come back down to London this weekend to pack my things."

"Well, give me a call when you're back in the

cottage, dear, just so I know that you're all right. And make sure you lock the door—"

"Don't worry, I'll be fine," Poppy reassured her.

"I just don't like the idea of you being out there, all alone at the cottage; a girl in the middle of nowhere—"

"Nell!" Poppy gave an exasperated laugh. "It's not in the middle of nowhere! It's in a busy village—and I've also got male neighbours on either side."

Nell snorted. "You mean that author chap?" she said, her tone saying exactly what she thought of Nick.

"Yes, and there's also Bertie—Dr Bertram Noble—on the other side. And he's got all sorts of weird and wonderful inventions, so I'm more than amply protected," said Poppy, laughing.

"Hmm..." Nell didn't laugh. "I thought the police arrested Dr Noble?"

"That was a mistake," said Poppy quickly. "I told you, that was just Sergeant Lee jumping to conclusions."

"Still, you don't know much about this Dr Noble, do you?" said Nell suspiciously. "How do you even know he's really who he says he is? What kind of doctor is he anyway?"

"He's not a medical doctor—he's a scientist. The 'Dr' is just his title. He used to be a professor at Oxford University."

"Oh?" Nell didn't sound impressed. "So why isn't he there anymore?"

Poppy thought of the magazine article she'd read and the mystery surrounding Bertie's past. There were still many questions unanswered, so many things she wanted to know... but they would have to wait for another day.

"I don't know—maybe he got tired of academic life or just decided to retire early or something," she said in a dismissive tone. "Anyway, the good thing is that he's got a little terrier and you know what good guard dogs they are. So I'm sure if there was any danger, Einstein would sound the alarm." Although the little dog had singularly failed at his job last night, she reflected wryly.

Still, mention of the dog seemed to mollify Nell and her old friend soon bade her goodbye. Poppy put her phone down, leaned back against the pillows, and let out a sigh, wishing that she had a magazine to help kill the time. She was just wondering if she could convince the ward nurse to let her pop to the hospital shop when there was a commotion by the entrance to the ward and, a moment later, she saw a familiar old man trot into the room, followed by a harassed-looking nurse.

"Sir! Sir! You can't just wander in here by yourself—you need to report to the nurses' station first and tell us who you're visiting," the nurse said irritably.

Bertie waved a hand. "No need to bother you," he said, busily going from bed to bed, and peering at each of its occupant. "I'm Dr Bertram Noble and I know who I'm looking for."

"Bertie!" cried Poppy, sitting up in delight. "How nice of you to come and see me."

The old man hurried up to her bedside. "Came as soon as I heard the news, my dear. I'm so sorry I wasn't home last night—it distresses me to think of it! I'm sure Einstein would have heard you otherwise, and sounded the alarm. But as luck would have it, we were at my friend Peter Saunders's house; he has the most—"

"Wait—*what?*" Poppy interrupted him. "Whose house?"

Bertie looked at her in bewilderment. "Professor Peter Saunders. He's an old colleague of mine who still lives in Oxford and he'd invited me over for dinner and a game of chess."

"Bertie, did he leave you a note recently? Something about a book you'd lent him?" Poppy asked urgently.

The old inventor looked even more bewildered. "Yes, that's right—how did you know, my dear? He's going on holiday to the Costa Brava soon, on the Spanish coast, and I lent him a book on the region."

"He also mentioned something about a 'secret' in his note," persisted Poppy. "He promised not to tell anyone. What was he talking about?"

Bertie frowned. "A secret? I'm afraid I don't know, dear. Perhaps I'd been telling him about one of my experiments…"

Poppy gasped. "Oh God—I happened to see your

note and I thought 'Pete S' stood for 'Pete Sykes' and that the note was from the murdered man."

"But I'd never even met Pete Sykes—why would I get a note from him?" asked Bertie with childlike simplicity.

Poppy shook her head, still chuckling. "Never mind, Bertie. It was just a massive misunderstanding on my part."

He handed her a brown paper bag. "Here you are—I brought you some grapes."

"Oh, how sweet!" said Poppy, smiling.

Bertie leaned towards her, saying in a loud whisper: "I modified them myself. They taste just like homemade chicken soup—but in easy little globes that you can pop in your mouth. So much more convenient than having to drink from a bowl."

Poppy paused in the act of pulling off a grape and hastily let go. "Er... that sounds great, Bertie. I... um... actually, I think I'll save them for later."

The nurse had followed Bertie over but, after eyeing him suspiciously for a few seconds, finally retreated to the nurses' station on the other side of the ward. As soon as she was gone, Bertie grinned at Poppy and said, "Someone else wanted to say hello too."

He leaned forwards again, parting the front of his jacket. Poppy had thought that he seemed unusually tubby and now she realised that what had looked like a bulging belly was actually a little sling beneath his jacket. A moist black nose and pink tongue emerged suddenly from the folds of the sling and Einstein the terrier gave her face a wet slurp.

"*Eeuw!*... Uh... hi, Einstein," said Poppy, gingerly wiping her cheek. She looked hastily around to see if anyone had noticed the dog, then lowered her voice and said:

"Bertie, you know animals aren't allowed in here! You could get in big trouble."

"Well, I couldn't leave him tied up outside on the street," said Bertie indignantly. "And when I heard that you'd suffered a head injury, I just had to come in and give you *this*."

He reached into his jacket once more and produced a strange contraption—a circle of metal spikes and wires that looked like a cross between a crown of thorns and a TV antenna. Before Poppy could stop him, he'd reached up and placed it on her head.

"Er, Bertie—"

"Don't worry, my dear. I've tested it on myself and it works perfectly! Well, it did singe my hair but only slightly," he assured her. "And I've made adjustments to rectify that. Now, I just need to find a socket..."

He held up a plug on the end of a long wire attached to the circle on her head and turned, scanning the wall next to her bed. Poppy gulped and hastily reached up to remove the circle from her head, but before she could, a voice screeched:

"Dr Noble! What do you think you are doing to my patient?"

The nurse rushed up to them, an expression of outrage on her face. She snatched the crown of wires off Poppy's head and waved it indignantly at Bertie. "What on earth is this?"

"It's my Neural Cranio-Analeptic Equaliser," said Bertie proudly. "It helps to heal the brain after a head injury, by synchronising the neural pathways using minute electromagnetic pulses that—"

"What?" the nurse stared at him. "What nonsense are you talking about?"

Bertie bristled. "It's not nonsense! If you don't believe me, I'll show you..."

"No, wait, Bertie—!" cried Poppy, but it was too late.

The inventor had plunged the plug into the socket on the wall. There was a loud crackling sound and then a *BANG!* as sparks flew from the circle of wires. The nurse squealed and flung it away from herself. It flew across Poppy's bed and hit the blood-oxygen monitor next to her. There was an even louder cackling sound and suddenly every machine in the room started beeping shrilly. Patients in other beds sat up, looking around in bewilderment. The fire alarm started ringing. Einstein stuck his head out of Bertie's jacket and began barking at the top of his voice. Poppy winced. The noise was deafening.

"What have you done?" wailed the nurse. "Turn it

off! Turn it off!"

Without waiting for Bertie to answer, she lunged across him and yanked the plug out of the wall. The beeping ceased instantly; the fire alarm went silent. Before Poppy could breathe a sigh of relief, however, she heard an ominous gurgling above her head. She looked up. The next moment, water gushed out of the overhead sprinklers and drenched everyone in the room.

"Aaaarrggghhhh!" screeched the nurse. Her hair was plastered to her head and water streamed down her face. She turned to Bertie with a murderous look in her eyes. "You... you—!"

"Well, it might need a *bit* more tweaking," said Bertie thoughtfully, gathering the circle of wires and stuffing it, plug and all, back into his inner jacket pocket. "Hmm... perhaps I need to reduce the conductivity... aluminium instead of copper wires— although that introduces the problem of thermal expansion, of course..."

Muttering to himself and completely ignoring the nurse's furious spluttering, Bertie trotted out of the ward and disappeared. Poppy was slightly sorry that he hadn't said goodbye to her properly, but on second thoughts—after a glance at the nurse's still-livid face—decided that it was probably a good thing that Bertie had made himself scarce so quickly.

It took over an hour to restore peace to the ward; Poppy was careful to keep a low profile and that meant she had to give up her idea of popping to the hospital shop for some magazines, since the last thing she wanted to do was face the nurse again. The long hours stretched into the afternoon and she found herself looking up eagerly each time a visitor entered the ward, hoping that it might be someone who'd come to see her.

Not that there is really anyone else, she reminded herself morosely. With her mother gone, there was really only Nell who cared about her. She had no other family—cut off from her mother's side and with no idea of who her father even was—and she had no close friends: her nomadic life with her mother meant that it had been impossible to put down roots anywhere and develop deep friendships, whether at school or at work. She had never thought that she'd minded it before, but now, for the first time, Poppy felt very alone.

Then she gave a self-deprecating smile. *Stop wallowing in self-pity!* It had been very nice of Suzanne Whittaker to come and see her that morning, even if it had just been a form of professional courtesy. And for all the mayhem that he had caused, Poppy was incredibly touched that Bertie had come to visit. He might not have been her father but she had a feeling that he could become a friend. A very good friend. As for family... well, she did have a cousin. Poppy grimaced as she thought of Hubert Leach and decided that, actually, she wouldn't have wanted him to visit her anyway. In fact—

A tall, dark-haired man entered the ward and Poppy felt her heart skip a beat, then she was annoyed with herself as she watched him walk over to another bed. No, it wasn't Nick Forrest—and why would he come anyway? He wasn't due back until tonight and even if Suzanne had told him what had happened, he was hardly going to cancel the rest of his book tour just to rush back and see her. They barely knew each other.

Her thoughts were interrupted by a doctor arriving to do a ward round and she was delighted when he gave her the "all-clear". Hurriedly, she got dressed, collected her few possessions, and prepared to leave the ward. As she was passing the nurses' station, she paused to get her discharge documents and was relieved to see that the previous nurse had gone off duty. The new woman smiled at Poppy and handed her some papers, then glanced at her name on the forms and said:

"Oh! Miss Lancaster—there's something here for you. I think the last nurse forgot to give it to you."

She reached beneath the counter and lifted up a beautiful bouquet of roses, wrapped in gilt paper and ribbons. Poppy caught her breath.

"For... for me?" she said in disbelief.

The woman nodded and handed it across. "Yes, there's a card addressed to you."

Poppy took the bouquet carefully, staring at it in wonder. She had never been given fresh flowers before and had certainly never been able to afford a luxurious arrangement like this. She had never seen a rose bouquet like this before either: these were not the stiff, whorled, artificially perfect blooms that she normally saw at florists—no, these roses came in all shapes and sizes, from fat buds of antique cream to big cabbage-like blooms in shades of pink, mauve, rose, and lilac. They reminded her of the roses she'd glimpsed at Hollyhock Cottage— romantic, old-fashioned cupped roses, filled with fragrant petals and heady with perfume.

She buried her nose in the bouquet and inhaled deeply, feeling like she was in a dream. Then she noticed the card tucked in amongst the leaves. She opened it and chuckled as she read the two words:

from Oren.

CHAPTER THIRTY-FIVE

Poppy watched the water gush out of the kitchen tap and into the old galvanised-metal jug she had found in the greenhouse. When the jug was full, she lifted it out of the sink and lowered the bouquet of roses carefully into the water. She would have liked to have put the bouquet in a proper vase but there were none to be found in the cottage. Still—she set the jug at the end of the kitchen counter and stood back to admire the effect—the rustic old container suited the roses somehow; the muted tones of the faded blue metal complemented the soft pinks, creams, and lilacs. For a man who professed to care very little about flowers, Nick Forrest certainly knew how to choose a bouquet.

She was just wondering whether to untie the ribbon still wound around the rose stems when she heard the sound of knocking at the front door. She looked up, startled. She wasn't expecting anyone—other than perhaps a smug ginger tomcat come to welcome her home. But clever as he was, she didn't think Oren had mastered the ability to knock yet.

She went to the front door but hesitated with her hand on the doorknob as a sense of *déjà vu* struck her. There had been a knock on the door yesterday, just like this, and she had stood in the same place, ready to fling the door open. The memory of Charles Mannering's terrifying attack was still uncomfortably fresh in her mind.

"Who is it?" she called nervously.

"It's your cousin, Hubert," came a familiar nasal voice.

Poppy felt a mixture of relief and dismay. Opening the door, she found Hubert Leach standing on the doorstep, a smarmy smile plastered on his face.

"Cousin Poppy!" he cried, reaching out an arm as if to hug her.

Poppy hastily moved back, out of reach, and Hubert took advantage of her retreat to step into the house.

"I'm so glad I caught you. They told me you were in hospital—sorry, I couldn't come to visit... busy, busy... you know how it is!—but you're obviously out now and looking well. Anyway, I just *had* to come and see how you were... oh, and I brought you these."

He thrust a bunch of limp carnations at her.

"Oh... er... thank you," said Poppy, taking the flowers. "Um... would you like a cup of tea?"

As she stood in the kitchen waiting for the kettle to boil, Poppy couldn't help looking surreptitiously at her cousin from underneath her eyelashes. She felt slightly ashamed now that she had suspected him of being involved in Pete Sykes's death. Okay, Hubert was brash and rude, but there was a big difference between being a boor and being a murderer. There *was* still the mystery surrounding his odd conversation with Dr Goh, though...

"Hubert, can I ask you something?" she spoke up, interrupting him as he started rambling on about some exciting news he had for her.

He stopped, looking surprised at her tone. "Uh... sure."

"Was Dr Goh my grandmother's GP?"

"Dr Goh...?" He looked completely bemused.

"Is he a good friend of yours?"

Hubert looked slightly shifty. "Well, I wouldn't call him a friend, exactly. We're both on the board of OGS."

"OGS?"

"The Oxfordshire Galanthophiles Society."

"Oh." Poppy was slightly nonplussed. "Um... I overheard a conversation you were having on your phone—with Dr Goh. You asked him to express concerns about something and said that you'd make it worth his while."

Hubert flushed. "Oh... uh... that." He cleared his throat and said defensively, "It wasn't anything... *ahem...* illegal..."

"Bribery can be a criminal offence," said Poppy. "It's sort of like the reverse of extortion, isn't it? When you offer money to—"

"What? I wasn't offering Dr Goh money!"

Poppy blinked in confusion. "But... but you said you'd make it worth his while. What were you offering him then?"

"Bulbs! *Galanthus woronowii* 'Elizabeth Harrison', as a matter of fact. It's a rare yellow snowdrop," Hubert explained at her blank look. "Very hard to find. Even harder to bulk up."

"Ohhh... I thought you were offering him money to lie about my grandmother's—" She broke off guiltily.

"I wasn't asking Goh to lie!" said Hubert indignantly. "I just wanted him to... uh... express some doubts. About Martin Veeland. He and I are both in the running to become the next president of OGS, you see. The nominations are next month and... and it's obvious Veeland would make a lousy president. I mean, the man is just a chequebook gardener! Gets all his plants from eBay," said Hubert contemptuously. "But he's got good connections and I could see all the board members voting for him, just because of the bloody old boys' network. So I was just trying to even the odds—get some of the board members on my side."

"And... and Dr Goh wasn't my grandmother's GP?"

Hubert looked bewildered by the seemingly random question. "Eh? No, Goh's not a GP. He's an opthalmologist. Why?"

Poppy felt embarrassed and very stupid. She had completely misinterpreted the eavesdropped conversation! She gave Hubert a weak smile.

"Er... nothing. It was just a mistake. So... you said you had some exciting news for me?" she said quickly, to distract him.

His face brightened. "Ah—yes!" He spread some documents out on the kitchen table. "Look at this! It's a second offer for Hollyhock Cottage and gardens, from a company called Blackmort Developments, and they're offering *double* the amount of the first company. Can you believe that? Twice as much money!"

He rubbed his hands, obviously thinking of his whopping agent's commission on the increased amount. "It's simply too good to miss. And they're prepared to transfer the full amount—minus a modest agent's fee to yours truly, of course," he gave a little cough, "—in cash to your bank account as soon as you sign the contract. So I've taken the liberty of drawing up the sales agreement and all I need is your signature... *here.*"

Hubert thrust a pen at Poppy and slid one of the pieces of paper in front of her. She looked down and her eyes widened at the number on the page in front of her. She had never seen a pound sign with so many zeros after it in her life! Her head swam slightly. With that kind of money, she could buy fresh roses every day... get a whole new wardrobe... go on a round-the-world cruise for a year...

She picked up the pen and her hand hovered over the dotted line. She thought of the glittering lights of Hollywood... of her father, waiting to be found... of a glamorous new life in America...

...and then she thought of a garden deep in the heart of rural Oxfordshire, with climbing roses and towering hollyhocks, and fragrant lavender lining the path to a little cottage nestled among the flowerbeds...

Poppy put the pen back down and pushed the paper away from her. "No," she said.

"N-no?" stammered Hubert. Then his face cleared. "Ah, you mean you prefer the first offer? Well, I suppose it's not as much money but it's still a very good price—"

"No," said Poppy again. She took a deep breath. "I mean—I'm not selling the cottage. For any price."

Hubert's mouth fell open. His jaw worked up and down but no sound came out. Finally, he croaked, "You're having me on, aren't you, cousin?"

"No, I'm perfectly serious," said Poppy. She stood up from the table. "I'm staying in the cottage."

"But you can't. Don't think I don't know the terms of the will," snapped Hubert. "You can only live here if you continue the family business."

"I... I'm going to. I'm reopening Hollyhock Cottage Garden Nursery."

"What? But you don't know the first thing about running a plant nursery!" sneered Hubert.

Poppy raised her chin. "I can learn. The Lancasters have plants in their blood—and I'm a Lancaster."

"You... you can't do this!" spluttered Hubert furiously. "You have to sell the cottage—then at least I'd get something out of the commission! The estate should have come to me! ME!" He jabbed his chest. "Mary Lancaster had no right giving it all to some illegitimate brat who'd never even met her! You owe it to me to sell the place, so that at least I get some share of the proceeds—"

"*I* don't owe you anything," said Poppy, drawing herself up to her full five feet, two inches. "I'm sorry that you lost out in the will, Hubert, but that's not my fault. My grandmother had the right to leave her estate how she chose—and she chose to give it to *me*."

She paused, then added softly with a smile, "Maybe because she knew that I would honour her memory. She knew that I wouldn't sell the cottage and gardens to some property developer to chop up into townhouse units—no, she knew that I would fulfil her dream: make Hollyhock Cottage my home and the garden nursery my living."

She gathered up the papers from the table, stuffed them into Hubert's lifeless hands, and steered her cousin to the front door. A few minutes later, she stood on the front porch and watched as he stalked angrily down the path and out into the lane, slamming the gate behind him.

Peace descended in the garden. A soft breeze stirred the leaves in the trees and bent the tall grasses and weeds growing by the path. A few loose rose petals fluttered past, like pretty pastel butterflies chasing each other in the wind.

Poppy took a deep breath and looked around. Her heart sank as she took in all the weeds, the thorny brambles, the overgrown bushes... It was going to need a *lot* of work to restore the cottage garden to its former glory. She had no money, no plan, and no experience...

She felt a flash of panic. *Oh my God—have I done the right thing?* She could have taken the money and by this time next week, she would have been on a cruise ship, sipping a cocktail in the sun. Instead of which...

Then she glanced down and her heart gave a different kind of lurch. There, by the side of the path, was a mound of lush green leaves surrounding a cluster of flowers. They were a vivid cherry-red, shaped a bit like lilies, with strikingly marked petals that seemed to glow in the late-afternoon sun, and they were absolutely, breathtakingly beautiful.

Poppy dropped to her knees beside the mound and reached out to touch a silky red petal, a smile of wonder breaking across her face. It was the alstroemeria—and it was flowering! She laughed; it obviously hadn't suffered any ill effects from having its pot smashed on someone's head, followed by a hasty planting by a complete beginner gardener.

She stroked one soft green leaf and felt a sense of achievement and pride, such as she'd never felt before, as she looked at the first flower she'd planted. She glanced round again—at the overgrown beds around her—and this time, instead of despair, she felt excitement fill her. She couldn't wait to fill the garden with beautiful flowers—all planted by herself!

As she was about to stand up again, her fingers brushed against something in the soil next to the alstroemeria. Poppy picked it up: it was the tip of a stem, dry and withered, with tiny dessicated leaves and flower petals that still showed a faint lavender colour. It must have fallen off a plant which had been flowering a few months ago and it had lain forgotten in the neglected garden, drying slowly into a thing of faded beauty.

It's a sprig of heather, Poppy realised, seeing the resemblance to the pin she had been given by the charity volunteer on the street. And with that thought came the memory of the woman's voice:

"Flowers have meanings associated with them, you know... Heather symbolises transformative change—from the mundane to the extraordinary."

Poppy stared at the dried sprig of heather and a

smile spread slowly across her face as the truth hit her. She'd thought that she needed Hollywood glamour, a rock-star father, a round-the-world cruise and more, to make her life extraordinary.

But she'd been wrong: the extraordinary had been here all along... in a beautiful cottage garden in England.

THE END

ABOUT THE AUTHOR

USA Today bestselling author H.Y. Hanna writes funny and intriguing British cozy mysteries, set in Oxford and the beautiful English Cotswolds. Her books include the Oxford Tearoom Mysteries, the 'Bewitched by Chocolate' Mysteries and the English Cottage Garden Mysteries—as well as romantic suspense and children's mystery novels. After graduating from Oxford University, Hsin-Yi tried her hand at a variety of jobs, before returning to her first love: writing. She worked as a freelance writer for several years and has won awards for her novels, poetry, short stories and journalism.

A globe-trotter all her life, Hsin-Yi has lived in a variety of cultures, from Dubai to Auckland, London to New Jersey, but is now happily settled in Perth, Western Australia, with her husband and a rescue kitty named Muesli. You can learn more about her (and the real-life Muesli who inspired the cat character in the story) and her other books at: **www.hyhanna.com**.

Sign up to her newsletter to be notified of new releases, exclusive giveaways and other book news! Go to: **www.hyhanna.com/newsletter**

ACKNOWLEDGMENTS

Thank you to my lovely beta readers: Basma Alwesh, Connie Leap and Charles Winthrop, for always finding time to fit me into their busy schedules and for investing so much time and energy into my books. Their thoughtful feedback is always so helpful in making each book the best it can be. I am always grateful to my editor and proofreader, too, for being such a great team to work with.

And last but not least—I can never thank my wonderful husband enough for always being there for me to lean on. I could never do this without his unwavering support, encouragement and enthusiasm. He is one man in a million.

Made in the USA
Columbia, SC
08 November 2020

24126930R00188